I0727360

Once Upon a Witch

DEMELZA CARLTON

Three tales in the Romance a Medieval Fairy Tale series

Feather: Swan Maidens Retold

DEMELZA CARLTON

A tale in the Romance a Medieval Fairy Tale series

One

"If we don't do it naked, we disrespect the old deities," Swanhild declared, pulling off her shift.

Raphael glanced around, then reluctantly removed his tunic. "That may be, but if Father Fazzio finds us, like he did the others, the whole town will hear of it, and we'll be listening to interminable sermons about chastity and purity for the next month." As his eyes rested on Swanhild's, the lust heating them said a month's worth of sermons was a small price to pay.

"Father Fazzio is afraid of the old pagan groves. He would never venture so far into the forest, and even if he did, the old gods would hide us from his sight, if we worship them properly."

Raphael lay down on the grass, and stretched his hands out in supplication. "It is you I wish to worship, not some god, old or new. Come here."

Swanhild laughed, stretching her arms above her head to better show off her breasts, before she perched herself astride Raphael's hips. He was ready for her, as always, but she took pleasure in teasing him, rubbing herself against him, until he could take it no more.

Today, he seemed to be feasting his eyes on her breasts, as she worked her way to a climax. It came fast today, and she arched her back as she cried out to the forest canopy above.

Raphael was rock hard beneath her, but still he didn't enter her.

"You're so beautiful," he breathed, reaching up to cup her breasts. "Marry me, Swanhild."

"No," she said, grinding against him again. She closed her eyes, pressing down harder. Surely she couldn't be about to climax again. Oh, but she was. She cried out for joy.

"Marry me, so that we may do this every day and every night," he said, staring up at her adoringly.

Swanhild laughed. "How is that different to what we do now? Come, Raphael, I am about to climax for the third time, and I am doing all the work!"

"The forest floor is fine in summer," he said, caressing her breasts. "But when the autumn rains come…or the cold winter snow, I want to be warm…inside…" Finally, he thrust into her, timing it perfectly to send her over the edge of another climax. "With you, in our bed. I want you to be my wife, Swanhild."

Something about the angle he'd chosen sent

waves of pleasure through her, building to another, impossible peak.

"I care nothing for autumn, or winter. What I want is you, her and now, in this moment, just as we are…now!" For the first time, they'd timed it perfectly, reaching their peak together. With more practice, they might manage this every time.

She cried out his name, but his shout sounded more like, "Marry me, Swanhild!"

She shook her head as they broke apart, and headed to the small spring that inevitably graced these holy groves so that she might wash.

Wash, dry, dress – it was a ritual of its own, one she'd completed three times today, twice in this grove. But they would have to leave soon, to make it home before dark, and any more lovemaking would have to wait until tomorrow.

She hoped he'd come up with a more acceptable marriage proposal before autumn, instead of his heat of the moment demands that would mean nothing when they were clothed once more. At least, to most men they meant nothing, or so her mother had said. Promises made in passion were worthless — and her mother would know, for her father had often promised never to beat her again, only to do so the next day.

But Raphael was nothing like her father, she reminded herself, as his gentle healer's hand closed around hers. One day he would choose the right moment, and she would see his eyes light up when she said…

They'd reached the edge of the forest, and Raphael had dropped to his knees, setting his basket down. He placed hers beside it, so that he might take both of her hands in his.

"Swanhild, I love you more than the sun in the sky, or the life-giving air that lets us draw breath. I love your body, I love your mind, I love your magic, and I love the sound of your voice. I would give my life to spend whatever moments I might have left with you. I know a witch and an apprentice apothecary are an unlikely match, for while we are apart, we compete for the same customers every day, but when we are together…ah, we are so much more. You are my dearest friend, my only love, and I beg you to become my wife. Please, Swanhild, whether it is today or tomorrow or next year, or a hundred years from now, promise you will marry me, because I love no one else, and I never will."

She stared into his eyes. This was the moment.

"Yes," she breathed.

Raphael's mouth dropped open. "What did you say?"

Swanhild laughed. "I said yes. My dress is ready, and we only need to tell my mother, before we may set a date. You'd better make good on your promise to make love to me morning and night, though, or I shall have to take you out into the forest and leave you for the old gods to deal with!"

He rose to his feet and wrapped his arms around her. "Whatever you desire. With you as my wife, I will give you anything you desire."

She laughed. "Then you may start now, with a kiss."

One kiss turned into several, and the sun had set by the time they emerged from the trees, hand in hand. But the darkness didn't bother them, for what could possibly mar such perfect joy?

Two

"Where have you been? I feared the worst!" Mother seized Swanhild's shoulders and stared at her. "Are you feverish? Have you started to cough? Any painful swellings?"

Swanhild had been a witch long enough to know what those symptoms meant. Her mother thought she was late home because she'd caught the plague. "I'm fine!" she snapped, trying to pull out of her mother's grasp, but she wouldn't be shaken.

"Good, good," Mother said vaguely, staring out into the night. She shook herself. "Then we must keep you that way. There is not a moment to lose!"

She dragged Swanhild out the door and down the road, until her boots splashed into the lake. Cold water washed over the top of them, swirling around her toes and threatening to slip off her shoes. She mustn't have fastened them properly, for it seemed her feet were swimming in shoes that had fitted fine in the forest.

And why was Mother suddenly growing taller?

Water seeped through her sleeves. Swanhild flung her arms up, out of the water, but they didn't feel right. Lighter, somehow. And she could see both arms at the same time, one on either side, filling her sleeves…no, slipping out of her sleeves…

Realisation hit her like a punch to the gut. "Mother! Why are you using magic on me?" she cried.

"It's the only way to save you. All the swans

in the kingdom are protected by the Queen, so you shall be safe from hunters, too."

"What do you mean…what are you protecting me from?" Swanhild tried to say, but only a horrible honking sound came out. Like a swan protecting her nest. "Mother!"

"Fly, fly away. When the plague is gone and it is safe to return, then you may resume your true form. Stand upon this shore, and if it is safe, you shall transform. But not before. Begone!" Mother flapped her arms, as if to shoo Swanhild away, deeper into the lake.

Some primal fear seized Swanhild's innards, and she found herself flapping, too. Wheeling around, lifting, gliding…her feet left the water and she flew across the surface of the lake, fleeing from her home and everything she'd ever known.

She wanted to turn, to head back, but the instinct to fly from danger was too strong.

One day, she would come back. Conquer and command this silly swan form to take her home. For it would be safe to return, she was certain of it.

Three

Raphael knew he should go home. He should tell his master, Gojko the apothecary, that he wanted to get married, and ask if he might end his apprenticeship early so that he might start earning enough to support a family. Well, just a wife at first, but the amount of time he spent naked with Swanhild, a family wouldn't be far off.

Instead, he lingered outside Swanhild's house. Gojko would not be pleased if he went inside the witch's house, for that is what the master called Swanhild's mother, Tola. On anyone else's lips, the word would not have sounded so sour, for even Tola herself was happy to claim the title of being the town witch, but when Gojko said it, it was with the same venom he reserved for demons, fleas and rats.

Hence he wanted to be certain Gojko would approve the end of his apprenticeship before confessing that he planned to marry Tola's daughter. Perhaps the man would be more accepting of the two women if he knew that both possessed real magic, as well as knowing as much about healing and herbs as Gojko himself, but Raphael doubted it. Gojko was a bitter old man who liked to hold a grudge, and Tola had once saved someone's life when Gojko had given up treating them, convinced no potion could possibly work when all he knew had failed.

So Tola became that foreign witch who did deals with the devil, at least in Gojko's house, and Raphael was not allowed to speak of her.

Yet here she was, bursting out the door of her own home, dragging Swanhild behind her as she hurried down to the lake.

So Tola hadn't liked the idea of Swanhild marrying him. For what else could anger the woman so, except today's news?

Raphael stepped into the shadows, so Tola wouldn't see him, before following the pair. There was no way he'd allow his future wife to face her mother's magical wrath alone.

Tola dragged Swanhild to the very edge of the lake, then pushed her in. Swanhild stumbled forward at her mother's push, but she didn't lose her footing in the knee-deep waters.

Light glinted off a blade in Tola's hand.

Raphael opened his mouth to cry out a warning to Swanhild, then almost choked as Tola turned the blade on herself, slashing it across her arm before shifting the blade to the other hand and slicing her other arm, too. The knife tumbled from her fingers into the sand at her feet, and Raphael found he could breathe again. Tola meant to cast a spell, not stab her daughter.

Only then did Swanhild turn to face her mother, her feet still in the lake. She crouched down, staring up at Tola with a look of horror on her face.

Her arms stretched out, splashing the surface of the water as if trying to drive it away.

And then…she changed.

Arms became wings, and her gown slipped off faster than it had when they'd made love in the forest.

"Mother! Why are you using magic on me?" she cried.

For a moment, Raphael saw the woman he loved, crouching in the water, wings outspread, and then she was gone. A swan sat there in her place, flapping her wings and honking like she was trying to drive away a predator from her nest.

Horror froze his tongue.

The swan who had been his betrothed wheeled around and took flight across the lake.

Despair freed it.

"Mistress Tola, how could you do such a thing to your own daughter?"

Tola started to turn, then staggered around to face him. "I would do anything to save her."

Raphael saw red. "What in heaven's name would be so bad about her marrying me? I would support her and care for her and love her all the days of my life!"

"Can you cure the plague, boy?"

The plague? Like the one that wiped out Altino?

"Of course not. No one can," Raphael said. That was why Mistress Sara had insisted no strangers would be welcomed in their town. And no matter what Elder Ahab or Father Fazzio said, there wasn't a man, woman or child in Mirroten brave enough to disobey Mistress Sara.

Tola fell to her knees. Only now did Raphael see the dark rivulets of blood running down her arms. She'd sliced open her veins, he was sure of it.

He rushed forward. "Mistress Tola, you must let me help you, or you shall die!"

She held up a bloodied hand. "I must do no such thing, boy. If you have any sense, and you hope to live long enough to marry my daughter, you will stay as far away from me as you can. I nursed poor Ysabel until the plague killed her, but not before she passed the pestilence to me, her father and likely the priest, too. Death comes to us all, but I shall choose the time and the place, not some disease. I give my life for my daughter, so that she may live." She coughed, and brought up blood, spitting it on the ground, away from Raphael. "Tell Sara to run. Far and fast and to somewhere she can close the gates to everyone. Her family's fortress, high in the mountains, maybe. Tell her to wait as long as she can to return. A year. Maybe two. Until news reaches her that it is safe. Then, you may return here, and Swanhild…Swanhild…"

She tipped over on her side, her breathing laboured.

"Mistress Tola, if you would but wrap the sleeve tightly around your arm, it might slow the bleeding. You may yet live."

Tola began to laugh, which only made her cough. "Sara will need you with your unquenchable hope when she goes. You see she gets somewhere safe. When it is safe to return home, Swanhild will come here, and if you truly love her, you will be here waiting when she does. And my daughter…you see you make her happy, boy. For if you ever beat her, I'll send the devil himself to rip out your intestines and whip you to death with them."

"And I thought you'd come back as a ghost and turn me into a frog," Raphael said. Oh, he was a fool. He should have thought of it sooner. "No, wait. Turn me into a swan, like Swanhild. Then we'll both be safe together, and when we come back…"

"Not enough magic left in my blood to turn you into anything, boy. You'll have to take your chances with Sara and whoever else you can save. Now go! Get those long legs up to the church and light a candle for Ysabel, and anyone else whose soul might help carry your prayers to heaven. For you'll need all the luck in the world to survive this." Another cough, weaker this time. "Go or I might try to change you into a slug after all. I might have enough magic for that…"

Raphael swallowed. "And how will I be able to face Swanhild, when I see her again, if I let her mother die alone?"

Silence was his only answer. Not even the sound of Tola drawing one last breath, for she'd released hers already.

Her dying words, her last wish…had been for Swanhild. He had to survive, to bring word to Swanhild of her mother's last moments, her love for her daughter. And he had to make her happy.

"Yes, Mistress Tola, I swear on my own life, I will," Raphael said. He was reluctant to leave her there, but there was nothing he could do for her now. Father Fazzio was the one who delivered last rites, and saw to it that bodies were buried in the churchyard.

So he legged it up to the church, where he met Tobias at the door.

"Where have you been?" Tobias hissed. "I told Father Fazzio you were coming, that you would never miss Ysabel's vigil, but now he's gone up to see Gojko to get you! Quick, get inside, so we can tell him you arrived just after he left."

Inside the church, where he could light a candle for Ysabel, and Tola, and maybe a couple for his parents, too. Because if the plague had truly come to Mirroten, like Tola said, then she was right that every prayer counted.

Raphael nodded and led the way inside.

Four

Swanhild could think of nothing but the rush of wind beneath her wings, buoying her up and away to…ah, that was her destination. Instinct had her angling down, toward a bevy of swans sitting on the shore. No, sleeping on the shore.

This was a safe place to sleep.

She landed roughly, suddenly aware of how much her arms…no, her wings ached. But here she could rest, because the other swans knew it would be safe.

She should stay here, with them, until she could return home.

Yes.

She settled on the damp sand, tucking her head under her wing.

Here it was safe for a swan like her to sleep.

If she'd been herself, Swanhild might have worried about Raphael, or her mother, or what the future would hold. But a swan saw no further than the next meal, and there was waterweed aplenty in the shallows, so the swan who was once Swanhild slept, as serene as the mirror-like lake that gave Mirroten its name.

But Mirroten was anything but serene.

Five

At the end of the vigil, when people started to slip out of the church, Father Fazzio stayed standing in front of the altar. He coughed, then said, "All the young people of Mirroten, I ask but a moment of your time. Children and youths and even adults who are not yet married. Boys and girls alike. I ask you to go home, pack a bag for a week's travel, and return here, within the hour. I have a quest, a most holy quest, for all of you. You have been

chosen to go on a crusade to save Mirroten —
but you must make haste! Quickly, now. Go
and pack a bag, then bring it right back here!"

He shooed them out of the church, his eyes
fever-bright with the sort of madness Raphael
had only seen in those near to death. When the
priest coughed again, Raphael was sure of it —
Tola had been right. The man was infected by
the plague.

Raphael drifted out of the church, his mind
awash with worry. He didn't surface until
someone seized his arm and yanked, hard,
bringing him face to face with Silvana, the girl
whose father owned the mill. She did not look
pleased.

Raphael held his hands up in surrender.
"Whatever it is, it wasn't me!"

She made a disgusted sound. "Of course
not, you fool. I'd let you go with all the other
sheep if I thought this was your doing. Unless
you've given the priest some potion that drove
him to this madness?"

Raphael shook his head. "Never! Mistress

Tola said he's infected with the plague."

Silvana swore. She turned to Tobias. "Did you know this?"

Now it was Tobias's turn to shake his head. "No, this is the first I have heard of it. Where can he have caught it?"

"Mistress Tola said Ysabel had it first, and it spread to her father…and to Father Fazzio."

Silvana's brow furrowed further. "Does Mistress Sara know? Someone must tell her."

Raphael did not consider himself a coward, but he knew he did not have the courage to bring bad news to Mistress Sara. "Tobias? She's your mum…"

Silvana shook her head. "I shall tell her. You two, go get your things, and get back to the church. Do what you can to keep the others away from Father Fazzio and his foolish crusade." She stabbed a finger at Raphael, "They will listen to you because you're the apprentice healer, and they'll listen to Tobias because he's Sara's son. Don't let him send anyone anywhere."

Raphael found himself nodding in agreement. Logically, he knew Silvana was younger than him, and he had no need to follow any order she gave, but something had changed in Silvana since her mother died. He couldn't quite define it, but something about her reminded him of Mistress Sara. Whatever it was, it spoke to something deep inside him that knew she wasn't a woman he should disobey.

So he headed home, to find Gojko had gone out, so there was no one to question him gathering his meagre belongings into a sack, which he then slung over his shoulder as he headed back to the church.

The benches where Mistress Sara and the other council members sat during mass had been moved aside, so only the stone floor came between Raphael and the altar where Father Fazzio stood. The children who'd already arrived – and yes, some of them were definitely children, for the youngest could not have been a day more than six years old –

stood huddled in the corner nearest the door, half hidden behind the holy water font.

Raphael waited a while before Tobias finally returned, with a frown upon his face and a bulging sack in each hand. When they were younger, Raphael might have taunted him for having so many things. Now, he was torn between bitterness and embarrassment that he'd even been tempted to say something so petty. Whatever Tobias had, he would gladly share, if Raphael had need of it, and if Raphael ever had anything worth sharing, he'd do the same for Tobias.

"What's wrong?" Raphael asked instead, when his friend's frown only deepened.

"I couldn't find Mother. She wasn't at home, and the fire had almost died out. It's not like her…"

Raphael shrugged. "Maybe she had to go help someone, right after the vigil, and she didn't have time to go home or mend the fire. It's not like we'll need it tonight, for it's still summer. Ah, so that's why Silvana said she'd tell her about Father Fazzio's crusade — perhaps she knew where your mother went, and she's gone to find her."

Tobias relaxed. "You're probably right. It's just…Mother worries so, and I hate to worry her if she returns and I'm not home. She – "

Father Fazzio coughed loudly, drawing all eyes to him. "Come closer, children. Elder Ahab has something to tell you."

Between his red eyes and pale face, or what little Raphael could see of it over the handkerchief clamped to his mouth and nose, Ahab looked very sick indeed.

"Come closer," Father Fazzio said again.

They only huddled closer to each other in the corner.

Raphael sighed and stepped forward, until he stood as far from Father Fazzio and Elder Ahab as Tola had allowed to him to stand before stopping him.

Would two yards be enough to save him from the plague?

The others seemed to think so, as they

clustered around him. Only Tobias stood at his side – everyone else stayed behind them.

"Elder Ahab?" Father Fazzio prompted.

Ahab coughed into his handkerchief before he spoke. "We have been blessed by the Lord, blessed as no other town has been. And if we are to thank Him properly for this blessing, it must be with grateful hearts that fully accept Him and all he offers us. He sent us a sinner whose soul is so heavy, it is a wonder he can walk beneath the weight of such evil.

"But we will see through his evil, and turn it into good! My Ysabel…poor, sweet, innocent Ysabel, who surely dwells with the angels now, died to save us from our sins, so that we might see the truth. That the sinner among us also will be our guide to salvation!"

Raphael struggled to keep a straight face. Ysabel, may God rest her soul, was not the second coming of Jesus, and the pied ratcatcher was hardly the devil. Mistress Sara would not have engaged his services if he was an evil man.

Perhaps this madness was a blessing, taking the minds of those with the plague so that they slipped into death unknowing, not fearing their fate…

"This assassin, this Zoticus, will be brought to see that only two choices lie before him. He can lead a crusade so that his sins, grievous though they are, will be forgiven, or he can be executed immediately, and his soul will go straight to hell.

"And you, the innocents of Mirroten, will go with him to remind him that it is not just himself he saves, but all of you, and the Holy Land itself!" Ahab flung his arms wide, gazing rapturously at the rafters, as if waiting for heaven to rain something down on him.

Tobias folded his arms across his chest. "I can't leave the village, let alone go all the way to the Holy Land. Mother will never allow it. And who would look after the goats, Uncle?"

Ahab stared at Tobias, a tear trickling from one red-rimmed eye. "I fear Sara has fallen under his evil spell already, but she will be made to see the truth. You must stay here until she does. You will be safe here in the church — the devil can't touch you here." He stared at them for a moment, then added, "You will all stay here, lest your families who have also fallen under his spell try to dissuade you from your calling. You will not leave this church until you depart on your most holy crusade!"

Raphael wet his lips. "Sure, Elder Ahab. We'll stay here and pray. Tobias and I will see to it. You should…go and rest. Father Fazzio, too. We will keep vigil." At least until no one was watching, and then they'd make good their escape.

"Such a good boy! Father Fazzio, is he not a good boy?" Ahab beamed.

Father Fazzio frowned. "I feared he might have been led astray by the carnal wiles of the witch girl, but perhaps you are right, and he is redeemable, after all. Yes, it is most fitting. You shall remain here, in prayer, until it is time to leave."

Raphael's blood boiled. The carnal wiles of

the witch girl? How dare the priest talk about his betrothed like that!

Tobias kicked him. "Thank you, Father. Get some rest. Raphael and I will watch tonight."

The priest and the elder exchanged a brief, muttered conversation that Raphael couldn't quite make out, until both men nodded.

"I've taught you well, Tobias. Now, it is your turn to lead everyone, for while the assassin will be your guide, everyone here looks to you. Do not disappoint me," Ahab said. He swept out of the side door of the church, followed by the priest.

Raphael didn't dare breathe until he heard the door close behind them both.

He turned to Tobias. "Right, wait until we're sure they've gone, and then you go peek outside to see if there's anyone who will see us sneak out."

Tobias nodded. "We can't go on a crusade. We'll go somewhere else instead."

The church doors slammed shut, followed by the ominous scrape of the heavy bar being dragged across the doors.

Little Bernard burst into tears. "They've locked us in!"

Tobias and Raphael checked all the doors, but the boy was right. They were locked in.

"What do we do now?" Tobias asked, keeping his voice low.

It didn't matter. Too many worried eyes were watching, ears straining to catch every word. In the absence of Mistress Sara and the rest of the Elder Council, they looked to Tobias to lead them. And when Tobias deferred to Raphael, as if being taller and older by a few years was enough to make him a wise leader…

Raphael managed a weak smile, as he might for a patient he did not dare tell they were dying. "We do what we said we'd do – we pray. Pray that we find a way out of this, and survive the plague."

Six

Honking and flapping and splashing. Danger. Swanhild woke in panic, her only desire to take flight. Yet with the other swans crowding around her, wings beating and ready to buffet her, there was no escape. She didn't understand. This drift of swans had tolerated her for as long as she could remember – why were they driving her out now?

Too close…too many…no space…she could scarcely move without hitting another bird. Could no longer open her wings because there were too many other bodies in the way.

She squirmed, trying to get out from under the writhing mass of feather encased flesh. Swanhild managed to make her way to the top of the pile, extended her wings, tensing to fly away, when it hit her. A weight that would not let her go.

The other swans panicked, attempting to escape from the weight, and she fell, her feet sinking into the muddy river bank.

A net. Hunters – one, two, three. Danger.

She recognised that much, but when she tried to bite her lip to activate her magic, she could not. No amount of biting drew blood from her beak, and try as she might, the magic would not work. If there was a way to escape, she could not find it – through magic or otherwise.

She opened her mouth to scream, but her despairing honk was only drowned out amid the cacophony from at least a dozen other birds who could not possibly understand what had befallen them.

To be saved from the plague, only to die to hunters? But swans were under the Queen's protection. They couldn't hunt her. This was treason.

Swanhild flapped and fought, not caring whether she hit hunter or swan, her intent only to break the net and free them all, until one of the hunters threw a blanket over the net, and darkness smothered her senses.

Seven

Raphael waited until most of the children had fallen asleep before he pulled Tobias aside. "Did any of what Elder Ahab and Father Fazzio said make sense to you?"

Tobias shook his head. "What I've heard about the last crusade was that it was a failure. Sending children to the Holy Land…it's madness, is what it is. I mean, if it was you, and me, and maybe some of the others who are almost men, maybe we could join someone else's crusade, but...even if everyone in Mirroten went, it would not be enough to fight an army. The last crusade was full of seasoned knights, and most of those never made it home!"

Through his mother, Mistress Sara, Tobias heard much news from the outside world. Raphael knew next to nothing about crusades, except that he never wanted to go on one. What use was an apothecary in battle?

"Mistress Tola said we should leave Mirroten. Go up to the mountains. Maybe even to the monastery," Raphael said. "To keep us safe from the plague."

Tobias made a rude noise. "You and me, monks? I don't think so. My mother would never let me. And you...aren't you going to marry Swanhild? When you ever find the courage to ask her, that is!" He gave Raphael a playful punch.

Raphael rubbed his arm. Tobias was stronger than he'd realised – neither of them were children any more. "She's already gone, because her mother told her to." He couldn't bring himself to tell Tobias that Tola had turned her into a swan. "If we don't follow after her, we might be too late, and catch the plague. It's here already, Tola said. Ysabel had it, and her father, and Father Fazzio, too. Maybe that's why he's gone crazy. Does plague addle your wits?"

Tobias shrugged. "How should I know? You're the healer. I herd goats. Now, if you ask me about the ailments a goat can catch, I can talk about them all day. Put you right to sleep, too."

"Maybe that's not a bad idea. Sleep, I mean, not goat stories. Father Fazzio will be back on the morrow, and we must not get too close to him, especially not if he has the plague. Perhaps we can distract him, while the others escape, and we can catch up."

Tobias nodded. "It's a long journey up to the monastery. It takes Gojko weeks, usually. We'll need plenty of rest, for we'll be carrying the younger ones by the end. We'll need pack animals, supplies for the journey…and what about when we get there? What's it like?"

It had been years since Raphael had visited the monastery with Gojko, but he doubted it had changed much. "They have just enough for their needs. No more. The lands belong to Mistress Sara, so that's all they are allowed to take. Sometimes they fast for holy days, so there's no food but what we bring for ourselves. I wouldn't even know how much food to take for us, let alone everyone…"

"Mother will know. When we go, we must take her. No one will go hungry with Mother in charge," Tobias said.

Raphael could not argue with that. Mistress Sara had arranged for his apprenticeship after his parents died, so he knew firsthand how she cared for those who had nothing and no one.

"In the morning," Raphael said. "In the meantime, we get some sleep, so we're ready to outfox Father Fazzio when he comes."

"Good night!" Tobias said.

Raphael replied in kind, but he knew sleep

would struggle to find him that night. His thoughts flew with Swanhild, wondering where she was, what she was doing, and whether she was thinking of him. Whether she'd come back.

She had to. They were betrothed. She had to come back and keep her promise. Or else…what had he left to live for?

They would share a thousand days like today. No, more. He would not let it be their last day together. He and Swanhild would marry, and Mirroten would one day be safe again. He just had to survive until that day.

Eight

Swanhild wasn't sure she wanted to open her eyes. Wherever she was, it smelled like a henhouse that had been ravaged by foxes – all feathers and fear, floating over the stench of sour sawdust.

"You have your money. Now go."

The ground swayed beneath Swanhild, like she was aboard a boat and not on solid ground at all. Soft bodies tumbled against hers, warm and limp in unconsciousness. Then she was falling, along with them, before the thud to earth knocked the breath from her.

Now she opened her eyes, to find herself in a stable of some sort, like the low-roofed lean-to shacks the poorer people of Mirroten used to house their goats at night.

An enormous man in rough clothing stood over her, holding a crate bigger than he was.

Swanhild tried to push herself to her feet, but her hands felt peculiarly powerless today. Somehow, she managed to stand upright, but she barely came up to the man's waist. She glared up at him, and tried to say, "I don't know what you think you are doing with me, but I swear you will regret it." But all that came out was an angry hiss.

She'd made her point, though – the man dropped the crate and seized a pitchfork, pointing the tines at her.

Someone laughed – a giant standing behind Pitchfork Peasant. "That one reminds me of your wife. Maybe she'll do for the Queen's dinner."

The man with the pitchfork advanced, driving Swanhild back. "No, she's half-starved. Better to pick a plump one for the Queen, and fatten the rest for later."

The second giant leaned down. "This one, I think." He lifted a limp, feathered body from the pile, his meaty hand clenched around the swan's neck. The bird began to awaken at his touch, its wings unfolding, but the man tucked it firmly under his arm, preventing its flight. He carried it outside. A moment later, Swanhild heard the thwack of an axe hitting wood.

Then the giant returned, holding the now headless bird by its feet, so that blood dripped from the severed neck onto the earth.

"Scatter some grain for them, then shut the door. The sooner we're done for the day, the sooner we can go to the kitchens for dinner," he said.

The pitchfork man did as he was bid, leaving Swanhild alone with the darkness, her only companions the swans that had begun to rouse at the prospect of food.

None of them seemed perturbed by the death of one of their number. Perhaps the birds were too simple minded to understand the danger they were in.

But Swanhild was not simple-minded. She had little appetite for grain, either, not if it meant fattening them to be feasted upon.

She settled in the darkest corner of the tiny stable, the furthest place from the door, desperately praying she would escape before the same dark fate befell her.

Nine

Only eleven swans remained, oblivious to their impending doom as they gobbled up the grain on the ground. She'd tried to tell the others the dangers they faced, but the language of swans was much simpler than that of humans, and her loud honks had only conveyed that there was danger, not the how or why or even what it might be. She'd flown into a rage then, honking and flapping at them to drive them away from the food, but the foolish birds had then decided she was the danger, to be driven off with beaks and wing buffets until she took refuge in her dark corner, stinging in so many places from the feathers she'd lost in the altercation.

Well, if the stubborn birds attacked the only person who wanted to save them, perhaps they deserved to die. But Swanhild was determined to live, so that she might return home, where Raphael waited.

Several days ago, Swanhild had given in to her hunger pangs and eaten sparingly, so while the stupid birds gorged themselves, she alone heard the approaching footsteps. Swanhild tucked herself into the corner behind the door.

It had to be the butcher, coming to kill another bird for the kitchen. He always came after the birds had been given their evening meal, standing in the doorway as he decided which bird he wanted, before swooping in to seize his hapless victim. He'd shut the door behind him, but it was not thick enough to stop Swanhild from hearing the bird's last, panicked moments, before the thwack of the axe ended the poor creature's suffering.

She had planned this for days, but some instinct told her this was the moment she would put her plan into action. Her instincts had never been wrong in the past, and she had to trust them now, for they were all she had.

The door swung open, and a shadow blocked the afternoon light.

Swanhild crouched even lower, willing him not to notice her, as one of the other birds unknowingly enjoyed its last meal. They might not have the wits to save themselves, but their sacrifice today might save her life.

The butcher made his choice, a swan so greedy it had flopped down in the middle of the grain, eating everything within reach of its long neck. He stepped inside the stable and reached down to collect his prey.

Swanhild saw her chance, and darted for the door. She exploded into sunlight, blinded, but she didn't stop. She had only to run and flap her wings fast enough, and she'd be free.

Faster, faster, she'd never flapped so hard in her life, but desperation drove her. She had to fly, had to fly…Her wings caught the breeze and she nearly cried as her feet left the ground. Higher, higher…

She collided with something that said, "Oof!" as her wings wrapped around the unexpected obstacle. Together, they fell, with most of Swanhild on top, but one of her wings trapped underneath whoever she'd hit.

She squirmed and honked and struggled to get free, but then an arm wrapped around her. "You will do nicely," a female voice said.

Then Swanhild's head was enveloped in a cloud of sweet-smelling dust. She sneezed – once, twice, three times – but still those arms held her fast.

"No. Must…get…free…" Swanhild swore she was the one speaking, but it wasn't her voice saying the words. How…

But darkness lurked amid the dust, stealing Swanhild's senses and her hard-won freedom in one swoop.

Ten

Scraping and swearing roused Raphael from a weary doze. Tobias, the lucky bastard, was still snoring, though most of the others were on their way to awake.

Raphael gave Tobias a shake. "On your feet. They're coming, and we need to be ready."

"Ready for what?" one of the younger girls asked. In the dim light, Raphael couldn't be sure who she was.

"Tobias and I will distract them. When I

give the signal," Raphael demonstrated, "I want you to sneak out behind them, and get as far from the church as you can. Get to the mill, hide in the cellar there if you can. Wait for Silvana, or one of us, before you show yourselves. We'll take you somewhere safe, or Silvana will."

Most of them nodded.

"What if Mistress Sara comes?" the little girl with the questions persisted.

Raphael and Tobias exchanged a glance. Tobias's mother was a law unto herself.

This time Tobias answered, "Then you do whatever Mistress Sara says. Like you would any other day. Mistress Sara will keep us safe."

Raphael dearly wanted to believe it. Mistress Sara would do anything to keep the people of Mirroten safe. How, then, had the plague managed to arrive, despite her best efforts to prevent it?

The church doors flew open, and sunlight streamed in, haloing a lone man.

Raphael stood and squinted at the

silhouette. He didn't look like Ahab or Father Fazzio.

"That's not Mum," Tobias whispered, sounding disappointed.

The man moved, and Raphael glimpsed his face.

"It's Master Zoticus, the assassin," Raphael hissed. "Stay as far from him as you can. Don't move unless we give the signal. Until then, stay behind us."

Tobias swallowed, then looked at Raphael. Together, they stepped forward, neither wanting to break the silence.

Finally, Tobias said, "You may tell Elder Ahab that our vigil has not changed our resolve. We will not go with you on a crusade to the Holy Land."

Raphael hoped the assassin couldn't hear the quiver in Tobias's voice.

"Good," Zoticus said. "Because one crusade is more than enough for any man. I'll not be going on another. Anyone with any sense will not be heading for the Holy Land, but in the opposite direction. Up into the mountains, maybe, until the plague has passed."

Wait…what?

Raphael glanced at Tobias, who was too busy frowning at Zoticus to notice.

"You mean on a pilgrimage, to see some holy relics?" Tobias asked.

"Like the Cloister of the Holy Innocents? To see the jewel encrusted skeletons?" Raphael blurted out.

Now Tobias looked at him. "You've been there?" Naked envy coloured his tone.

Of course, that only made Raphael uncomfortable. Tobias was the one with everything, while Raphael was just an orphaned apprentice. That he could possibly have done something that inspired jealousy in Tobias, of all people… "Master Gojko journeys there once a year to trade herbs. They have some rather unusual ones that only grow high in the mountains, and because the Rialto traders can't go any further up the river, he buys extra to take to the Cloister. I used to go with him when I was younger, but now he leaves me to tend the shop while he's gone."

There. That should explain why Raphael had never mentioned it to his friend. Something so long ago, barely half remembered, hadn't been important enough to talk about until now.

"Could you take us there?" Zoticus asked, his gaze almost painfully sharp as he directed it at Raphael.

Raphael stared at his feet, wishing he'd paid better attention. "Maybe. Once you're on the right road, it's hard to get lost." Actually, the monastery would be the perfect place to flee to – far and fast, like Tola had said. "Why? Who's going to the monastery? It'll be autumn soon, and the high passes won't be open much longer. One decent snowfall and you're stuck there until spring." And safe from the plague, though not from assassins. Surely Zoticus had no intention of hiding in a monastery, though. Did they even allow assassins in such a holy place?

Zoticus didn't seem worried. "We all are, if we want to survive this plague."

So the assassin would be coming. Raphael didn't see how he could stop him, so he would have to resign himself to the man's presence.

But Tobias ruffled up like an angry rooster. "Why should we go anywhere with you? This is our town. We're not rats, to be driven out and drowned."

The assassin winced.

Ha, he was human enough to be hit by that barb, at least.

Then his eyes became steely again. "Because Lady Sara told me to take you."

Lady Sara?

Raphael met Tobias's eyes. No, he hadn't missed the title, either. That meant Zoticus knew Sara owned Mirroten, but was not familiar enough with her to know to drop the title. Maybe this was his mistaken way of trying to curry favour with her. Assassin or not, he'd seen how the man behaved toward her in the council meeting. He'd entered her service willingly, even if he wasn't entirely happy with her current orders.

Tobias lifted his hand to make the signal to the others, his eyes asking the question of Raphael.

But Raphael shook his head. All that Zoticus had said made sense, and it would be wiser to work with him than disobey Tobias's mother. If he was wrong… "You take it up with her. I wouldn't dare argue with Mistress Sara," Raphael said.

Tobias was reluctant, but finally he nodded. "I'd better get the goats. I'll never hear the end of it if I leave them behind." He dashed off.

The assassin stared after him. "Do you think he'll come back?"

Raphael couldn't suppress a grin. "Of course. Tobias said he was going to get the goats. It might take a while to get them all moving, but even he knows better than to cross his mum." And that should be warning enough to tell Zoticus that he shouldn't cross Mistress Sara, either.

The assassin nodded, as if he'd gotten the message. "Take everyone here down the road to the first traveller's camp to wait for me. We'll meet you there, with or without the goats," Zoticus said. He strode off after Tobias.

The others looked at Raphael. Somehow, he'd been left in charge.

"Right, gather your things. Don't leave anything behind, because it might be a while before we can come back. We're going on a pilgrimage," Raphael said. He hoped he managed to sound more excited than he felt. Because if any of the others knew about the emptiness inside him now Swanhild was gone…they wouldn't follow him anywhere.

Eleven

"No, you must lift the bread to your mouth, not bring your face down to the food!" The smack of flesh hitting flesh, before a yowling wail filled the air. "You will not eat unless you do it properly, or the King will know. No!"

Something felt wrong, Swanhild was sure of it, though she did not know what. She rested on softness, not the earth of that tiny stable or even her straw mattress at home. Only Mistress Sara had such a mattress, filled with feathers instead of straw. But the voice she heard did not belong to Mistress Sara, or anyone else Swanhild knew.

"You must learn, or you will not eat at all!" Another slap, followed by a longer wail.

Swanhild doubted Mistress Sara had ever struck anyone in her life. And she would give anyone in Mirroten the food from her own plate, rather than let them go hungry.

Even the thought of bread set Swanhild's stomach grumbling. Too long, she'd subsisted on the smallest specks of grain. If there was bread about, she was too hungry to resist.

She rose. Stone walls surrounded her on all sides, with the floor and ceiling made of the same grey stone. Beds were lined up against the wall behind her, with the rest of the room empty but for a table with benches on either side. Blank faced children sat along the benches, tears dripping from reddened eyes, as a long-necked woman towered over them from the head of the table, her arms folded across her chest, her glare enough to wither the smile off anyone's face.

Not that Swanhild had smiling in mind. Her sole desire was escape. While the woman was occupied with her children, perhaps Swanhild could reach the door and…

An arm wrapped around Swanhild, yanking her back. "And where do you think you're going?" the mother asked.

Swanhild was no child – not any more. She'd be a mother herself, soon after she and Raphael married. So she turned and returned the woman's glare. "I am going home. I do not belong here." Then she reached for the door.

Swanhild's hand stretched out – a real hand, not a wing – and surprise froze her for a moment. The moment was long enough for the woman to seize her by the ear and drag her over to the children's table, where she was forced to sit on the end of the bench.

"This is your home now, and you belong with me. You are my daughter, and you will behave properly – you all will! – or I shall find other swans that deserve to be princesses, and you shall be killed for the table, as you deserve."

The children wept and wailed, but Swanhild remained stony. This woman surely had to be the Queen, but if she was, the Queen had taken leave of her senses. "How could we possibly be your children?"

The Queen slammed both hands on the table. "I brought my true children here, to the King's hunting lodge, to keep them safe from the plague ravaging the countryside. Their stupid nurse, may the devil scourge her for eternity, permitted them to play on the beach by the lake, where infected rats had washed up. Having seen the priest burying bodies in the churchyard, they played at funerals themselves, burying the plague rats like common gravediggers. One by one, they sickened and died, followed by their fool of a nurse. I bore the King fifteen children, and I've outlived them all. Well, I will not bear him any more, nor will I be executed for treason, which he will surely do if he finds out what happened.

You will all be his children, or some other swans will take your place. You will behave as befits royalty, and you will live in luxury, or you shall die."

The Queen had gone mad with grief, Swanhild decided, but that didn't make her any less dangerous. A woman who had lost everything feared no consequences any more.

Swanhild wanted to ask a hundred, nay, a thousand questions, but the Queen's brittle composure threatened to crack at any moment.

"You will eat your dinner, and you will sleep. I shall see you in the morning," the Queen said, sweeping out of the room.

Swanhild heard the clunk of her barring the door on her way out. Her gaze swept the room, landing on a bronze mirror she hadn't noticed before. A mirror that showed a reflection very unlike her own, yet it moved as she did. She'd gone from her full grown self to a slip of a girl, budding breasts only just beginning to poke at the front of her gown. Only her eyes gave her away, for they weren't filled with the blank despair the other children shared. No, her eyes held dark foreboding, because every moment she stayed in this form, she committed treason with each and every breath. Pretending to be a noble, let alone a princess, was punishable by…actually, she wasn't sure what happened to them. It had to be bad, though, for no one dared do so.

Until now.

Then again, was it not treason to disobey the Queen, too?

Swanhild slumped in her seat and reached for the bread. She ate without tasting it, praying that she would survive the Queen's subterfuge, long enough to escape and return home to Raphael.

All the swan princesses' eyes turned to her, watching as she ate. Then, almost as one, they took some bread and joined her in her meal.

Twelve

The Cloister of the Holy Innocents soared high above them, a castle that might be impregnable if it closed its gates. But just like in Raphael's memory, the gates stood wide open, ready to welcome travellers and pilgrims alike. He remembered the place a-bustle with monks in their robes, doing whatever chores they'd been assigned for the day.

But now…he saw no one.

Someone shouted for a healer, and Raphael

turned to offer his assistance, only to be forced aside as Master Zoticus, still shouting, bulled past him into the great hall, carrying someone.

Raphael headed toward the herb gardens, and the back door to the kitchen, where he knew the still room was located. If there was a healer here, that's where he'd find them.

He found the still room well stocked, but empty of anyone but himself. From the dust on the workbenches, it looked like they'd left some weeks ago, and not returned.

"Raphael! There you are. You must come to the great hall at once. Master Zoticus wants you." Silvana beckoned.

"Master Zoticus the assassin wants me? But I'm just an apprentice apothecary. He can't possibly…" Raphael began.

"He wants a healer, and you're the best we've got. Come on!"

A good healer didn't go in blind. Perhaps some of the herbs in here could help. "What's the matter? Who's injured?"

Silvana swallowed, looking pale. "It's

Mistress Sara. She's coughing a lot, and Master Zoticus just put her to bed in the best bedchamber. Come with me, I'll show you."

Raphael's mind went blank. Not Mistress Sara. They couldn't lose Mistress Sara! He hurried to catch up with Silvana.

The best bedchamber was larger than his parents' house had been, with a massive bed that held Mistress Sara.

The assassin stood beside her, his expression full of dark shadows.

"I've brought Raphael." Silvana shoved him forward. She said something about dinner and departed, leaving him alone with the assassin and Mistress Sara, who looked weaker than he'd ever seen her.

He swallowed. If he was indeed the best healer they had, he'd do everything in his power to help her. They were lost without Mistress Sara.

"I found the stillroom. There are many herbs hung up there, most of which I recognise, and shelves full of jars that could contain anything. It will take some time, but within a few days, I should be able to make something to help Mistress Sara. What would be best for her cough is oil of rue, but that will take weeks..." He'd set to work straight away. The sooner he started, the sooner he would have what he needed. Unless he was very lucky and there was some in the still room already...but he'd have to search the place thoroughly if he had any hope of finding it.

The assassin pulled out a bottle that looked like it had come from Tola's shop. Yes, the label was written in Swanhild's own hand. He held the bottle over Mistress Sara's lips for the briefest moment, before corking it.

For one dreadful moment, Raphael wondered if he'd just witnessed the assassin poisoning Mistress Sara, and whether he'd be next.

But Swanhild would never have sold poison to an assassin. Something dangerous, perhaps, but he'd only given Mistress Sara the tiniest amount, as if he knew what dose to use safely.

Was the assassin a herbalism student, too?

The assassin — nay, Master Zoticus, for the man had a name and he'd best get used to using it, if they were to live in the same castle for some time — Master Zoticus stared at him for a moment, as if wondering why he was still there.

Raphael wondered the same thing. His stare was more than a little intimidating.

"Do what you can," Zoticus said, tapping the bottle. "I have enough oil of rue to do for some days yet."

Raphael nodded. "I'll see what I can find in the stillroom, and distil some more, as soon as I can."

He hurried back to the stillroom. If Mistress Sara's life depended on his skills, he'd best take a full inventory of the stillroom by nightfall, before the contents of Swanhild's bottle were gone.

He sighed, wishing with all his being that Swanhild was here beside him. No one brewed potions as skilfully as she did — it was her they wanted, not him. But she was far away, likely flying through the air or drifting across a lake, safe with not a care in the world.

Thirteen

"You are a princess, not an animal! Lift the cup to your lips to drink!" the Queen scolded, cuffing the child so hard, the girl's nose went into her drink and she inhaled some of it. Coughing and spluttering, she overturned the cup, and soon all of them were splashed with water. Not to mention the nearly untouched food on the table.

"What is wrong with all of you? Why are you not eating? This is a feast fit for the King

— how can you not eat it? The servants are starting to say how strange you are. If they suspect..." the Queen continued, shaking her finger at them all.

Swanhild shook her head. If she, a human turned into a swan, had trouble understanding the Queen's constantly changing demands, what hope did these ordinary birds have? No wonder they would not eat or drink, if they were to be beaten for doing so. Beating children was bad enough. To beat innocent birds…birds who were supposed to be under her protection…

Swanhild snapped. She jumped to her feet. "Would you eat, if you were confined to this chamber instead of soaring through the skies, or drifting through the cool waters of a lake, catching your own meal?"

The Queen squinted irritably at her. "I've told you many times. If you cannot behave, I will find other, more pliable..."

"No, you won't," Swanhild said. "We're wild birds, used to being free. To be kept within these walls will kill us, and every other creature you transform into copies of your children. You must see this is foolish. You must set us free. Free to fly again, and feed as swans do!"

Not that she wanted waterweed, for she was growing quite partial to the cakes the Queen commanded the kitchen castle to make for her children. But the other birds were growing painfully thin...

"If you could fly, would you want to be confined so?" Swanhild persisted. She sensed a change in the Queen's demeanour, a slight slump of her shoulders, but the Queen's mood was as changeable as the wind, so it might mean nothing. Or it might mean she'd find herself as the target for the Queen's wrath. So be it. At least she could defend herself, unlike the others.

"No. I can not fly again, but if I could...and even though I can't, I still...these walls..." The Queen's eyes shimmered, with what looked like tears. "Very well. When night falls, meet me at the top of the tower. All of you. If you are good, and eat your dinner, then perhaps I shall permit you to fly again."

With a swish of her skirts, she left the room, closing the door behind her. Before Swanhild could reply, she heard the scrape of the key in the lock, and the Queen was gone.

Swanhild slumped into her seat. The others just stared listlessly at the table, as if they had not understood the exchange. Perhaps they hadn't.

"Here," she said, reaching for some bread. "Hurry and eat before she comes back. Never mind how, just make sure the food is all gone. It's the only way for any hope of getting free."

Swanhild wanted to believe it, but by the time the Queen returned, she might have forgotten her promise, or the sight of them might make her lash out again. Still, she had to hold onto hope. She had to get home to Mirroten. To Raphael.

Fourteen

Raphael stood on the threshold of Mistress Sara's chamber, clutching the vials so tightly it was a wonder they didn't break, but he didn't dare enter.

Something about the way Master Zoticus leaned over Mistress Sara, his eyes closed but such an intent expression on his face, screamed that the assassin was using magic. Not that Raphael could sense the stuff the way Swanhild could, but he'd seen the look on her face when she fell into one of her finding trances, as she sent magic out searching for what she wanted.

Raphael had never heard of a male witch before. Like Swanhild and her mother, he'd only known witches who were women. But there was no mistaking the fact that Master Zoticus was using some sort of spell on Mistress Sara. Whether for good or evil, though…

If he was doing her ill, Raphael should interrupt him, and stop him if he could. But if he was casting some sort of healing spell, something that would help Mistress Sara, the slightest distraction might make the spell go awry, and Raphael would never forgive himself if Mistress Sara took injury because of him. And yet…

He wished Swanhild were here. She'd use her magic and search the assassin for evil intent, and know whether he was Sara's friend or her foe. After the council meeting, Swanhild had insisted they should trust Zoticus, for he meant them no harm, she'd said. She'd even sold him some of her oil of rue, when she knew just how much they'd need every drop over winter.

If she were here now, Swanhild would still say the same thing – to trust the assassin.

So Raphael forced himself to stand in the doorway and watch, as his master Gojko had commanded him to do when entering any sickroom.

Zoticus had his hand pressed against Sara's throat, but lightly, as though taking her pulse. If he'd meant to do her harm, that hand looked strong enough to strangle her, but he did not. He would not, for the way his other hand clasped hers spoke of affection, tender feeling, like a man might show for his unwell wife, as he worried for her wellbeing while the healer made his assessment.

Wait…Mistress Sara and Master Zoticus, a match? No, surely not! Mistress Sara was too old for such things, with her son Tobias nearly a man grown. She and the assassin might be friends, but to imagine Mistress Sara sneaking off into the forest with him, like Raphael did with Swanhild, well, the thought was simply absurd.

An unexpected chill made him shiver and look up to find the assassin's eyes on him. Cold and calculating, as though he could read Raphael's thoughts and did not approve of them. Most of the adults in Mirroten would have disapproved of what he and Swanhild did, but it wasn't his fault they weren't married yet. He'd have made her his wife years ago, if she'd only agreed back then.

"What is it, boy?" Master Zoticus asked.

Raphael held out the vials with a shaking hand, hoping they would be shield enough to protect him from the assassin's wrath. "I found some oil of rue in the stillroom. I do not know how well made or even how old it is, so I would advise caution, only a drop at a time. While you have the stuff Swanhild made, I would use that. In the meantime, I shall make some more, if you wish it, of course."

Zoticus nodded slowly. "How much longer did you have on your apprenticeship?"

"I had hoped...and my master said...that I would be good enough to become a master by year's end. The sooner the better, for I am betrothed to be wed, and Swanhild will not marry me while I am a mere apprentice. Or, at least, she won't...if..." Raphael trailed off, not wanting to finish.

"You're betrothed to the witch girl? I have not seen her since we left Mirroten. Where is she?"

Raphael swallowed. A man who could use magic and maybe even read minds would want nothing less than the truth, however strange it sounded. So, Raphael told him how Tola had turned Swanhild into a swan.

"And what of the mother?"

These words came even harder still. "Dead. She bled out from casting the spell on Swanhild. I tried but she would not let me help her. She said she was already infected with the plague."

Master Zoticus nodded. "A great pity, which will grieve Lady Sara. Does anyone else know about Tola and Swanhild?"

Raphael shook his head.

"Then I must ask you not to tell anyone. We managed to save few enough from Mirroten, and I'm sure all of them left someone behind whose fate they fear, but do not know. Faced with the certainty that their witch is dead, and likely others with her, may be more than they can withstand. Let their fate remain a mystery, until it is safe to return to Mirroten."

Raphael did not want to agree. He rarely kept secrets from Tobias, or Silvana, and to be forced to hold this weight of grief inside, it was like his parents dying all over again, and it was only a matter of time before he ran away into the woods to give way to that grief, just as he had then. This time, though, there would be no Swanhild to come and find him, and without her, it was hard enough to see a way forward...

"You're needed here. You're the only healer they have. Well, the only one they trust, at any rate. I probably know more than you, but they know and trust you, more than they will ever trust me. With Lady Sara ill, it will be up to you, and Tobias and Silvana, to take charge of this place. To see in the last of the harvest, and ensure enough is stored to last everyone through the winter. I need you, to mix up whatever potions Lady Sara requires to bring her back to full health. Her recovery will take time, for she is not young any more."

"But I'm only an apprentice." Nowhere near skilled enough to save Mistress Sara or anyone else from the plague. "And no healer can save someone from the plague."

"Lady Sara does not carry the plague. It's an inflammation of the lungs that ails her. An affliction I can heal, but only with your help. Potions, herbs, poultices…will you make them exactly as I instruct you to, which whatever ingredients you can find? If you will help me nurse Lady Sara back to health, I will proclaim to anyone who will listen that you are no longer an apprentice but a master of your craft.

An apothecary in your own right, ready to set up your own shop and support your own family, when your swan girl returns. And she will, for birds are peculiarly immune to this plague. She will return, but not before it is safe for all of us to return to Mirroten again, and when she does, she will be looking for you. Will you be there when she does?"

It was Tola's dying wish, but Raphael could not deny that there was no future for him without Swanhild. She was everything to him, and he would do anything to ensure that they would meet again, and be wed, like she'd promised.

"Yes, Master Zoticus, I will do as you ask. Unless…unless Mistress Sara commands me to do otherwise. I can't disobey Mistress Sara."

To Raphael's surprise, the assassin laughed, and as he did, he became just a man, not some terrifying monster who might end his life in an instant. The man Swanhild had seen, and likely Mistress Sara, too, for Sara usually knew people better than they knew themselves.

"Yes, we would be fools indeed to even consider disobeying Lady Sara. A formidable woman indeed. The world would be a better place with more like her, but I fear she is unique. A woman to be treasured, as she deserves."

For a moment, Raphael thought he saw the same look in Zoticus's eyes that he felt in his own, when he gazed at Swanhild, before it was gone, so quickly he must have imagined it. He must have, for Master Zoticus was too old to fall in love with Mistress Sara.

"Is there anything else you would like me to bring you from the stillroom, Master Zoticus?" Raphael asked.

"Perhaps an infusion to help Lady Sara breathe. Something that will strengthen her, too," Zoticus said.

Raphael bowed, and headed back down to the stillroom to do his master's bidding.

Fifteen

Swanhild followed the Queen to the top of the tower, hearing the shuffle of the other swans' footsteps on the stairs below her. She wished she hadn't eaten so much, but if she was to escape tonight, best that she go with a full belly, for it wasn't as though swans could carry packs when they flew.

A chest sat in the shadows of the battlements, which the Queen knelt to unlock, before throwing the lid open to reveal…feathers.

No, not just feathers, Swanhild realised as the Queen lifted the first layer up high, but feathered cloaks, so artfully fashioned that when the Queen gave it a shake, it flared out and looked like wings in flight.

Surely she couldn't mean for them to don these cloaks and actually fly…

"My godmother fashioned these for me, each a little larger as I grew, until I reached the height I am now. They are all imbued with magic, transforming the wearer into a swan for as long as the full moon is in the sky. But should sunlight touch even a single feather, the entire cloak will erupt into flame, burning the wearer and sending them plummeting to earth and a painful death." The Queen gave the cloak one last shake, before sweeping it around the shoulders of the smallest swan child. She fastened the bone button at the child's throat, then stepped back. "There!"

There, indeed. The cloaked child flapped her arms, once, twice, three times, and they were no longer arms but wings, her neck stretching, stretching, as before Swanhild's eyes, the child turned back into a swan.

Swanhild wanted to weep. The bird looked so pathetically grateful to be herself again, but it was only for a night. By dawn tomorrow, they'd all be back to being children again, at the mercy of the mad Queen.

But for one night…she might go home to Mirroten, and at least see Raphael again.

"Wearing one of these cloaks, you may fly where you wish while the moon is in the sky, but you must return here to this tower before dawn, or you will die a fiery death. Do you understand?" the Queen said.

Swanhild nodded, and the others did, too.

"And when you return, you will be good little children, and make King Bela believe you are truly his daughters. If you behave yourselves, I will allow you to fly on the night of the next full moon, just like tonight, but only if you can convince the King. Can you do that?"

Swanhild doubted it. Anyone with eyes to see would surely notice that there was something odd about these children who did not speak or behave like anything but scared savages. And yet…if they did not agree, the others would surely die, and she would never see Raphael again…

"Yes, Your Majesty," Swanhild said.

"Yes, Mother," the Queen corrected.

Swanhild swallowed. If this was the Queen's price…so be it. "Yes, Mother."

She helped the Queen dress the others, until only she remained, with the largest cloak of them all. It was too big for Swanhild, for the Queen was far stouter than she, but she threw it about her shoulders anyway, fastening the clasp with feverish fingers.

Swanhild closed her eyes and stretched her arms out. She took a deep breath, flapped her arms once, twice, then lifted them a third time…

Tingling began in her fingers, spreading up her arms, before moving across her whole body. Lightness invaded her very bones, until she felt she might float away. This was nothing like her mother's spell, that first time, filled with shifting and strangeness and pressure. No, this was…magical, like stepping into a forest clearing and suddenly being enveloped in a shaft of sunlight, and the whole world seemed to effervesce like a complicated potion made just right.

Swanhild felt as if she could simply step off the top of the tower and float all the way down, feather light. She could. She would…

Almost without thought, she stepped up onto the battlements, arching her shoulders to spread her wings as wide as the crenelations would allow. The world…nay, the very universe demanded that she fly.

An updraft rising from the sun-warmed courtyard below beckoned, and Swanhild could not resist. She leaned forward and stretched out her wings.

The wind lifted her, like she weighed nothing more than a feather, and she floated for a moment before another updraft sent her higher still. With a cry of triumph, Swanhild soared, circling the tower far below.

From up here, she could see the shining expanse of the lake, with the moon's reflection laying out a path home to Mirroten. While the other swans spiralled upward toward her, Swanhild flapped her wings and arrowed toward the water.

She heard the others land in the lake behind her, in the shallows where the forest grew right down to the water's edge, and the waterweed was thickest. That would keep them occupied, while she headed for Mirroten.

Swanhild glided down in the lee of the dock, hoping the shadows would hide her from anyone watching the water. Swans might be under the Queen's dubious protection, but some of the boys in the village would happily chase and torment anything smaller or weaker than themselves, and not even a few strong wing buffets would deter those little brutes from their sport.

She waded ashore at the spot where Mercurio had set up his stall. Only scant days could have passed since he'd packed up and left, for she could still see the circles in the sand from the casks he'd used to prop up his counter. Either that or she'd been a swan so long that he'd had time to travel to Rialto and return.

It mattered not, she decided, as she strode across the sand to the grassy bank above. No one moved in the streets, and the nearby houses were dark. Was it so late in the evening? It could not be midnight yet. Or perhaps everyone was in the church, or the council hall…

Hope died a little when she reached the church, and a little more by the time she arrived at the darkened council hall. Everyone in the town was simply gone. Or dead from the plague…

No. Swanhild couldn't bear to even think it. She took flight across the lake, rousing the other swans from their post-supper roost and into the air alongside her, to fly back to the Queen and her tower.

Sixteen

"Tobias has asked me to take over Mistress Sara's care," Raphael found himself saying, the moment Master Zoticus stepped into the stillroom.

Zoticus did not look surprised, or even miffed that Raphael hadn't waited for him to ask. "Yes, he said as much to me. Locking the door to Lady Sara's chamber and placing his own body across the threshold every night is unnecessary, though. He is your friend.

Perhaps you should speak to him about it, and try to dissuade him?"

He already had, but Tobias wouldn't listen. He was so worried the assassin might hurt his mother, he was blind to what was really going on between them. Now Mistress Sara was awake, she'd made it perfectly clear that she had no problem allowing the assassin in her bedchamber.

So he'd gone to a greater power for help. "Silvana will do a better job, I think. She came asking for some special herbs, the sort girls use to prevent pregnancy, this morning. She said they were for someone else, but when I tried to tell her how much to use and when, she brushed me off, as though she knew what she was doing. She can't have been with anyone but Tobias, and she wouldn't...not outside Mistress Sara's door..."

Zoticus grinned. "Good man. Seeing as you're in the habit of making wise decisions today, I'm going to ask you to make another one. Given the improvement in Lady Sara's health, do feel that you could take on the responsibility Tobias has asked of you?"

Raphael's jaw dropped. "You mean…be Mistress Sara's healer, not just an apprentice? But you…"

"I believe you can do it, and your friend is struggling to step up and lead the people of Mirroten, as he must while his mother is still ill. If he no longer needs to worry about whether she will recover, it will set his mind at ease enough to focus on what is important – his real responsibilities. So, what do you say? Are you enough of an apothecary to do what is necessary?"

"I guess so…but if something were to go wrong, and Mistress Sara were to grow sicker instead of better…" He'd never forgive himself for failing her.

"Worry not, for I will be watching."

Raphael almost laughed with relief. A scant few weeks ago, such words from the assassin would have made him worry more than ever, but he thought he knew Master Zoticus well enough now to be sure the man was always watching. Watching like an eagle from its eyrie, scanning the landscape for suitable prey, but otherwise unruffled until its quarry caught its attention. Who his quarry was, Raphael could not be certain, but he was sure it was not himself, or Mistress Sara, or any of the people who'd come from Mirroten.

"Thank you," Raphael said.

"No, thank you. Lady Sara is much improved, and both she and I owe you our thanks for your skills in the stillroom. It takes a master to know one herb from another, how to prepare them, and to make sure the dose is right. When you return to Mirroten, and you wed your swan girl, you will have no problem supporting what I'm sure will be a large family with your burgeoning apothecary business."

A large family with Swanhild? Oh, he hadn't even dared hope…but…

"Do you think it will be safe to return soon?" Raphael asked eagerly.

Zoticus shook his head. "I am no expert,

but the witch was, and she said it might be years before it will be safe in Mirroten once more. We will not know until the monks return to the monastery. And when they do, you will be the first person I send to Mirroten, to see what you have left to go back to."

Swanhild, or so he hoped. He didn't dare think otherwise. She had to be there when he returned, or he had nothing left to hope for.

The next morning, as the other swan children dozed fitfully in the carriage on their way to court, Swanhild bitterly regretted her cowardice. She should have checked inside the houses. She might have been in the form of a swan, but that didn't make her any less of a healer, and if people were ill inside, she might have been able to help. Or…something. At least she would have known whether Raphael was alive or dead. Or Mother. Or if they were all simply gone somewhere safer.

She could think of nothing else as the Queen settled them into the royal nursery, where Swanhild had her hands full trying to train the other swan children to at least behave like children. They never spoke, but they seemed to understand her, though how, she did not know. Servants came and went, bringing food and clothes, or taking away laundry and dirty dishes, laying fires and sweeping away ashes. They didn't seem to mind the swan children ignoring them, which Swanhild found hard to believe. When she'd pointedly thanked one of the maids for clearing away after a meal, the girl had ducked her head, refusing to meet Swanhild's eyes, as she bobbed a curtsy before fleeing the room.

Perhaps it wasn't the swan princesses the maids feared, but the Queen, whose chambers occupied the lower levels of the tower that also held the nursery. A nursery that had become as much a prison as their chamber in the King's hunting lodge.

Swanhild lost count of the days, for they all blurred into one another, locked within stone walls, as they were. It felt like months before the Queen brought out her chest of feathered cloaks and summoned them to the top of this new tower.

But when Swanhild stepped out onto the battlements, her breath caught in her throat. This castle sat atop a mountain, topped by towers that soared up into the very clouds. She could see the whole valley below, the town spread out on both sides like the most marvellous children's toy, all the way to a line of mountain sentinels, armoured in stone and snow.

Home was on the other side of those mountains, she knew with a certainty that resonated deep down in her bones. Raphael lay in that direction, too, though whether he lived or not, she could not say. This time, if the Queen permitted her to fly, she would spend the night scouring all the houses in Mirroten, to see if Raphael or anyone else could be found.

Swanhild scarcely felt the wintry breeze as she arrowed over the mountains, toward the lake. Snow lay on the ground here, as smooth and untouched as though it was freshly fallen, though the icicles hanging from the eaves told a different story. The snow was untouched because no one had walked on it, for there was no one left to do so.

Still, she resolved not to waste what time she had in Mirroten. It took her some time to work out how to use her wings and beak to nudge open the door to her mother's house, but once she was in, the others were easier. There was no sign of Mother, and the other houses along the road were just as empty, all the way down to the mill. That's as far as she managed to get on that first night – it wasn't until spring had taken the town firmly in her grasp that Swanhild reached the final house in town she intended to check – the great house where Mistress Sara lived with her son, Tobias.

Like all the others, the house stood empty,

but it was the barn that drew Swanhild's attention the most. The two carts Sara usually kept there were gone, along with all her horses and their entire herd of goats. What a fool she'd been, checking all the houses instead of the barns...if the goats were all gone, they must have left with the people who owned them, or at least Tobias.

Swanhild wanted to laugh, but the only sound that came out of her beak was honking. Still, it was funny to think of Sara and Tobias, as distant from the Queen as chalk and chestnuts, for they would never strike an animal or a child, or lock one up for weeks at a time.

Wherever they had gone, she prayed that they were safe, from the plague and whatever else might befall them, and that they would return soon. For, despite a layer of dust, and the chill in the air, most of the houses looked like their residents had merely stepped out for a moment, fully intending to return.

And when they did, Swanhild would return,

too. She'd persuade her mother to reverse this spell so she might be herself again, and she'd marry Raphael, just like she'd promised.

She would, she swore softly to herself. For she could not bear to even think of a future without them.

Eighteen

When Silvana and Tobias moved out of the monks' dormitory they'd shared with the others, and Zoticus left the tower room to sleep in Mistress Sara's chamber, Raphael took the tower room for his own. Oh, he'd had offers from some of the girls, and if not for Swanhild, he might have been tempted, so it was best that he sleep alone, somewhere they would not find him. And if it had the best view of the gates and the road up the mountain, all the better.

He spent every spare moment up there, feeling like he, and not Zoticus, was an eagle in an eyrie, but in the end, it was Zoticus and Sara's daughter, a wilful little mite named Rossa, who saw the party of monks first.

Nevertheless, Raphael's longer legs carried him down to the bailey faster, so he was the one to tell Zoticus of their approach. Zoticus was already at the gates, as if he knew they'd be coming today, and his only response to the news was to tell Raphael to pack his things, ready to travel home to Mirroten.

The sun was still high in the sky when Raphael rode out of the gates on the back of the bishop's own palfrey, no less, for the bishop had no further need of the beast.

Raphael did not glance back, for he hoped to return with good news soon enough. Now, he set his sights firmly on Mirroten, and his reunion with Swanhild. He had a promise to Tola to fulfil.

Nineteen

"The king has summoned you! All of you! You must dress for court…and don't forget the crowns! They must wear their crowns!"

The Queen flew about, like a panicked bird not sure of the way out, slapping child and servant alike as she gave orders to everyone.

Fine gowns were found, then picked over, before being approved and dragged over the heads of swan princesses who'd begun to panic themselves in the pandemonium in the nursery.

The whole room was a froth of fur and silk and wool, with so many preservative herbs flying about that Swanhild had sneezed more than once, to the terror of the smaller girls.

Finally, it was Swanhild's turn to be dressed in her finery, a confection with so many layers of silk and lace, she worried the dress might try to fly away on its own, for the slightest puff of wind sent the skirts dancing.

"A crown! She must have her crown!" the Queen cried, and a circlet was pushed so forcefully onto her head, Swanhild's knees threatened to buckle.

While the Queen and two maids busied themselves, stabbing pins into her hair as they pulled it this way and that, Swanhild dared to look at the others. They were all dressed now, looking like the princesses the Queen pretended they were. Each girl wore a thin silver circlet with a jewel on her brow, which didn't look half as heavy as the crown weighing down her own head. Swanhild reached up to investigate…

"Don't touch it, you silly girl!" the Queen screeched, slapping Swanhild's hands away. "You'll undo all our good work, and the King is waiting!"

The Queen, dressed in her own finery and topped by a heavy crown that Swanhild suspected was a twin of the one on her own head, led the way to a hall so huge it could only be the King's throne room – as evident by the man seated on an ornate chair on a dais at one end.

When they reached the foot of the dais, the Queen halted, then hissed, "Bow before the King!"

Of course, none of the swan princesses had ever been taught to curtsy, so they merely stood there, looking confused, and not a little frightened at what the Queen might do to them.

The Queen uttered an oath under her breath, then began to clout each child over the head until they fell to their knees. By the time she reached Swanhild, she had already dropped into a deep curtsy, which she hoped looked as subservient as any maid.

"What's that one's name?"

Swanhild raised her head, to find the King pointing at her.

"That is Princess Odette, your oldest daughter," the Queen said.

"She will be sixteen this summer, yes?" the King asked.

Swanhild blinked in surprise. The child she'd seen in the mirror did not look anywhere near sixteen.

The Queen seemed to be equally unsettled. "She is still young, Your Majesty. Too young to leave the nursery, I am certain."

The King shook his head irritably. "No, I'm certain she is sixteen, at least. Born the same year as the Emperor's son and heir, though he would not consider a betrothal between them. It matters not. At Midsummer, she will wed Prince Tristan, and when I am gone, they will rule this kingdom together, as king and queen."

"But she is so young…"

"No younger than you were when we wed, Klava. Young enough to be fertile and give him many heirs to the throne, just as you have. Though I hope Odette and Tristan will at least have a son." The King's eyes seemed to accuse the Queen of some terrible crime, of failing to bear him a son.

If the King only knew that the sex of a child was determined by both parents, not just their mother…Swanhild couldn't help but grin.

"See? The girl approves. You know you are old enough to marry, do you not, Odette?" the King asked.

Curses — the King had seen and misinterpreted her smile. Oh well, better make the best of it. "If my betrothed stood here before me, I would gladly marry him today, Your Majesty," Swanhild said. Of course, she meant Raphael, not some northern prince, but the King wasn't to know that. She grinned even more widely. "And spend all night working on conceiving a son, of course." Or a daughter. Swanhild didn't much care about the sex of her first child with Tobias, as long as they spent plenty of time in bed together before the baby was born.

The Queen glared daggers at Swanhild, but the King merely laughed. "Daughter, you are exactly the sort of queen this country needs. Your mother would be wise to listen to you, child." He rose and made shooing motions. "Now, take the children back to the nursery. I will send for her when Prince Tristan arrives to take possession of his new bride."

The Queen turned her back on the King and swept out of the hall. "Come, children," she called.

Swanhild had the most peculiar urge to open her mouth and tell the King everything his wife had done, but she knew as well as the Queen did that pretending to be a princess was just as much treason as any of the Queen's crimes, and the result would be death, either at the Queen's hand or the King's.

Swanhild sighed. She'd have to find some

way out of here, before they forced her to marry Prince Tristan. Even if he was the handsomest, kindest, most skilled lover in all the world, she would never break her promise to Raphael.

Now she just had to find a way to keep her promise and her head.

Twenty

That night, Swanhild was surprised when the Queen led them up to the top of the tower, where the chest of feathered cloaks lay open to the starry sky. The moon had not yet risen, but the glow on the horizon signalled that it would appear soon.

Much like every other full moon night when she'd been allowed to fly, Swanhild helped the others into their cloaks until there was only one left for the Queen to hand to her.

Tonight, the Queen clutched it in her hands like she didn't want to let go.

"Odette, you must tell me something, and you must tell me the truth. Swear it!" the Queen said.

The Queen's madness had made her forget the girl before her wasn't really her daughter. Swanhild sighed.

"Swear you will tell me the truth!"

Swanhild wet her lips. This could not end well. "I swear it."

"You have already found a mate, have you not? One you fly to meet, every full moon?"

A mate? It was a strange choice of words, but if Raphael was anything, then yes, in the most animal sense, he was her mate, her partner in life, and when they finally said their wedding vows, it would be a mating, of sorts.

She'd sworn to tell the truth, but what would the Queen's madness make her do to Raphael, if he still lived? Swanhild could not place him at the mercy of this mad woman.

"Do your hearts beat as one? Have your

bodies already become one? Does your heart belong to him, and not some prince?" the Queen demanded.

Swanhild swallowed. "My heart belongs to someone who is not the prince the King wishes me to marry."

"I knew it! I will not let history repeat. I will not…" the Queen muttered feverishly to herself. She settled the last cloak about Swanhild's shoulders, as lovingly as if the girl had truly been her daughter. "Tonight, you must give yourself to him. The male who holds your heart. Give all of yourself, over and over, until there is no doubt in his heart or your own. Then, return here to tell me it is done. Only then can I set matters straight."

As if Swanhild could find Raphael in a single night, when she'd been looking for him since the day she first turned into a swan. So many months, with no sign of where he might be or if he was even alive. She opened her mouth to say something, anything, but before she could form the words, the Queen fastened the cloak clasp at her throat and the transformation silenced her.

So Swanhild gave the Queen a nod, before diving off the tower into the swirling winds that had carried the other swan princesses away to the lake.

Twenty-One

In all the years he'd lived there, Mirroten never looked so quiet as it did right now. Raphael half expected people to walk out of their doors, to greet him, but there was no one left. Every house stood empty, with neither a man nor a mattress to be seen.

He found the answer to the mystery in the churchyard. A massive mound rose on along the fence on one side, topped by a stone cross. Grass had grown over the top, withering to straw now after the warm summer. Someone had buried all those who'd perished of the plague some time ago, then left the town empty. Maybe even the monks who were, even now, settling in to the monastery that had sheltered them for so long.

Raphael had known the disease would take its toll, and immeasurable lives would be lost. He'd known, but…it hadn't really hit him until now, seeing that grave as big as a house, that was now home to Gojko and all the townspeople he'd tried to save from so many ailments over the years. Until the plague had come and wiped them all from the world.

He fell to his knees and wept. Wept for all those lost, unmourned until now. When their children returned to Mirroten, they would mourn them, too, but today, Raphael alone held that crushing weight of grief, and was forced to collapse beneath it.

Hours later, he staggered into the church, determined to light a candle for their souls. Flint, tinder, fire, and then finally a taper…it seemed such a tiny flame for so many souls, so after lighting one candle, he lit them all, every candle he could find in the church until the altar was a blaze of light. Even that wasn't enough, and Raphael stumbled out into the street again, looking to the skies for something, anything, a sign that this was all part of some plan, that so much sacrifice could not have come without some reward. Or why had so many died?

A gust of wind blew past him through the open church doors, snuffing all the candles out in one breath. Much like the plague had taken the lives of the people Raphael had tried to pray for, though the words would not come.

Wings flapped, high above. A flock of some night birds, ghostly white, drifted overhead, toward the lake.

Swans. They must be swans! Raphael's heart soared, and he sprinted for the beach.

Twenty-Two

Swanhild circled the town, looking once again for signs of life, like she did every time she came to Mirroten. All the snow had melted away in the spring thaw, and she knew as well as anyone in Mirroten that once the spring sun had dried the roads, they would show no footprints until the next autumn rains fell.

Just like every other night, the only light came from the full moon above.

Swanhild shook her head. The Queen was

mad, as she knew well. No matter how much she wished he was, Raphael wasn't here.

She coasted in to land, skimming the water as she slowed before settling in the shallows. If she'd known flying was so much fun, she might have asked Mother to transform her into a swan sooner. Or a more agile bird, like a falcon or something. When she saw her again, she would ask.

Once again she felt the urge to walk through town, checking her house and the apothecary shop, in the faintest of hopes that she might find some clue to where they'd gone. She knew there'd be none, for surely if there was anything to find, she'd have seen it by now, but hope burned eternal. She would walk the streets of Mirroten one more time.

She stepped out of the water, surprised to find that it was the same patch of shore where Mother had first turned her into a swan. Swanhild had the strangest sensation that if she but took off her cloak, she would be herself again, and the world would be as it was before.

So strongly did she feel it that she reached for her throat to unclasp her cloak, only to discover that her wings were useless. Hissing a curse, she set to work on the clasp with her beak. She could feel the bump where it should be, but no matter how hard she pecked and tore at it, it wouldn't budge.

She hissed again and set off for her mother's house. She'd find something there that would help her take her cloak off.

"Swanhild? Is that you?"

She turned, at the sound of a name she hadn't heard in far too long, from the lips of someone who couldn't possibly be…

"Raphael?"

Twenty-Three

A single swan stepped out of the water, walking up the beach with a measured step that reminded Raphael of Swanhild. This swan had a strange band about its head that gleamed in the moonlight, almost like a crown.

It unfolded its wings, feathers spreading like fingers as it reached for something on its breast. It tried a few times, but whatever it wanted to do, it appeared that it couldn't, and the frustrated bird hissed something that had to be a curse, exactly like Swanhild would.

"Swanhild?"

She'd twisted her head around to try to reach whatever it was that her wings couldn't grasp, so it took her a moment to right herself. One piercing eye regarded him as she honked softly three times.

"Let me help you with that," Raphael said to the swan, dropping to his knees before her. She spread her wings wide, as if warning him away. He half expected her to buffet him with her wings, like a normal bird would do, but instead she puffed out her chest, and touched the offending part with her beak. In the moonlight, he could see what looked like an ivory brooch, gleaming against her feathers. He fumbled with the clasp, wishing he'd thought to bring a lamp so that he might see better, but finally he managed to yank the thing free.

The swan flapped her wings, then uttered the most horrible cry. Her features blurred, before it was no longer a swan but Swanhild standing before him.

"Raphael! Are you really here?"

He had no words, but he could and did wrap his arms around her. His lips found hers, and he drank her in like the first draught he'd had in three years. Nay, in forever, for that's what their time apart had felt like.

They could not shed their clothes fast enough, and it was but the work of a moment before he felt her body against his on the sand, ready and willing and wanting. She pushed him onto his back, straddling his hips as she took him the way she liked best.

The heat of her around him, moonlight gleaming on her breasts as she rode him to the peak of her own pleasure, was more than he could bear, and his cry of joy mingled with hers as they came together.

Still breathless, she leaned forward to kiss him, then rose. "I want to do that again, and again, and again, until neither of us can walk any more. But next time, I want to do it in a bed."

Raphael grinned. "The only mattresses left

in town are the ones in Mistress Sara's house. I'm sure she would not mind."

Swanhild looked surprised. "She lives, then? And the others?"

Raphael nodded. "All the other survivors took refuge at the Cloister of the Holy Innocents, a castle high in the mountains. Not everyone survived, though. I'll show you tomorrow. Tonight it's just us here, and we can do as we wish."

"I wish to make love with you, to feel you inside me, until I forget everything else but you and me," Swanhild said.

Raphael laughed. "Then I will become as one of those desert djinn, and grant your wish, in one of Sara's soft feather beds."

"Oh, yes!"

Twenty-Four

When Swanhild awoke in an unfamiliar bed, her body ached in places she'd forgotten existed. And she could think of nothing but Raphael. His lips, his hands, his body, his voice…caressing her until she begged for more, for she would never ask him to stop. Such a beautiful dream…

"I brought your clothes. We left everything on the beach. Oh, and some water to wash with. I thought you might want to dress before

I showed you the churchyard."

She looked up, and he was there. "Every night, I dreamed of you, wishing you were there with me. Is it…are you…is it over now?"

He sat on the edge of the bed and leaned in to kiss her. His lips tasted salty-sweet, and she wanted…

"It is indeed over, my dearest friend, my only love, my soon to be wife. Come back with me to the castle, and we will make the priest marry us, so that we may do this again every night, and you need never dream of me again, for I will be right beside you, only a whisper away."

Tears sprang to Swanhild's eyes. The mad Queen had been right after all. Raphael was really here, and hers, and nothing and no one would ever part them again. Not king or queen or even her own mother.

"Is my mother…is she…?" Swanhild began, not sure how to finish.

"Dress, and I will show you," Raphael said.

He'd brought her the silk and lace court

gown, that decadent thing that seemed so out of place on her, or here in Mirroten. And yet, that's all the clothing she had, so she slipped it over her head, tying the many laces herself until it fitted her just as it had before the King. The crown lay beside her pillow, a heavy half circle of silver that rose up to a jewelled point in front. It belonged on a princess, not on her humble head, but she put it on anyway, for it would not do to lose such a valuable jewel, even in Mistress Sara's house.

Her shoes were silk court slippers, hardly suitable for Mirroten's roads, but they were better than going barefoot. Or being a swan.

She twisted her hair up onto the back of her head, pinning it to keep hair and crown in place, before venturing out to where Raphael waited.

His eyes lit up at the sight of her. "You look like a princess, or an angel. Having seen you naked, I had not thought you could ever appear more beautiful to me than that, but looking at you now…where did you find such a gown, Swanhild? Or that crown? Will you wear it to our wedding?"

So much to say, and Swanhild knew that once she started, she would not stop, but she did not want to tell her tale more than once. "First, show me to my mother. Then I will tell you both about the gown, and the crown, and my life as a swan."

Raphael nodded gravely, and led her to the church. To the rounded hill where once there had been flat ground, topped with a stone cross with edges so sharp they cut her fingers when she gripped it. Swanhild watched a blood droplet well from her fingertip, before closing her eyes and sending her magic sight out to find her mother.

The magic flew out wide, before coalescing back around Swanhild, sinking to the ground around her slippered feet. Then it sank into the mound, and she knew.

"My mother?" She let out a sob.

"I'm sorry, Swanhild. The spell she cast to turn you into a swan took too much out of her. She was already weak from the plague. After Ysabel, she was the second person in Mirroten to die. With her last breath, she made me promise to protect you, and I will. I swear I will."

A grave so large held more than one body — it must hold half the town, if not more. So many friends and their families, people she had known all her life. Gone.

Raphael took her in his arms as she wept for all she had lost. All they had lost. So much, so many, and yet they were still here…

And when she had cried herself out, she sat down with him and told her tale.

Twenty-Five

Somehow, while telling their stories, they'd managed to walk back down to the beach. There were no swans on the lake now – they'd evidently flown back to the Queen, to be safely inside by dawn. Some other swan princess would marry Prince Tristan now, Swanhild supposed, seeing as she wasn't going back. The prince wouldn't know the difference, for they'd never met, and the Queen surely wouldn't care, for she'd gone three years pretending swans were her children after the real princesses had died. The only person Swanhild really felt sorry for was the King, who evidently didn't know the death of their children had driven her mad.

And the swans. Not the brightest birds, but they didn't deserve to live out their lives as the Queen's captives. Someone should go to court and tell the King to let them go.

"Oh, here's your cloak, where we left it on the beach last night. I must have missed it when I collected the rest of your clothes. I'm never seen a feather cloak before. It looks like a great deal of work, every feather sewn to the cloth…" Raphael picked up the cloak and shook the sand off it.

Swanhild reached out to take it from him, then stopped. It was nearly noon, with not a cloud in the sky. Sunlight shimmered off the feathers, which absolutely did not melt or burn or do any of the things the Queen had said it would in the sun.

"That lying, scheming bitch," Swanhild breathed. "She held us prisoner in a cage of her own lies!" She took the cloak from Raphael and settled it across her shoulders. It was warm from the sun, but that was all. They could have escaped her at any time by simply not returning. The other swans still could, if she only told them.

But that would mean leaving Raphael.

Quickly, she told him what she'd come to realise.

"You must go, and save those swans. We've waited three years. What is a few more days?" he asked. "While you go back to save them, I will go get everyone and bring them back to Mirroten. When you return, we will have our wedding here, with all the town as our guests."

"Yes," she said, before doubt seized her. What if something went wrong? She did not want to wait another three years. "If I have not returned by the time you come back, come to court. Bring Mistress Sara, if you can. She will know what to say, and how to say it, to the King and the Queen. The King must know what she has done."

Raphael touched his lips to hers. "You will return, and we will be married. Nothing will go wrong. But if it does, I will challenge the Queen herself before I will let her keep you captive again." He fastened the clasp, and stepped back.

Magic tingled over Swanhild's body, as she transformed into a swan for what she hoped was the last time. Into the water she went, flapping her wings to generate enough lift to launch her into flight.

She circled around Raphael once, twice, three times, memorising his every feature as she prayed she would see him again soon, before she flew off.

Twenty-Six

The Queen was waiting at the top of the tower when Swanhild landed. But instead of unfastening her cloak, the Queen picked her up and carried her down the stairs to her chamber.

"I knew you would return, Odette. I knew! Tell me, did you mate? Did you mate for so long that you lost track of the time?"

Unable to say anything that wasn't a wordless honk, Swanhild simply nodded. The

Queen, married to a man she had no problem lying to, would not understand what it was share a love like the one she and Raphael had. And the joy of their lovemaking…even as a human, she did not have the words to express it so the woman would even have a hope of understanding.

"Then it is time I told you my tale. A tale of my mate, the mate who was stolen from me, by the man I was forced to marry," the Queen began.

Wait…what?

"When I was young, younger than you, a witch came to our court. An enchantress, a very powerful kind of witch, who could work magic and enchant things like you wouldn't believe. For my fifth birthday, she offered me a gift – a spell, or enchanted object, that would do whatever I wished. I'd always loved the swans that lived in the river beside our castle, so I asked her to give me a cloak that would allow me to transform into a swan. She made the cloak, and warned me that I might only use it at night, when no one would see me. When I returned the next morning, I was so loathe to turn back into a girl again, that she promised I might go out another night, and the next, until I spent every day as a girl, and every night as a swan.

"Until I grew too big for the cloak, so it no longer covered me. I wept and I raged for days, until my fairy godmother, which is what that witch told me she was, made me a new cloak, bigger and wider, until I outgrew that one, too. Over and over again, until I was a woman grown, and ready to find my mate.

"I met him on the river at dawn, the biggest, handsomest swan you ever saw. He swam close behind me, and nipped at the base of my neck. Before I knew it, he took me, the weight of him sending me so low in the water for a moment, I thought I would sink, before he was done. Three times, he took me, as the sun rose, before I could bring myself to part from him and fly home. The next night, I could scarcely wait for the sun to set before returning to him. He had made me his, pinning me beneath him as he took his pleasure, and I could think of nothing else but him, on me, in me, like nothing I had ever felt before.

"Until one day, my father told me I was betrothed to some king in the mountains, and that I must leave that very day, for the King had arrived to claim me. I begged my fairy godmother to help me, to stop the marriage, for I had fallen in love with a swan, my mate, and together, we hatched a plan. She gave me two potions – one that would turn a swan into a man, and one that would dispatch a man direct. I was to wait until our wedding night, when I was to pour a cup of wine for the King, and mix the poison into the wine so that he might drink it, and die. The other potion I was to mix with one of the King's hairs, before pouring three drops over my mate. My mate would then transform into the King, and together we could dispose of the King's body, before reigning together side by side, as king and queen. I was already carrying my mate's child – twins, actually, though my son did not survive.

"My mate followed us in the air, all the way to the King's castle, biding his time as the celebrations began. For days, the court feasted and danced, while the court tailors made me a gown fit for a queen. I was constantly surrounded by courtiers, never able to don my cloak and see my mate. Finally, the day of the wedding arrived. We said our vows before the priest in the cathedral, amid so much singing, my head ached before we were even halfway through.

"Then came the wedding feast. I sat beside the King and smiled, for I knew my wait was almost over. I would see my mate again, and we could be together.

"Course after course came out. All manner of dishes, more than I could count, until they brought out a platter that was the chef's specialty – roast swan. Only the biggest, plumpest swan would do for the King's wedding feast, and they'd assembled him with all his feathers, he looked so lifelike, though beneath that finery, he'd been roasted well past death.

"I screamed at the sight of him, nearly fell over in a faint, and the King, he just laughed, as if it was a great joke, before pulling my mate's head clean off his butchered corpse, to show me that the bird was dead. As if that could comfort me!

"They carried me to bed, those courtiers who pretended to be my friends, but I would not speak to anyone until my fairy godmother came. I asked her to bring me my vial of poison, so that I might drink it myself and join my mate in death, and she brought me a vial, but all it contained was a sort of sleeping potion that left me helpless on the bed. Then she told me that we must make a new plan. I must allow the King to take me, and be his obedient wife, so that when my mate's child was born, the King would think it his own, and my mate's child would inherit the throne.

"My son did not survive the birth, but my

daughter did. And I vowed when you were born, Odette, that no son of his would survive, so that the throne would be yours when the King was dead. So I birthed child after child for him, but only the girls lived. Now you are a woman grown, nay, a woman mated, just like I was, and I shall give you the choice I never had. You will get to live out your life with your mate, and I shall take the poison I wished for on my wedding night, so the King will never know how to find you!"

At such a story, Swanhild could scarcely think. No wonder the Queen was mad, if this was her tale. So she did not have time to resist before the Queen snatched her up and carried her to the nursery, where eleven other swans milled about, honking in distress. The Queen dropped her in the middle of them, and they flapped and honked, stray feathers flying through the air like fog so Swanhild could not see until it was too late.

A vial tinkled to the ground, shattered into a hundred shards, followed by a thump as the

Queen's body landed atop it, gasping for a breath she could not take, for the poison had stolen it from her. "Fly, Odette," she gasped out before her eyes closed for the final time.

No - no! Swanhild shouted, or at least she tried to, but all she could do was honk, so honk she did, until a servant came running. Her scream alerted everyone else, until finally, the King himself entered the nursery. He took one look at his Queen, then a longer look at the room full of swans, before he shook his head.

"Someone see to the Queen. Someone shut the swans in that room, so they cannot escape. And then find me whoever transformed my daughters into swans and make them change them back or I shall have their head for this!"

It all happened too quickly for Swanhild to form any sort of plan. The Queen was carried out, the door was shut, and she was stuck in a room with eleven panicked swans. Worse, all her worst curses all sounded like either a honk or a hiss.

Twenty-Seven

As Raphael had feared, when they returned to Mirroten, Swanhild was nowhere to be found. He headed straight for Mistress Sara's house, where she insisted he join them for dinner.

After he'd told them Swanhild's tale, he asked, "So, will you help me find her, Mistress Sara?"

"No," Zoticus said, setting down his cup. "Lady Sara's needed here, in case any more of the late Bishop's men try to take Mirroten from her. But I'd intended to pay a visit to King Bela and his court, if only to tell him about the late Bishop, so I'd be happy to help you find your lost bride. In fact, I have just the thing to get us there, too…I found it while I was going through my things. It's been so long since I'd seen it, I'd forgotten about it, which is just as well, seeing as this thing has a habit of toppling cities. Not to mention the Emperor would kill to get his hands on it. Would you believe I found it in a Rialto canal? I think if we arrive at night, so no one sees us, and I put it back into my bag when we arrive, we might be able to risk it."

None of this made sense to Raphael, but he wasn't going to refuse Zoticus's help. When he saw what Zoticus had found in a canal, though, he did wonder if the man had gone mad.

"That's a wooden horse," Raphael said, walking around it, hoping it might look like something more than a worn children's toy if he but looked at it from the right angle, but nothing changed. "I don't see how it will help us."

Zoticus climbed onto the horse. "That's because you've never seen it fly." He touched something on the horse's neck and it rose several feet into the air.

"We're going to fly a wooden horse to court to rescue Swanhild?" Raphael asked. Maybe he was the one who was mad, for even considering this.

"Well, unless you can cast portals like an enchantress, it's the quickest way to reach it. And you did say the King thinks your bride is his daughter, and he wants her to marry some prince…"

Raphael grabbed the horse's tail, and hauled himself up behind Zoticus. "I lost her once. I won't lose her again!"

Zoticus laughed. "Never underestimate a witch, boy, or any woman who truly knows her heart. If she wants to marry you more than some prince, she will stop at nothing until things work out in her favour. You'll see. If we arrive in time…"

The horse whooshed upward so fast, Raphael suspected he'd left his stomach and the rest of his innards on the ground below. But then the creature surged forward so quickly, it stole his breath, too, so it was all he could do to hang on until they reached the King's court.

Twenty-Eight

"Wake up, boy, we're here," Zoticus said.

Raphael blinked blearily up at him. Somehow, he'd fallen asleep on the ground, and the flying wooden horse he'd been dreaming about was nowhere to be seen.

Zoticus grinned and patted the small pouch at his belt. "You'd never know what you can fit inside a magic pouch until you own one, and sometimes, I even surprise myself. Tell yourself you dreamed it all, and it'll be easier. If word reached the Emperor that you knew where to find the enchanted horse, you'd spend the rest of your life in one of his torture chambers, and Mirroten would need to find itself a new apothecary."

Raphael shook his head. One moment, he thought Zoticus was an ordinary man, skilled with weapons and herbs, until he said things like that, and reminded Raphael that the assassin's life was stranger than anything he could imagine. "How are we to get into the King's court?" he asked.

"Well, me, I'll probably just walk in and ask for an audience. King Bela and me go way back. I'm sure he still owes me a favour or two, and then there's the matter of that bishop believing he could claim Lady Sara's lands. You, however, might have a harder time of it. Or you would if the King weren't looking for a man of your talents right now. You see, the whole city is buzzing about the King's latest proclamation. He's looking for a man who can transform a swan into a woman, and from what you've told me, I think you're the man he's looking for. Your job is to persuade him."

Raphael's heart sank. "And what if I can't?"

"Then I believe the King will throw in his dungeon for a few days, along with all the other charlatans, which I imagine he'll release once he meets you."

"Why?"

"Because he's not really looking for a man who can turn a swan into a woman. He's looking for whoever turned his daughters into swans, and when you point at the Queen, I imagine you'll have his attention."

That didn't sound like a good idea, either, but Raphael didn't have anything better, so he forced himself to trudge after Zoticus into the city. The sun had risen by the time they'd trekked all the way up to the castle from the city gates, and the doors to the throne hall were wide open. A crowd of courtiers and common petitioners stood inside, for the only seat was the throne on the dais, where the King sat. A wooden cage rested at his feet with what looked like a swan inside.

"Swanhild!" Raphael blurted out, ready to rush forward to release her, but something caught the back of his tunic and stopped him short.

"That's not your bride, boy," Zoticus said. "It's just an ordinary swan. Nothing magical about it. The King's gone through a dozen birds already, and this one here's lucky number thirteen. Several have been poisoned by charlatans' potions, a couple were burned, one managed to break out of its cage and fly out of the hall, and I don't know what happened to the others. Nothing good, as I understand it. Which is why he's using normal swans to test people, before he lets anyone near his daughters. He's got no sons, you see, so he needs those girls to marry and give him an heir."

Raphael didn't want to think about what the King would do when he found out that his daughters were all dead.

"You go up to talk to the King. I'll speak to

the herald, so he'll announce me when it's my turn. Don't worry, I'll find you when it's time to leave," Zoticus said, strolling through the crowd as if it didn't exist. People just seemed to move to give him a path.

Raphael had to weave through people to approach the dais, the crowd growing thicker, the closer he got.

Two swans met unfortunate ends before Raphael could reach the steps before the throne, and three more corpses were carried away by servants before Raphael could get a close enough look at the swan to see that it didn't have the cloak clasp on its breast that Swanhild had. Zoticus was right – this was an ordinary swan, and not a princess.

Raphael took a deep breath. This was to save Swanhild, he reminded himself. "Your Majesty, you're wasting your time. If you really want to see someone transform a swan into a woman, first you need to find a woman who was transformed into a swan."

The King looked straight at him. "What's

your name, man?"

"Raphael, Master Apothecary of Mirroten," he said proudly.

"Mirroten? The plague town? There's no one left in Mirroten!" someone shouted.

The King waved them into silence. "I ask again. What's your name, man, and where are you from?"

"I am Raphael, Master Apothecary of Mirroten, and anyone who tells you the town is empty is a liar, Your Majesty, for Lady Sara holds those lands still!"

The Kind looked disgruntled. "Yes. Well. Be that as it may, there is the matter of this swan. Master Apothecary, can you turn it into a woman?"

"No, Your Majesty, for it is nothing but an ordinary swan. But if you have a swan who only wears that form because of some spell, who was once a woman, then I may be able to help you."

The King beckoned to one of his guards. "Take him to the dungeons. He knows something. Have him questioned."

Two guards seized Raphael by the arms and started to drag him away before he could protest.

"Master Zoticus," the herald boomed, and everyone, from the King right down to the guards bracketing Raphael, froze.

"Master Zoticus," the King said, as the man himself strode into view. "To what do we owe this honour?"

"I've come to swear fealty. I believe it's customary, when one of your landholders marries, and while the lands are my wife's, I thought it might be nice to come and do a bit of swearing anyway." With that, Zoticus knelt, rattled off the vows, and rose to his feet again.

The King appeared perplexed. "You have a wife?"

Zoticus beamed. "Oh, indeed I do. One of your most loyal landholders – Lady Sara of Mirroten. Why, would you believe the Bishop of Rialto tried to spread a plague across her lands, and take them for himself? Of course, being the virtuous lady she is, God was on her side, not the vile Bishop's, and struck him down for his crimes. Before more than a dozen witnesses, too."

The King did not look pleased. "How fortunate for Lady Sara."

"Oh, no, it's me who is the lucky one! Her people would do anything for her. When she welcomed me into Mirroten, they accepted me as one of their own. In fact, I think I might just retire there with my lovely wife, and maybe raise a family." He smiled. "And how is your family, Bela? Are your daughters well? What about your wife?"

The King rose abruptly. "This audience is over. Master Zoticus, if you will join me…"

The guards remembered themselves, and resumed dragging Raphael out of the hall.

Zoticus snapped his fingers. "You two. Release my apothecary. He may be of service to the King."

The guards let go of Raphael so quickly, he landed on his backside. Before they could seize him again, he was on his feet, dusting himself off, running to catch up with Zoticus and the King.

He reached them just in time to hear the end of the King's tale: "…and she was dead. Dead! All my daughters turned into swans. I could not make any sense of it, and, worse, there is not a single person who witnessed what happened who can explain it to me!" The King shook his head. "I offered untold riches – his own weight in gold, and a princess for a bride, if any man could change them back, but all I get is burned feathers and dead birds and fools! If your apothecary can do something for them, I will double the reward. Give him a place at court. Anything to the man who can give me back my daughters!"

He gestured at the door in front of him. "They're in there. Please, Master Zoticus, if you or your apothecary can help me…I will be forever in your debt. I will give you anything you ask. Lands. Titles. Anything."

Zoticus waved Raphael forward. "You hear

that? The King wants to be indebted to you. That's not the kind of offer you refuse. Especially if you're looking to get married and start a family."

Raphael took a deep breath and pushed open the door.

Twenty-Nine

Swanhild felt like she'd been flying around forever. First to the window, then to the door, but she couldn't open either of them, for the door was bolted from the outside and her wings were not strong enough to push the window shutters open. Yet she had to find a way out, to free the other swans, and fly back to Raphael.

If she could only take her feather cloak off, she could throw open the shutters, but no amount of pecking at the clasp would make it release her from her feathered prison.

She cursed the Queen, whose madness had imprisoned her here, and she cursed the window shutters, for every time she flew at them, feathers tore out of her wings, so that she could almost see her skin where only feathers should be.

No…it looked like human skin, an arm beneath the feathers. What if…

If she could tear the cloak off, instead of unfastening the clasp, would that help her return to her true form? It was worth a shot…

She flew at the window, slamming her body against the shutters again and again until her bones ached and feathers flew everywhere. Too many – she could not stay aloft on what was left, and she plummeted to the ground, landing on top of several other swans. The birds squawked and flapped, attacking her and each other in their panic.

Beneath their onslaught, something tore, and she saw her hand, then an arm. Swanhild threw herself at another group of birds, sending the whole room into a frenzy. Beaks tore at her, wings beat her, and Swanhild staggered to the window, hand outstretched. The shutter…if she could only unfasten the shutters…

But while one hand appeared human, she was still only the height of a bird. This would not do. She scrabbled at the clasp with her fingers, tearing the fabric in her haste to break free. The shredded cloak fell to the flagstones, a mess of ribbons with only a few feathers left and a hole where the clasp had once been.

With both hands now, Swanhild reached for the shutters, and threw them open wide. Then she seized a swan and tossed it out the window. Then another, and another, until all eleven of them had formed up into a sort of flock, waiting for her to join them.

Her heart twinged in her chest. With her feather cloak in ribbons and her mother dead, Swanhild would never be able to transform into a swan again. Never soar through the skies, drift across a lake, ride the updrafts into the clouds…

But the other swans would, as was right, and they would all be free. Free of the mad Queen and this prison of lies.

If only she could unbar the door holding her here, so that she might return home to Raphael. Ugh, she'd settle for someone cleaning up all the feathers. It was enough to make anyone sneeze.

Behind her, the door swung silently open.

Thirty

The door opened, but all Raphael could see was a storm of feathers, flying in all directions. Then the cloud cleared, and standing in the middle of the room was…

"Swanhild?"

She didn't seem to hear him at first, for she was facing the window, but the third time he said her name, she turned around. "Raphael?"

"What in heaven's name is going on here? Who are you and where are my daughters?"

the King demanded.

Swanhild winced, then dropped a curtsy, as prettily as any courtier. "Your Majesty, I am Swanhild of Mirroten. Perhaps I can shed some light on the matter." She ducked her head. "First, my condolences on the loss of your Queen. She was quite driven mad with grief, I believe, when the plague killed her daughters."

"But…the swans…" the King blurted out.

"The swans you saw in here were not your daughters, but birds that had been bespelled to look like your daughters. When the Queen died, the spell wore off, and they were trapped in here, until I released them. The poor birds were quite frantic. If they were stuck in here much longer, they might have hurt themselves."

"So where are my children?"

"I believe if you sent someone to your hunting lodge on the lake near Mirroten, you will find where they are buried. They died of the plague, Your Majesty, for which there is no cure. I am a herbalist, and my betrothed is an apothecary, and while we do all we can, we cannot cure the plague." She bowed her head. "I am so sorry for your loss."

"But…but…my children…"

Zoticus stepped up to the King's shoulder. "Bela, I think this is where you command your servants to bring you a cask of your strongest wine, and together we drink to the memory of your wife and children. I've pieced together much of this tale already, but you deserve to hear it all. And these two should go home to Mirroten, where they have a wedding to celebrate and probably plenty of herbs to prepare before the winter. In fact, that vile Bishop of Rialto was responsible for your daughters' deaths, even as he tried to rob my wife. Would you like to hear how he died?"

Zoticus threw an arm around the King's shoulder as he began his tale, shooing Raphael and Swanhild away.

Raphael looked at Swanhild, who shrugged.

"So, we go home?" she asked.

"If the King lets us leave, yes."

"And what then? We just settle down in Mirroten, and live our lives again? After all that has happened?"

Raphael wrapped his arm around Swanhild's shoulder. "First, we get married. Then, we spend at least a week in bed together. Maybe even two. Then, we start our new lives together. And, after all that's happened to us, I mean to spend the rest of my life making you happy. I made a promise to your mother."

"Did she threaten you with the devil, or her ghost?"

"She didn't have to. I love you more than the moon and all the stars in the sky. I love every part of you, inside and out. You are my only love, because I love no one else, and I never will. I mean to make love to you every morning, and every night, and spend every hour between making you happy. If you'll still have me, Swanhild."

"Yes. A thousand times yes."

Curse:
Rose Red Retold

DEMELZA CARLTON

A tale in the Romance a Medieval Fairy Tale series

One

When Boris laid down his sword at the end of
the day, it felt so much heavier than when he'd
buckled it on this morning. Was it the weight
of the lives he'd taken, or the blood the blade
had drunk during battle?

"I brought water for you to wash, Your
Highness," Igor said, sloshing the contents of
his bucket into the bowl before the squire

dropped the bucket on the floor. "Do you want me to help you out of your armour, too?"

Boris was perfectly capable of taking his own clothes off, and any other day he'd have said so, but they'd been fighting since dawn, and there wasn't a bit of his body that wasn't complaining of weariness. "Please," he said instead, lifting his aching arms to give the boy better access to the buckles on his breastplate.

His previous squire wouldn't have asked — he'd have simply made himself useful, but Kyrilu had earned his knighthood a year ago now, and he now served Boris's brother, Yarik, in the north. Igor still had some growing to do, as well as a lot of learning, before he'd be as good as Kyrilu.

"It'll need a good clean and polish before the morrow, for we march for home in the morning," Boris added.

Igor's thin shoulders lifted in a massive sigh. "Yes, Your Highness." He'd learned not to complain, but his sulky expression said he wanted to.

Boris hid his smile. He hadn't liked cleaning armour at Igor's age, either, but he'd known blood could eat at steel like rust, weakening what needed to be strong. Armour had saved his life more than once, and Boris appreciated the value of well-maintained gear.

"Tell the cook I'm ready for supper, too," Boris said. "After that, I won't need you until breakfast."

Igor nodded and dashed away.

Boris barely had time to finish washing and don fresh clothes before his knights began to arrive to deliver their reports of the day's battle.

"I lost six of my men today in an ambush, but we found the Bisseni camp."

Which wouldn't have had much of value in it. The food they'd stolen from the villages south of here was likely long gone,

"All our dead are buried, Your Highness. Far fewer than the enemy dead. My men are still working on the pit to bury all of them."

Boris wasn't sure the Bisseni would

appreciate the good Christian burial his men gave them, but as they were dead, they weren't likely to complain about it.

"We're down two horses, but only minor wounds among the men."

Two warhorses would be costly to replace, but the knights who'd lost them could surely afford it. As they'd all head home on the morrow, it wasn't likely they'd need new warhorses until next year's campaign.

"My scouts report no more Bisseni within a day's ride."

No Bisseni they could see, anyway. The mountain dwellers could be hiding under a rock just outside camp, and they'd never know until someone decided to use the rock as a latrine.

"Your supper, Your Highness."

Igor was getting better at not spilling the stew. The pot was still more than half full.

"Two of the Bisseni got away, vanished into the mountains."

If only they'd stay in the mountains, instead of coming to raid their villages. Then Boris and his men could stay at home, polishing benches with their ever-broadening butt-cheeks as they feasted on this victory until the next enemy dared to invade their borders.

Boris suppressed a smile. He and his men were not made for polishing benches, or growing fat from feasting. Much like his father, who would have ridden out with them, had his health not prevented it.

"Where to next, Your Highness?"

Boris raised his head to find all his men watching him with an air of expectation. Good men, loyal men, who had earned a victory feast a dozen times over during this gruelling campaign.

"On the morrow, we pack up and head for the capital. God willing, we'll be feasting in Prislav before we know it!"

A ragged cheer rose up, followed by a chorus of thanks. To him, to God, to the saints and whoever else they prayed to in the heat of battle.

"Your father would be proud, Your Highness," said Sir Cyril, the oldest of his knights.

Boris acknowledged the older man's praise with a grave nod. "Indeed. As am I, to have fought with so many good men, in my father's stead."

The men trooped out, leaving Boris with his now empty supper bowl. He couldn't remember eating a bite, he'd been so busy. Probably for the best — those newly dead warhorses had likely gone into the stewpot.

The court in Prislav might not be his favourite place to be, but at least his father's kitchens served more than old horse.

Even better would be a meal at home, with his wife and daughter. Would baby Lida be walking and talking yet? She'd barely learned to smile before he left. How would she have changed in the months he'd been away? He couldn't wait to find out.

Boris blew out the candle and lay down to dream of family dinners instead of fierce fighters who wanted him dead. He was going home.

Two

"And this is my heart," Mother said, placing Rossa's hand on her breast. Through the layers of linen and wool, Rossa could barely feel the thump of her mother's heart. Not like when her hand was against her own skin.

If she could just reach through the wool and linen…

Rossa bit down so hard on her lip that it hurt. She opened her mouth to cry out, but then she felt it. The deep drum of her mother's heart, as it squeezed and expanded inside her.

Fascinated, she focussed on the heart, and the blood pumping through it. Streaming out in a thousand directions, keeping her mother alive. She could look, but not touch, the memories from her ancestors told her. To touch was to kill, and an enchantress never used her magic for evil.

"They come! They come!"

The shout from above, followed by thunderous footsteps racing to the bottom of the tower sent Mother's heart fluttering like a bird's wings.

"What is it, Raphael?" Mother asked.

The healer man who lived in the topmost tower room stuck his head through the tapestry into Mother's chamber. His eyes were fever-bright. "I don't know, but there's a large party coming up the road. Maybe they've come to tell us it's safe to go home!"

His head disappeared and Rossa heard his feet on the stairs once more.

Mother said a bad word. "Stay here in the

tower, Rossa. I will come fetch you when it's safe."

Rossa nodded.

Mother left.

Rossa grew tired of sitting alone in Mother's chamber, so she pushed the tapestry aside and climbed to the top of the tower, where Raphael kept watch. She wasn't sure what he watched for, but she knew it made him frown and sigh a lot.

But when she reached the top, she couldn't find Raphael, and she was too short to see out the windows.

She repeated Mother's bad word. Several times. But it didn't lift her any higher. She said the bad word again, then headed down the stairs. She'd be able to see the road from the bailey.

It was a long climb for her short legs, but Rossa kept going. She wanted to see the party.

There was no one in the great hall, but someone had left the doors open, as if they knew she was coming. Giggling, she broke into a run. After only a few steps, she tripped on the uneven flagstones and went sprawling.

Pain flared in her shin, and Rossa let out a yowl.

"Rossa?"

That was Mother. Mother would take her to the stillroom and cover her in smelly herbs and bandages and she'd miss the party. Rossa jumped to her feet and raced for the doors.

"Rossa! Get back here! Rossa!"

Mother could not run as fast as her. This was a race, and Rossa knew she would win.

Daddy was in the bailey, and he always caught her. Rossa ran straight for him. Sure enough, he scooped her up in his arms, sending her soaring like the eagles higher up in the mountains.

But there was a horse coming, heading straight for Daddy. Focussing on the still-stinging graze on her shin, Rossa held up her hand to stop the horse.

The horse rose up on his back legs, almost like he was dancing. The fat man on his back rolled off and landed in the dirt.

Rossa giggled. She'd never seen a man roll like a ball before. Oh, but the horse did not like dancing. Rossa reached out, touching the horse's back, so he set his hooves on the ground again. Only she hadn't reached with her hand, but with an invisible hand made of magic.

The fat man got up and said things to Daddy and Mother. Daddy stiffened, his arm tightening around Rossa while his other hand went for his sword.

Daddy only used his sword on evil men, he'd told her. To cut out their evil hearts. That meant the fat man was evil. Would his heart look different to Mother's?

Rossa reached out, just to look, not to touch. The evil man's heart was different to Mother's. It looked like it was straining, not strong enough to pump the blood, which didn't stream like Mother's. There was a dark lump trapped inside.

Was that what evil looked like?

Mother shouted for a healer, drawing Rossa out of her reverie.

The evil man had collapsed on the ground. As Rossa watched, his evil heart beat slower and slower until it ceased beating altogether.

Rossa didn't need to ask if the man was dead. Daddy wore one of his hidden smiles, the sort he wore when Rossa did something funny that Mother didn't like, and he had to hide his smile from Mother.

Rossa gave a little nod. She wasn't sure how, but her father had killed the evil man. Stopped his heart dead.

One day, she vowed, she would be just like him. Evil men would fear her, and good people would come to her for help. Just like Daddy.

Three

Boris woke with the dawn, as was his habit. The war might be over for the moment, but old habits died harder than a Bisseni berserker. His wife Vica lay asleep beside him, and little Lida was curled up in her cradle in the corner. A reminder of who he fought for and why he spent so long away – protecting his wife and child, as well as all the wives and children in his father's kingdom. They deserved to sleep safely in their beds, too.

His men, camped in the fields outside Rostov, would be awake. He'd made it a habit to break his fast while walking through the camp, exchanging words with not just his knights but their men, too. He could do that this morning, and still have time to return to the house and have breakfast with Vica when she woke.

Boris dressed, not bothering to put on his armour today. What danger had he to fear here at home?

The camp bustled with activity, quite the opposite of his quiet home. A rider galloped past him, headed for the command tent in the centre. Instinct made Boris change course to follow the lathered horse. Whatever tidings the man carried, they must be urgent.

When he reached the command tent, both horse and rider had gone, but a pensive Sir Cyril stood in conference with several other knights, frowning at the missive in Cyril's hand.

"Well met, Your Highness," Sir Cyril called,

spotting him first.

The other knights merely bowed and made way for him.

Boris nodded at the paper. "What news?"

The knights eyed each other, none wanting to speak the ill words aloud.

Cyril sighed. "Prince Yaroslav sends word from the north. Your father has succumbed to his illness, and your brother now sits upon the throne."

Grief caught Boris's heart in its mailed fist. "My father is dead?"

"It seems so, Your Highness. Your brother Sviatopolk is king now."

Boris started in surprise. "Sviatopolk? But I thought…"

Boris had never truly thought about which of his father's sons would take the throne upon his father's death, but for his father to name his bastard son Sviatopolk as his heir over any of his legitimate offspring seemed more than a little strange. As the oldest legitimate son, coming home from a successful military campaign, surely Boris himself would be the better choice.

Not that he wanted a throne. No, he wanted his father on the throne, so he could tell him about the campaign.

Now that tale would go untold.

"Your brother Yaroslav sent you a gift, the fruit of a successful hunt in the far north. A small token of his affection and loyalty, he says." Cyril gestured, and one of his men held out a bulky package.

Boris had no choice but to take it, and, with all eyes upon him, open it, too.

Creamy white fur spilled out, lined with lambswool. It was at once the most beautiful and the most impractical cloak Boris had ever seen. In battle, it would turn from white to red in a day, and then to black and rust after that. This was a cloak for court.

"Prince Yaroslav is coming south, to join his forces with yours so that he might set the rightful king upon the throne," Cyril said.

The rightful king was the heir his father had

chosen.

Had Father really chosen Sviatopolk to be king?

"We will fight beside you, Your Majesty," Sir Cyril said, dropping to one knee. The other knights did the same.

Boris shook his head and gestured for them to get up. "I'm your prince, not your king. I will not go to war against my brother, if he is my father's chosen heir. My father was a good and wise king, and he would have made his choice with as much wisdom and forethought as any other decision he made. I must ride for Prislav immediately, to see my new king and offer him my allegiance."

"We will ride with you, Your Highness," Cyril said.

Once again, Boris shook his head. "I shall go alone. King or not, Sviatopolk is my brother. We are family. If my father chose him as king, then I am honour-bound to serve him as I served my father. As are we all. I have no need of an army at my back to speak to my brother, even if he is now my king."

"Your Highness..." Cyril was too loyal a man to say the words, but his expression said he had grave misgivings about this course of action.

Bur Boris was decided. "Send the men home to their families. We will not campaign again before spring, unless the king orders otherwise."

"Yes, Your Highness."

The knights dispersed, leaving Boris to shake his head and sigh. He'd hoped for more than a night in Vica's arms – perhaps enough nights to sire a son – but it was not to be. He was a prince first, and a husband second. First he must serve his king and his kingdom, and then he might spend a quiet winter with his wife and daughter.

Home would still be here when he returned from court.

Nodding to himself, Boris trudged home to don his travelling clothes once more.

Four

"Ready?" Father asked.

Rossa nodded sharply. "How many targets today?" She would get them all this time, she swore. Without missing a single one.

Father tilted his head to the side, as though he needed to consider for a moment before he said, "Twelve."

Another nod, and she was off.

She caught sight of the first one, half-hidden behind a tree. She slipped around the other side of the thick trunk, then plunged her dagger into the target's neck, or where it would have been, had the target been a man and not a stuffed sack. An ambush like this one usually had more than one, in line of sight of each other…

Rossa pressed against the straw corpse, scanning the trees for his accomplice. Ah, there it was.

Carefully, she strung her bow, and took aim at the painted acorn, set high in the fork of a tree on the other side of the path. When she loosed her arrow, she didn't wait to watch it hit its target, as she knew it would. Instead, she shifted to a new position and scanned the forest for other targets.

High, low, behind trees and rocks, she took out her targets, disarming two traps and springing a third, rendering it harmless, until her count reached eleven.

One more to go.

She followed the game trail in a long loop, back to where they'd started, but she didn't see a hint of a target anywhere.

Had she missed one on her way, which now lay behind her, or had her father placed it at their meeting point, ready to ambush her when she thought she was safe?

While there were many who wished to engage the services of an assassin, hired killers were not well-liked, and their heads often fetched as high a price as the people they killed. So, her father would definitely have placed a target where it might shoot her in the back, when she reached the meeting point.

Rossa skirted the clearing, selecting a tree that would give her a good view across the dell where she knew her father waited, while its branches would hide her from the sight of anyone who might hope to catch her unawares.

Zoticus sat on a rock in the sun, calmly slicing up an apple with his dagger, before popping the slices in his mouth, one by one. The loud crunching sounds surely would have alerted any would-be assassins to his presence, and made him an easy target, but Father had so many magical protections, even Rossa wasn't sure she could fight him and win.

The twelfth target would be somewhere that gave it a clear view of the clearing, and the path Rossa would have taken, if she hadn't chosen to climb a tree. She scanned the clearing, then the treeline, then did it all again.

It had to be there. The twelfth one had to…there! Just as she saw a hint of red paint, it vanished. Yet something was there, moving along the tree branch…

She nocked an arrow to her bow, sighting along it as she exhaled. Her arrow flew across the clearing, sinking into its target before tumbling off into the undergrowth.

There. Mission complete.

Rossa slid down the tree trunk and skipped into the clearing. "I'm done, Father," she announced. She couldn't keep the pride out of her voice.

"How many did you take down?"

"All twelve."

"Ah, but you missed one," he said, rising.

On the rock he'd been sitting on, a patterned sack came into view.

Rossa knew better than to argue. He'd said twelve and she'd hit twelve, but here was a thirteenth to taunt her.

She drew her dagger and flung it at the cloth. The blade struck the centre of the target, then tipped over onto the ground, taking the sack with it.

"All thirteen," she said.

"And now you're a blade short, with only half a quiver of arrows, going to meet the contact who sent you on your quest. Not all men are honourable, and those who would hire one assassin to kill for them aren't above hiring others, so that they don't have to pay the first," Father said, drawing both daggers.

Rossa swallowed. She had one knife in easy reach, but to draw any of the others, she'd need to take her gaze off her opponent, which would be a costly mistake.

Perhaps if she could reach the sack and the

knife she'd thrown…

She edged away from her father, hoping to put the stone between them before he advanced.

A shrill scream rose from the trees behind her.

"What in heaven's name – " she began.

Before she could finish, she found herself flat on her back, without the breath to say another word.

The screaming had stopped.

"This is what happens when you kill an innocent, and leave them to suffer," her father said, holding up one of her arrows, which impaled both a painted acorn and a squirrel who had tried to steal it. The limp squirrel would never scream again.

Rossa shuddered and sat up. She dragged in a breath, then said, "But it was a thief, stealing my acorn!"

"Thieves are beneath an assassin's notice. So is anyone except the target who deserves to die. Unless you are hired to kill a thief, or the thief threatens your life, he is nothing to you. Justice will find him, without your help." Father slid the squirrel's body off the arrow, and tossed it into the trees. "And you never hurt innocents."

"Thieving squirrels aren't innocent. The monks up at the castle swear about them all the time," Rossa protested.

Father just frowned. "Collect your things, then we'll return home. A good assassin…"

"Never leaves a trace," Rossa finished for him, sighing. Her father might have finished arguing with her, but she knew she hadn't won. No one could beat her father, in a fight or an argument. Least of all her.

Father inclined his head. "You have learned so much, Rossa. If I'd only known half what you do now when I was your age…" Now it was his turn not to finish his sentence. Instead, he sighed.

There was darkness in his past, from long before he met Mother, Rossa knew, but he never talked about it. She'd asked Mother, who'd told her that everyone had regrets, and her father's were for the people he could not save, which is why he had chosen his line of work in the first place.

He trained her so hard so that when her time came to exact justice, she would have no such regrets – she'd save those who needed it.

But after today's debacle, her time wouldn't be for a while yet.

Rossa sighed and tramped back along the game trail to retrieve her arrows.

Five

Dusk smudged the sky when Boris trudged up the steps to the throne room in Prislav, not pausing to take off the white fur cloak. The usual crowd of courtiers and petitioners was gone, so the king had finished hearings for the day. But the route to the royal apartments lay through the throne room, so he crossed the empty hall and kept going.

As Sviatopolk was a bastard, he'd had much more modest chambers in the palace than those given to Boris and his legitimate brothers, so it didn't surprise Boris at all to find his brother had already moved to the king's apartments.

What did surprise him was that his brother sat alone, his head and shoulders bowed with the weight of the kingdom he now carried.

"Is the crown so heavy, brother?" Boris asked.

Sviatopolk lifted his head. "Boris? Oh, you do not know how good it is to see you, brother!"

The two men embraced, and as Sviatopolk leaned against him for just that moment, Boris wondered if it was the weight of kingship he felt, a burden that was far more than one man could bear.

"How fared you in the campaign against the Bisseni?" Sviatopolk asked eagerly. "Father talked of little else in his final days. He made me swear I would not hinder you in your work, preserving our borders against those cowardly raiders. His greatest regret was not leaving a peaceful kingdom for his people."

Boris forced a smile. "The campaign ended in victory, or I should still be out there fighting them. What few Bisseni that were left fled into the mountains. They will not trouble us again for a while. And surely that cannot be all our father spoke of in his final moments. He named his heir, did he not?"

Sviatopolk shook his head.

What? A flash of triumph sparked in Boris's breast. He knew Father had not chosen Sviatopolk as his successor.

"I fear Father was too ill to know what he said at the end, for I scarcely believe it myself. In between his constant talk of you and your campaign, he made me swear to take the throne so you could stay in the field and fight. When the kingdom needs a king to make war on one front and another to sit on the throne and keep the peace with our neighbours, he had to choose, he said. So he said I should take the throne, so that you could command our armies. His final act was to declare the legitimacy of my birth, so that I might be crowned upon his death. I protested that you would make a better king, but he ordered me to be silent unless I wanted to go to war in your place. Heaven knows I am no warrior." Sviatopolk laughed.

As a bastard born of the king and a serving girl, Sviatopolk's blood had not been considered noble enough to cross swords with the other princes and young noblemen in the practice yard. Yet now he was the highest man in the land, with no sword skills to speak of. No, Sviatopolk would not have survived even his first battle against the Bisseni.

"So it is true? Father named you as his heir?" Boris pressed.

"For my sins, yes. I wish he had chosen someone better suited, but how can any son deny his father one last dying request?" Sviatopolk's eyes appeared haunted for a just a moment, before he managed a smile. "But you are here, and victorious, too, so we must have a feast to celebrate. I'll send word to the kitchens, and you shall sit at my right hand at the high table, so that we may drink to our father's memory, and the peace he did not live to see."

"I would be honoured, Your Majesty. And on the morrow, I will swear fealty to you, before the whole court," Boris said. His brother would not lie about such things. His father had chosen him to be king, with Boris as his general. Indeed, how could any dutiful son deny his father's last request?

Family did not betray family, after all.

Six

When Rossa sat down to dinner, she found her whole family present – including her half brother, Tobias, and his wife and children. Was it some important feast day, that she'd forgotten? She'd been so intent on her training, one day blended into another until even Sundays took her by surprise.

"Aren't you going to wish me a happy birthday?" Rossa's nephew, Bruno, demanded.

Ah, so that was the occasion.

Rossa shrugged. As her brother's only son and heir, Bruno was fussed over most days, so she felt little need to add to his over-inflated sense of self-importance.

"You're a terrible aunt," Bruno complained. "On my friend Peter's birthday, his spinster aunt gave him a whole new set of clothes, and new boots, with a purse of coins to hang from his new belt. And she spent a whole week before his birthday, cooking all his favourite foods."

"Peter the innkeeper's son?" Rossa asked. At Bruno's nod, she continued, "Dominique is not a spinster. She's a Rialto courtesan, who spends more money on potions from Swanhild and Raphael than the rest of Mirroten combined. Peter's new clothes were likely not new at all, but left behind by one of her clients." Rossa suspected Dominique would have quite the story to tell about the client who'd lost his clothes – she'd have to ask her to regale the tale when she next came home.

Bruno's brow creased with puzzlement.

Evidently his education had not included herbalism, or the customs and courtesans of Rialto. "You're still a mean aunt," he announced, before stuffing his face with food.

Assassins were not known for their kindness, so she said, "Good," before she reached for the meat.

Bruno swallowed with difficulty. "Peter says you're going to be a spinster because no one wants to marry you. You should be married already, he says."

"Peter says, or his older brother John says?" Rossa asked sharply. Though she wouldn't have put it past either of them to be making snide comments about her, after she'd repeatedly turned down invitations from both boys for most of the spring and summer. Last year, it had just been John, but now Peter was the ripe age of fourteen, he deemed himself enough of a man to pester her, too.

"They say if you don't marry soon, no one will have you, for all the good men will be taken," Bruno said. "You spend too much time in the forest alone. You'll never be as good as Master Zoticus. Better to be a proper wife and have babies. Some of them say you can't have babies because you're a witch, an evil witch."

Oh, that part was too good. "Ah, but I am a witch," she purred, wiggling her fingers. "Want to see if I can turn you into a slug without anyone noticing?"

"Mother!" The wail that came out of Bruno sounded like it came from a boy much younger than ten.

Conversation around the table stilled.

"What is it?" Silvana asked, the edge on her tone sharp enough to cut through bone. She didn't spoil her son, though Tobias did.

"Aunt Rossa said she'd turn me into a slug!"

"What did you say to her?"

"I only said what everyone says – she should hurry up and get married!"

Silvana's lips thinned. "And?"

Rossa recognised the danger in her sister in law's tone, even if Silvana's own son didn't.

"If she doesn't pick a husband soon, she'll

turn into an evil old witch!"

Silvana pointed at the door. "Lady Sara needs more kindling for the fire. Go outside and chop some for her. Now."

"But it's my birthday, and I haven't finished my dinner," Bruno whined.

"Do as your mother says, boy. Are you sure you're ten, if you haven't even learned that yet?" Father only had to look at Bruno for the boy to shrink. "What are you waiting for?"

Bruno bolted outside. Soon, Rossa could hear the sounds of an axe at work.

Silvana shook her head. "I'm sorry, Rossa, he's become impossible of late. Before the twins died, they kept him in order, but after…" She stared at Mother. "Was Tobias ever this much trouble?"

Mother laughed. "Tobias was never any trouble. He's always been his father's son, and if I hadn't been there at his birth, I'd wonder how such a placid child could have ever been mine. However, I do remember your father was quite the troublemaker. The things he used to get up to with my brothers…"

All dead now, Rossa knew.

"What the boy needs is some discipline and responsibility. Have you tried goats?" Father asked.

Mother bit back a smile, but no one else dared to laugh.

Tobias looked uncomfortable. "Since the avalanche took both his brothers, he won't go anywhere near the goats. He's terrified of them — has been since he was little, and one of them butted him so hard, he couldn't sit for a week."

Now it was Rossa's turn to smile. The boy had been taunting the goats, and she might have given the goat's horns a little magical help.

"You should have sent Bruno off to become a knight," Rossa said. In her father's stories, all knights deserved to be turned into slugs. Though he'd exacted a more permanent kind of justice on them, as was fitting for a man of his talents.

"He's a little old to be a pageboy, yet too

young to be a squire. Maybe..." Mother said, staring at Father. "Would you know a knight who would train him?"

Father looked thoughtful. "Several, actually, but I think he'd do best with the Baron of Maraschal. He owes me a favour for returning one of his breeding mares, among other things."

Rossa opened her mouth to ask for the tale, but her mother pointed at Tobias's two young daughters, and shook her head. Rossa shut her mouth with a snap, and resolved to ask him later.

"What sort of man is the Baron?" Tobias asked.

Father shrugged. "The Baron I knew is likely dead and buried by now, and one of his sons has taken his place. They were all honourable men, riding all over their family lands to settle disputes and see that their people were well defended. Their money comes from the exquisite horses they breed, local stock mixed with horses one of their ancestors brought back from the very first crusade, though they have some contacts in the Holy Land still. His daughter…why, I see her like in Rossa here. Young Melisende joined a crusade herself once, and held her own in battle, but she was a trained healer when she was at home, seeing to the health of all her father's people." Father grinned. "All the family work hard, especially when it comes to the horses. Bruno will learn to behave as a proper young baron should, or he'll spend his days shovelling horse shit."

Tobias didn't look convinced, but Silvana nodded sharply. "Will you write a letter to the Baron, please, Master Zoticus? The sooner we send Bruno to train, the better."

Father inclined his head. "You shall have it by morning, as long as Sara remembered to buy more ink from the traders today."

"Of course I remembered. I'm not so old that I would forget to visit any traders who come so far up the river. They would not let me forget, either – you spend more coin than the rest of the town combined." Mother sucked in a breath. "Oh, I almost forgot. A message came for you, too. I didn't dare break the seal on the scroll."

A frown crossed Father's face, before serenity reigned there again. "I'll read it after dinner. Whatever they want can wait."

Mother looked like she wanted to argue, but she stayed silent. Whoever's emblem she'd seen on the seal must be important. A king, an emperor…or perhaps the Pope? Father travelled less and less now, but he still took on some assignments. He might have more white hair than brown, but he was still a formidable fighter any man would fear.

One day, she'd be good enough to go with him. But if she asked today, she knew what the answer would be. He no longer said a simple, "No," anymore – he'd ask her if she thought she was ready to be an assassin, to take someone's life while keeping a firm hand on her own, yet to do it so subtly, so carefully, that no one but she would know she had done the deed.

If it weren't for that thieving squirrel…

Rossa sighed. One day. But not today, or tomorrow, either.

Seven

"To the late king, my father. May his place in heaven be assured!" Sviatopolk shouted, raising his cup.

Boris joined him in the toast, as did most of the courtiers in the feasting hall. Once again, his cup was empty. This would not have happened when Kyrilu was his squire, but Igor still had much to learn.

Boris gestured for a servant to fill his cup. After some time, Igor appeared, looking sulky, but carrying a pitcher of ale.

"A squire should be more attentive, boy. This is not the first time my cup has been empty. The king has proposed many toasts tonight, and if I had to refuse to drink on account of having an empty cup, it would be a terrible slight to my brother. Why, better men have been tried for treason, bringing such dishonour to their king!" Boris said, thrusting his cup forward.

"Perhaps if you did not drink so much, Your Highness," Igor said. "If you were more careful about what you drink – "

Boris slammed his hand on the table. "I will not be lectured to by my squire. I can hold my drink as well as any man here, and you'd do well to remember your station. Your job is to keep my cup filled, and if you do not, I shall find myself a better squire who can!"

Igor winced. "But, Your Highness – "

"Fill my cup or get out of my sight!"

Igor filled the cup, and Boris drained it, then held it out for more.

"Again!"

The look on Igor's face was one of pure pain, as though pouring the drink cut him to the core. Yet he did as he was commanded, before slinking away.

None too soon, for Sviatopolk was on his feet again, raising his cup to Boris.

"My late father said this kingdom must have both a ruler and a protector, and he was blessed to have sons who could do both. United, Prince Boris and I will bring a peace to this kingdom even my wise father could not. I pledge the health of Prince Boris. May we celebrate many more of his victories, against the Bisseni and any other enemy who dares to threaten us!" Sviatopolk roared.

Roars of agreement came from around the hall as everyone drank Boris's health.

He felt his face grow hot. His king had praised him, and he had not yet toasted his new king's health. He must make amends.

Boris rose up onto unsteady feet. The ale was strong tonight — he had not drunk too much of it, no matter what his squire said.

"To our new king. Long may he reign!" Boris said. He lifted his cup, then drained it in one big gulp.

The other men in the hall thundered their approval, shouts and stomps ringing from the very rafters as they drank to their king's health.

Boris sat down suddenly, finding his legs would no longer hold him up.

The ale must be terribly strong, for he could not remember being this drunk since…

The world went black.

Eight

When day dawned, Father had already left, and Mother had that steely look in her eye that said anyone who disobeyed her would rue it for the rest of their life.

So when Mother said, "We must finish shelling the chestnuts today," Rossa merely nodded and resigned herself to a day at home.

At least she'd be spared Bruno's company — Father had written the letter he'd promised, and Tobias and Silvana were preparing him for the journey to the Baron of Maraschal's lands. Tobias would take him on the morrow, and hope to be home before winter.

Rossa finished her breakfast, and headed for the smokehouse. The sooner she started, the sooner she'd be finished for the day. Maybe there'd be enough light to squeeze in some archery practice, when the chestnuts were done.

Mother had taught her to choose chestnuts the way her mother and grandmother had taught her, weighing each in her hand as she picked them. So Rossa knew what to look for when she sat in the middle of the smokehouse and summoned her magic.

Four baskets drifted into a line before her, ready and waiting. Rossa took a deep breath and sent her awareness out through the smokehouse. The ripest, ready to be released from their shells, rose from the racks where they'd been smoking for weeks, and floated to the nearest basket. Within moments, all four baskets were filled to the brim.

Rossa took two baskets in each hand, and headed outside to the table overlooking the lake that gave Mirroten its name.

"Good morning! I thought you'd be in the forest, training with your father," Swanhild said, already seated and waiting.

Rossa forced out a smile. "A message came for Father yesterday, so he left for urgent business this morning." She pulled off her soft slippers and tugged on her boots.

Swanhild's grin was as natural as the sky above. "Ooh, I wonder who his business involves."

"He's gone to the Emperor's court in Byzas. It could be anybody," Mother said, dumping the first basket of chestnuts into the pressing tub.

Rossa didn't wait for her to ask — she stepped into the tub and started crushing the shells with her heavy boots. Usually Silvana did this, but not today.

"So, do you think he's going to assassinate the Emperor, or work for him?" Swanhild asked.

"In that court, anything's possible, but from what he said last night, I suspect he's tangled in a squabble between two members of the royal family. He wants us to spend the winter up at the castle, just in case," Mother said.

Rossa stepped out of the tub, so that her mother could divide the crushed chestnuts between the baskets for peeling.

"I told him we'd go as soon as the chestnuts are sent to the mill," Mother finished.

Rossa's breath caught in her throat. Spending a whole winter at the castle in the mountains? She hadn't done that since she was a small child, hiding from the plague that had swept up the river, wiping out whole villages.

"Is Silvana going, too?" Swanhild asked.

"No, she's staying to take care of the town. Truly, I should pass the title to her and Tobias now, if I had any sense, and retire from the town council and everything." Mother's hands moved so quickly, prying the nuts loose from their shells, then tossing the nuts into one sack and the shells into a tub at her feet.

Swanhild laughed. "My mother would turn over in her grave to hear you say that! It wouldn't be Mirroten without Mistress Sara ruling over us all, she would say, before telling some story about how you terrified a grown man into doing your bidding. She would have loved to see you tame Master Zoticus."

That set Mother laughing, too. "Zoticus is the sort of man who can never be tamed. I never thought he could be content staying here in Mirroten, and he has gone away on his missions, as he calls them, yet he always returns to me. Maybe that's why Rossa hasn't fallen for any of the boys in town. She yearns for someone untameable, like I did."

"Is that true, Rossa?" Swanhild asked. "Is that why you spend so much time in the forest – looking for a wild man to take as your lover?"

Rossa choked. "I go hunting in the forest with my father!" They never encountered anyone else, except occasionally Swanhild, when the healer was out collecting herbs.

"So you don't know where the clearing with the ancient altar is? Remind me to show you sometime," Swanhild said, mischief twinkling in her eyes. "It would not do if you got lost on your way there with your wild lover."

"Don't say such things in front of my mother!" Rossa hissed.

"Your mother, who has gone quite a telling shade of red? Oh, Mistress Sara knows exactly where her ancestors performed their ancient fertility rites, for she's the one who showed my mother, who passed the knowledge on to me. If I'm not mistaken, your brother Tobias was likely conceived before that very altar."

Mother rose. "I'm going to get more nuts." She hurried off to the smokehouse.

Swanhild smiled. "There, now she's gone…what's his name? Your lover in the woods?"

"I'm not in love with anyone!" Rossa cried, clenching her fists. Magic bubbled up within her. If she shed so much as a drop of blood, she'd sent the whole table flying, chestnuts and all. She fought to control it.

"That's because the man for you is not here. He's…" Swanhild closed her eyes and bit her lip, sparking her own magic into life. She sat there in silence for a long moment before her eyes popped open. "Ooh, I can feel him, though he's far away. Over the mountains. At the castle, maybe, or the monastery? Maybe you will seduce a monk. Enchant him so completely, he forgets his vows of celibacy and pledges himself to your pleasure instead…"

Now Rossa's cheeks grew hot. "I would never ask a man to break his vows. And I could never love someone so dishonourable."

"Maybe a courtier, then? The king's court lies that way, across the mountains, too. When the winter is over, your mother might send you to court. You are a lady, after all. A pity there is no queen at the moment, or I would suggest your mother send you to be one of her ladies in waiting. Plenty of men you might meet when you keep company with a queen."

Swanhild's smile faltered a little.

She had spent time at court, before she married Raphael, the town apothecary, Rossa remembered. "Was that what you were?" she asked eagerly. "A lady in waiting?"

Swanhild shuddered. "No, I was…more like the queen's ward, for a time. Before she came to a tragic end. The king never did remarry. A most…unfortunate affair."

Rossa opened her mouth to ask for Swanhild to tell the whole tale, instead of just this tantalising glimpse.

"What is unfortunate?" Mother demanded, tipping a new basket of nuts into the pressing tub.

"Oh, I was just saying to Rossa that it is unfortunate we have no queen, or she could go to court to meet her wild man," Swanhild said. She grew thoughtful. "If he's a courtier, he would have to be most refined in the king's presence, and keep his wildness for the hunt or the bedchamber. You'd have to accompany a hunting party to see him truly in his element, I imagine."

Rossa fought her rising panic. She didn't want a man in her bedchamber.

"Zoticus would never allow his daughter to go to court without him," Sara said. "No suitor would dare look at her with him around."

Rossa dared to breathe again.

"Don't be silly. Rossa will fall for a man who not only has the courage to stand before her father, but who does not fear him." Swanhild held out her empty basket for Rossa to fill.

"But I don't...I won't..." Rossa began.

Mother burst out laughing. "There isn't a man alive who isn't afraid of my Zoticus. And if there is, he's a fool. Rossa would not choose to marry a fool."

"I don't want to marry anyone!" Rossa said hotly.

Swanhild patted her hand. "Of course not. None of us want to be bothered by a man, until the right man gets down on his knees. It usually takes him a few tries to work out what to do with his tongue, if he's not that experienced, but once you've trained him…"

"You're as salty as your mother!" Mother swore.

"I'm going to get more nuts," Rossa said, heading for the smokehouse.

Neither woman noticed, for they were too busy talking about…unspeakable things. At length. With obscene hand gestures and way too much laughter.

Nine

The sound of screaming sent daggers through Boris's head. By all that was holy, why had he drunk so much? And why in heaven's name must they scream so?

"Enough, woman," he grumbled.

But the screams only grew louder. He fancied he could hear his name amid the wordless shrieks.

Boris forced his eyes open, and felt as if the light were stabbing them, too. The light of a single torch lit the stone room, but it was enough to see a pair writhing on the floor together.

"Go bed the girl in your own chamber," Boris grumbled, lifting his hand to shade his eyes.

Or at least he tried to, but he couldn't seem to reach. His hand stopped short, and he squinted to see why. A manacle encased his wrist, fastened to a chain that he assumed was fixed to the wall behind him. His other hand bore a metal cuff, too, and equally heavy chains.

"Boris! Help me!"

Boris blinked. Vica? Some other man was bedding Vica? He roared and tried to reach them, but his chain was too short.

His struggles attracted the man's attention, though, so he left Vica alone to stride over to Boris. The stranger wore the livery of the castle guards, though he was no one Boris knew.

Boris's eyes darted to Vica. Blood stained

the front of her slashed gown, and tears streaked her cheeks, which already darkened with a blooming bruise no doubt inflicted by the villainous guard advancing on him.

"I will have you executed for daring to touch the Princess of Rostov," Boris declared, glaring at the man.

"Me and the princess are busy," the man declared, throwing a punch at Boris.

Between the mother of all hangovers and his chains, Boris was too slow to dodge the blow. Instead, the man sent him reeling against the wall, and the impact sent him back into the darkness, followed by the sound of Vica's screams.

Ten

It was late afternoon by the time Mother called a halt to peeling chestnuts, so she and Swanhild might make dinner. Rossa escaped before she was forced to help with the cooking, too. She'd rather be out in the forest, hunting fresh meat for the stewpot, than hunched over the stewpot, stirring it.

After all day sitting in the autumn sun, the coolness in the shade of the forest was as refreshing as the waterskin of well-water she'd brought with her. Rossa's feet found their own way back to the clearing where she'd last trained with Father.

Where a single squirrel had been her downfall.

The squirrel's corpse still lay where it had fallen, cold and stiff after a night on the ground. She bit her lip and sent a bolt of magic into the dead squirrel. The sort of magic she didn't dare practice in town, or where anyone might see her.

The squirrel moved, stiffly at first, then more like the living creature it had once been as the magic began to work.

"Take to the trees," Rossa whispered to it.

The squirrel scampered up the nearest tree trunk, then broke into a run across the branches above Rossa's head.

She dug her teeth into her lip again, conjuring missiles made of magic alone. One by one, she directed the dagger-shaped projectiles at the fast-moving squirrel. And again, and again…

The magic blades passed harmlessly though the enchanted squirrel, before splashing on the leaves and branches behind it. The magic crackled and spat for a moment, before it vanished, leaving the trees relatively unharmed.

It did not have to be so — she could conjure fireballs, blades of ice or bolts of magic so concentrated, they punched holes through things. Father sometimes permitted her to practice with magical projectiles, but he preferred her to be proficient in more mundane weapons, leaving her magic for a last resort. A secret weapon, ready to be called upon when she needed it.

She'd tried using her magic against her father once in a fight, and only succeeded in knocking herself out when the spell rebounded, magnified, thanks to one of the magical charms he wore. She'd since managed to replicate such a shield around herself — no charm needed — but it had taken the shape of a large bubble, a sword's length from her body, so that it stopped her from fighting at all.

As the waning evening light would, too.

Rossa sighed. Her mother expected her home by nightfall. Never mind that there was nothing in this forest that was a match for her magic – her mother's word was law, and Rossa knew better than to disobey.

Besides, if she was late for dinner, there might be nothing left – Mother had been known to give their leftovers to the less fortunate in town. Especially if they were headed up into the mountains soon.

Rossa took a moment to dispel the spell on the squirrel, then buried the creature's corpse in a shallow grave beside the tree it had originally fallen from. Thief or no, it had helped her today, however unwittingly. And yesterday, for her father was right – she did need to be vigilant, not just for thieves, but for innocents who did not deserve to die.

Tomorrow, she would do better. And with that thought, Rossa straightened her shoulders and strode home.

Eleven

When Boris awoke, the chains were gone. Had he dreamed them?

A straw pallet crackled beneath him as he rolled over, sliding out from under what he recognised as his white cloak and onto the cold stone floor. The blinding headache he'd had in his dream was little more than a memory.

And Vica…

No, Vica was home in Rostov, where she belonged, with Lida. He could not have seen her here in Prislav, with some other man.

He drew in a deep breath and let it out slowly, before taking another.

It smelled like a battlefield in here. Had Igor neglected to clean his armour again?

"Igor? Where are you, boy?" Boris demanded.

"I'm here, Your Highness." The boy appeared, his eyes wide with what looked like terror.

If the boy would only do his job, he wouldn't have to fear punishment, but Boris didn't say it aloud. Let the boy figure it out for himself.

"Fetch me something to eat and drink," Boris said. "And then clean my armour."

The boy swallowed. "I...I can't, Your Highness. I can only give you this." He held out a bottle, small enough to fit in the boy's closed fist. "I'm to tell you if you wish to live to seek vengeance, you must drink this. Word reached us today that your brother David is dead, too. Cut down as he prayed for your father's soul in the chapel."

David was dead? But David was just a boy, and his only surviving full-blood brother, sent to a monastery to spend his life serving the church. No one could possibly want to murder David, and what man would kill a prince at prayer?

"Your brother did this. If you want vengeance, you must drink this," Igor insisted.

Boris's wits were slow, but those he'd begun to gather told him not to trust Igor. He dashed the bottle from the boy's hand, and it fell into the straw. "I'll drink no more of your poison, traitor. You gave me the tainted ale at the feast."

The boy bowed his head, but he did not deny it.

"Tell me where I might find my wife."

Boris prayed she was safe at Rostov, where she belonged.

The boy's eyes grew wide. He swallowed. Words seemed to fail him as he raised a shaking hand to point across the room. "She's there, Your Highness."

So he had not dreamed it. Vica was here.

"Get out," Boris snarled at the boy.

Igor scrambled away, bolting through the door before slamming it behind him.

Boris sat up, and, when his head did not threaten to explode, he rose to his feet.

A bundle of bloody clothes lay in the corner, as though someone had flung them there.

Please, let it not be her.

He forced himself to step closer. One step. Another. A third. Until he was close enough to turn the bundle over.

By all that was holy…

No, by all that was unholy.

Vica's mouth hung open in a silent scream, likely at the dagger buried in her breast that had stopped her heart. Her lifeblood stained her gown in rusty brown, wet and cold, for her spirit had fled many hours ago, while he'd lain senseless.

He shifted her body until he laid her out on

the stone floor, then folded her arms across her breast. He should take the dagger out, and use it to take the life of his wife's murderer.

But what did he know about the man, aside from the guard uniform he'd worn?

Boris scanned the room, looking for some clue to the man's identity.

Only then did he see the second, smaller bundle.

His arms reached out of their own accord, before even his mind could stop him.

The bastard who'd killed his wife had cut Lida's throat, slicing so deep, he'd almost taken the little girl's head off.

Boris fell to his knees, cradling his daughter's mangled body to his chest, and wept.

Twelve

An eternity might have passed, or it could have only been a moment. Boris wasn't sure it mattered any more. He laid Lida's body beside her mother's, hands folded at her breast like the angel she surely was now.

He stared down at what had been his family, wishing with all his heart that he was with them now.

It would be so easy…

He had only to take the dagger from Vica's

breast, still coated with the blood that had once given her so much life, and plunge it into his own heart. Two hearts, together forever.

The dagger felt so light in his hand, as cold as the death that awaited him, just one sharp thrust away.

But the balance was off…this was some other man's knife, an inferior blade to his own. Boris threw it down, and it clattered across the stone floor to land in the straw pallet he'd slept on.

David would have shaken his head, and told him it was a sin to take your own life. If Boris killed himself, he'd never see Vica and Lida again.

Or David, who was dead, too.

Dead by his brother's hand, if Igor was to be believed. Was his brother responsible for Vica's death, too? And little Lida, who had never been a threat to anyone?

The only brother here in Prislav who could have had a hand in their death was Sviatopolk. Their cursed new king.

His brother's betrayal stabbed him sharper

than any knife. No, Sviatopolk was no brother of his. Not kin or blood or anything to him. He was as destined for death as any Bisseni raider who dared set foot on their kingdom's soil

Vica, David, Lida…had Sviatopolk killed their father, too? Such a vile traitor might do anything to secure the throne.

But he would not have it, Boris vowed. He cursed Sviatopolk's name, and cursed that he'd ever called the worm brother.

No more.

He'd bury the inferior blade in his brother's breast, and make him bleed. For Vica.

Boris headed for the pile of straw where he'd last seen the dagger. He donned the cloak, still miraculously white in a room so steeped in blood. Then he clawed though the bed, desperate to find the blade, but his hand closed around a bottle instead.

The bottle Igor had given him. For vengeance.

Boris uncorked it, and sniffed at the contents.

Liquid sloshed, sending the scent of bitter herbs wafting up his nose.

Vengeance did not smell like much more than a simple tonic, if that's what this was.

Yet there were poisons that could not be discerned by smell alone, like whatever Igor had put into his ale at the feast.

Ale Igor had told him not to drink, now he remembered. Did that mean this new elixir would help set things right?

Or send his soul spiralling up to heaven to rejoin his wife and daughter?

Carefully, Boris corked the bottle and set it on the floor.

He took a cloth and washed his wife's face, then did the same for his daughter. Long he looked at them, memorising every detail, for if he succeeded in this, he might never see them again.

But it would be worth it, to know they were avenged, and their souls could rest.

Until they were, his soul would never rest.

He leaned over and kissed Lida's cheek, like he'd done so many times before.

Never again.

Swallowing, he moved to kneel beside Vica, Princess Slavica of Rostov, a woman he'd been blessed to call his wife, if only for a little while. He touched his lips to hers, wishing fate had allowed them one last kiss. For letting her die instead of defending her, he did not deserve one, but men have always wished for more than they deserved, he knew.

Boris uncorked the bottle, and raised it high. "For you. For David and Lida and my father, but most of all for you, Vica. May your place in heaven be assured, as I send the man responsible for all this to hell."

He drank.

The potion was barely a mouthful, yet it burned his mouth like molten metal, coating his throat in liquid fire until he could not even scream at the agony.

Still it burned, invading his blood, spreading through his body like wildfire, until he could bear the pain no more and the world went white.

Thirteen

They hadn't been on the road for three days when Rossa noticed the first flakes of white on her horse's mane. "Mother, it's snowing," she said in wonder, holding out her hand to catch some.

Mother frowned. "It's far too early for snow. We must ride faster, to get there before the pass closes."

Reluctantly, Rossa put her glove back on and urged her mare to pick up the pace.

It was still snowing when they stopped for the night, settling in white drifts anywhere that was open to the sky. Mother found a clear spot under some trees to pitch their tent, and Rossa set to work. Everything was fine until she backed into a tree branch that dumped a load of snow on her.

Rossa swore, then bit her lip and cast a shield, pushing it out a few yards to encompass the tent, her mother and the fire her mother was attempting to light. "Stay," she told it.

And it did, like a big, invisible, dome-shaped tent that kept the snow out. It slid down the sides, instead, until it formed a wall high enough for Mother to notice.

"Did you do that?" she asked, wiping a sooty hand across her brow. The firepit remained ominously dark.

Rossa nodded. "I can light the fire for you, too, if you like. Just...don't tell Father."

Mother rose clumsily from her crouch. "And why in heaven's name would I not?"

Rossa ducked her head. "Because he doesn't

think magic should be used for mundane things. Cookfires and pitching tents and things that most people do without magic. He says…"

"Your father says a lot of things. And while I admit he knows more about magic than me, given both his mother and sister were enchantresses like you, I've seen him use magic for plenty of mundane things. In fact, every fire he's ever lit while travelling uses a magic candle that his mother gave him when he was a boy. A candle he keeps in his magic travelling bag, with all manner of other things." Mother sighed. "Perhaps he means that you should not take your magic for granted, to use such power without thinking about it first. To consider whether to use magic, or to stay your hand. My friend Tola, Swanhild's mother, always thought twice before using magic, because her husband used to beat her if he caught her casting a spell. Even after he died, she'd hesitate. She still warded her shop, though, and she used her magic to save Swanhild, though it cost her own life, in the end." She wiped away tears. "Oh, look at me, crying over the dead, though it's been nigh on twenty years since I last saw her. More, maybe, as it was before you were born. The last thing we talked about was your father, and how she thought I should…give him a chance."

If she was anything like Swanhild, Tola had probably said something far more crude than that. But she'd been Mother's friend, and Mother still mourned her, so Rossa kept her thoughts to herself.

"Your father slept in the tower room, and then Raphael did, when Zoticus moved into my chambers. I thought you might like the tower for yourself, this time. I sent word up to the castle to have rooms prepared for us, so it should be ready for you. But if you don't like it, I'm sure we can move your things somewhere else," Mother said.

Rossa remembered the tower room, and how Raphael would lift her up to see out the windows so she could gaze out over the countryside. When she was little, it had seemed like watching the whole world. Something God might do, and not mere mortals like her. Now, she knew she hadn't even seen the full extent of her mother's lands.

Mother, who knelt in the dirt to light her own fire, to cook their meal, because it never occurred to her to rely on servants to do what she could do herself.

As long as she didn't expect Rossa to cook. At best, she'd burn everything to cinders, and at worst, she'd poison them all, herself included. The last time she'd tried, Father had caught her in time to keep her from killing anyone. He'd said she was just like her aunt, who couldn't cook, either, and told Mother to keep Rossa out of the kitchen.

"I'm sure the tower room will be fine," Rossa said. It wasn't like she'd spend much time there, during her waking hours. She'd be training, much like she did at home. Because when her father returned, she intended to be ready. "Shall I light that fire for you now?"

Earth and damp and…was that wet dog he smelled? Wet fur, anyway, musky and earthy, like he'd been hunting too long in the forest.

Hunting?

Boris opened his eyes to darkness. No, dimness, for he could faintly see the outlines of walls that no sane builder would ever knowingly construct. Things stuck out of the wall and ceiling and sometimes even the floor, jagged like teeth that intended to devour him when the monster whose mouth he'd stumbled into developed an appetite.

Was he in hell, then?

No, hell would be hotter, instead of just a pleasant temperature.

He lay in a cave, then, upon a pile of half-rotted leaves, with a stream trickling in the darkness, real darkness, deeper inside. Now, if he could only find the dog…

Boris scanned the cave.

There, in the corner. Something that might be an emaciated dog, curled up in exhaustion, a bag of bones clinging to life.

Boris approached cautiously, not wanting to scare the beast so that it would bite.

Yet the closer he got, the less it looked like a dog, or any animal at all. A bag of bones, perhaps, but their owner had departed life a long time ago.

Boris picked up the sack and emptied it onto the ground. Metal clunked and clanged into a pile at his feet, catching what little light there was like no bones he'd ever seen.

Atop the pile was a crown he'd only ever seen on his father's head, on special events. His mother's crown lay in the tangle of items, too, along with what looked like a collection of the crown jewels.

Sviatopolk might sit on the throne, but he would never wear his father's crown, Boris thought with satisfaction.

The rightness of this thought, combined with the memory of his own hands stuffing the crowns into the sack, told him he'd been the one to steal these things, and he'd planned it to spite his brother.

Everything else was hazy, though, until he'd woken up here. His last clear memory was of drinking Igor's potion, which hadn't poisoned him after all.

Ah, but he'd said someone had ordered him to give Boris the potion, hadn't he? That mean Igor hadn't prepared the draught himself, and likely had no idea what it would do when Boris drank it.

A dog whined.

Boris shifted to a crouch, reaching for a sword that wasn't at his side, where it should be. He cursed his own stupidity for stealing the crown jewels, yet forgetting to procure a sword.

Another whine, as shadows crowded at the cave's entrance.

Not one wet dog, but a pack of them.

The thought had barely coalesced in his mind before Boris realised his mistake.

They weren't dogs at all, but a pack of wolves.

He scrabbled at his belt, only to realise that not only had he forgotten his sword, he'd neglected to don a belt, too. It was a blessing he'd remembered to put on clothing at all, for without the thick fur garments he wore, he'd surely freeze to death in the chilly autumn evening.

One wolf stepped forward, the leader of this war band, and it gave a snarl.

Boris stared at it, reaching down for the jewelled sceptre his father had once told him had been a gift from the Emperor of Byzas.

He prayed that his father, and the long-dead emperor who had given this gift, would grant his arm and the sceptre the strength to defeat these enemies, so that he might survive to take the crown jewels somewhere safe.

The wolf leaped.

Boris swung the sceptre.

The wolf flew over its packmates and straight out of the cave.

The rest of the wolves attacked as one.

Afterwards, Boris couldn't say what had happened. He'd felt rage and a haze had come down over his eyes, and when he'd been able to think again, two wolves lay dead at his feet, while a third tried to drag itself away when both of its back legs were clearly broken.

Boris considered the injured wolf for a moment, then seized the sceptre and brought it down upon the beast's head, ending its pain. No animal deserved to suffer so.

Only when he was certain the third beast was dead did he go back to examine the other two. Both bore deep claw marks, like some great beast had slashed at them until they'd punctured something vital. Yet the only beasts Boris had seen were the wolves themselves, which did not have claws like that.

If anything, he'd think a lion had been here.

Boris tried not to laugh. There were stories of lions in far-off lands, but he'd never seen one outside of books.

He shook his head and headed out of the cave, hoping he might wash the sceptre in the stream. It wouldn't do to have the crown jewels caked in blood.

He followed the tiny stream down the hill, until it widened into a pool big enough to immerse the sceptre in. He leaned over, wondering at the hulking shape he saw reflected in the water.

By all that was holy, it was a —

Boris overbalanced and fell in, shattering the reflection and driving all thoughts from his mind, except the most immediate question of how not to drown.

Fifteen

It was almost dark when they finally reached the castle, but the gates were open and the courtyard was filled with torches, lighting their way in.

"Lady Sara, it is an honour!" a woman said, bobbing a curtsy, and the shadowy figures behind her did the same.

"Salacia? It has been too long!" Mother, never one to stand on ceremony, hugged the woman. "What have you been doing all these years?"

"Well, after running the boarding house for the construction crew who built the new monastery, I married one of the masons who had a secret talent for brewing beer. We turned the boarding house into an inn for pilgrims who come to see the relics. Since they saved Mirroten from the plague, many more miracles are hoped for, and not a day passes without half a dozen pilgrims arriving. Well, until the winter closes the passes, which looks like it might happen early this year. That's had a lot of people heading home, so I've left my daughters to take care of the kitchens there while I claim the castle kitchens again." Salacia grinned. "I nearly cried when I reached the cellars — so much to choose from! And always the very best."

Mother frowned. "Has the harvest been poor here this year? Or are the monks taking too much? You have only to send word down to Mirroten. We would not let you go hungry."

Salacia laughed. "Oh, no, 'tis not that, Lady

Sara. But the best of the harvest always goes to the castle cellars. It's tradition. There's plenty left for the rest of us – even the pilgrims who come to see the relics at Holy Innocents on the Lake, as they call it. No, it's that the pilgrims expect plain food, not the fancy stuff that I used to make in the castle kitchens. With wine and spices and honeyed fruits from Rialto…why, it's almost like Christmas come early, though it's months off yet. But what am I saying? You must be tired from your journey. I'll have warm water sent up to your chamber and dinner will be on the table when you come down."

"Rossa can bathe and change in my chamber for now, as she used to," Mother said. "Right, Rossa?"

Rossa nodded.

Salacia's eyes widened as she stared at Rossa. "Why, I had it in my head that you would be little Lady Rossa, just like I remembered, not a real lady, old enough to be wed! Beg pardon, milady." She dropped another curtsy, considerably lower than the one she'd given Mother.

A real lady, old enough to wed. No, she was neither of those things. And if Mother could hug the woman, then Rossa was allowed to be informal, too.

Rossa summoned a smile. "Please, don't, um, Mistress Salacia. No one at home calls me that. I'm just Rossa. And no wedding for a while yet." If ever, she added silently.

Salacia beamed. "You're just like your mother. You should call me Sal, like you did when you were a little girl." She rubbed her hands together with what Rossa suspected was glee. "Ooh, you wait until some of the boys in the village see you! They'll fall all over themselves to impress you, I'm sure."

Rossa's smile faltered. That was the last thing she needed. "I'll go up and wash, I think."

"Of course, of course." Sal shooed her inside.

Thankfully, Rossa knew the way up to the

tower. When she reached the top of the stairs, she opened the window, scooped up a bucket of snow, and melted it with a well-placed fireball. More than melted it, what with those wisps of steam curling up from the water.

She washed quickly, wishing she could immerse her whole body in hot water, but that would have to wait until she found a suitable tub, and carried enough water up those stairs to fill it, as there wasn't enough snow on the windowsill to fill more than a bucket or two.

Rossa brought in what she could, then closed the shutters. It was too dark to see anything out there now, and the snow was still falling.

She surveyed her tower room, which felt smaller now than it had all those years ago. Perhaps it was the carved bed that took up most of the floor space – Raphael's narrow pallet had been enough for him then. Had he and Swanhild ever…?

Shuddering, Rossa trotted down the stairs for dinner, trying to shake such distasteful thoughts out of her head.

Sixteen

"Where's the rest of it?"

Boris blinked, but his eyes just didn't want to stay open. Nearly drowning and having to drag oneself out of a surprisingly deep pool took a toll on a man.

Something poked him in the belly. Hard.

"Where's the rest of it?"

That sounded a bit like Igor, but it couldn't be. No squire would use such a tone to his master. Not unless he wanted to be clouted across the ear and assigned latrine duties for the next month. Two stints of latrine duty had surely taught Igor some manners by now.

And yet, whoever it was persisted to poke him most painfully.

Boris flung his arm out, shoving his tormentor away, before he forced his eyes open.

An angry Igor sat on the ground, presumably where he'd landed, with the dripping sceptre in his hands.

The sceptre Boris had been forced to leave in the pond, so that he might save himself from drowning.

"Give me that, boy," Boris said, stretching out his hand.

Igor stuck the sceptre behind his back. "No! You give me what you stole from the king, so I can take it back. You should have just taken the potion and run, or not drunk the ale, like I told you! Instead, you stole the crown jewels, so he knew you weren't dead, and he won't rest...I won't rest...until I bring back everything you stole, and you!" His voice had crept up higher in his panic, as though he knew he was on an impossible quest, but it was too late for him to refuse it.

Better for the boy to give up, head to some other kingdom, and find a less treacherous king to serve.

Boris rose. "He is no longer my king." He snatched the sceptre out of the boy's hands, and held it up high, where he could not reach it. "You can go back and tell him the only time he will see the crown jewels again is when he submits to justice for what he did. I will wear them to his execution."

Igor began jumping like a flea, trying to reach the sceptre. "You don't understand! I must bring them to him! I must!"

Boris sighed. "Then you're the stupidest squire who ever lived," he said sadly. With one swipe of his arm, he sent the boy sprawling, out cold.

He took the sceptre back the cave, where he packed it into the sack with all the other treasures. Then, he headed deeper into the forest, where Igor would not be able to find him. Even his stupid squire would have to give up some time.

Seventeen

When day dawned, it took but a moment for Rossa to get her bearings and remember where she was, before she threw open the shutters, to see the world outside. Not just one, but all the shutters, though at the first touch of chill air she put up a shield to keep the warmth inside the tower, while still letting her look out.

Sometime in the night, it had stopped snowing, and the sky was now as clear and crisp as the icicles that would soon festoon the eaves around the castle. The world…well, the world was white, smoothing the ground while it frosted the trees and shrubs, blanketing the roofs of cottage and monastery alike. Only the lake stood out, bright blue depths like a single, giant eye, staring at the sky above.

But it was the forest that drew her gaze, trees stretching endlessly up into the mountains for many miles more than she could see. She wouldn't be surprised if the forest did not thin until it reached the plains on the other side of the mountains, where the king's court lay. Not that she or any other sane person would travel that way, when there were roads and rivers, both far more sensible ways to reach the capital. If her father ever deemed her ready to go there.

He would. Maybe not this week or this month or even this year, given it was waning into winter, but he would.

As long as she did not slacken in her training. And what was a little snow, except a new challenge to be faced?

Movement caught her eye, between the trees, way down below. A creature of some kind…no, several of them. A herd of deer, she realised, fattened for winter but still searching for just a little more to eat before the final frosts set in.

She and Father had talked of going hunting, before he'd been summoned to Byzas. Because winter stews and sausages wouldn't be the same without a little smoked venison to season them. Without Father here, she'd have to go alone, but she didn't mind. She was more than a match for any deer.

She dressed for the hunt in clothes that had once been her brother's, though Tobias was much broader in the chest and shoulders now. Sure, the tunic was a little tight across her breasts, but it would do for today. Tomorrow, she could buy new ones in the village, at whatever tailor or weaver shops existed here in the mountains. Mother would approve of her bringing her trade to the local businesses, and they'd likely make warmer vestments than what was needed in Mirroten. They'd need the warmth up here in the mountains.

Maybe it was time to get a new winter cloak, too. She fancied a fur one, though she didn't think there was anything big enough in these mountains with the fur to fashion a whole cloak from. So pieces, maybe, from a hundred thieving squirrels…

Rossa laughed softly to herself. It would take all winter to amass so many squirrel pelts. Then again, it wasn't like she'd have anything else to do up here except hunt…

Venison first, then she could think about clothes, she scolded herself, taking her bow and a quiver of arrows, plus a brace of knives, as her weapons for today. A quick stop to the kitchen, where Sal plied her with fresh bread, a waterskin and some of the last autumn apples, and Rossa was soon headed out the gates, to the freedom of the high forests.

She mapped the forest in her mind's eye, trying to match what she'd seen from her tower to the view down here on the ground.

The deer had been…that way, she decided, marching into the trees.

Her boots crunched through the snow, making her wish she'd chosen softer leather shoes instead. But they'd have been soaked in an instant, she knew, which was why she'd donned the heavy boots. Still, she was hardly a silent hunter, when anyone could hear her from miles away. Not even deer were that stupid.

If she intended to hunt today, she'd have to make it an ambush, lying in wait where no one would hear her. Of course, that meant guessing which way her prey would go, so that she might surprise them.

She cast her mind back to the view from the tower. Several streams meandered into the lake from the mountains, and the deer had been heading toward one. If she got there first and found a tree to hide in…her noisy boots would no longer matter.

Almost by magic, she found a fresh trail that led to the stream. Someone had tramped through the snow this way, breaking branches with the width of his shoulders, for she knew of no two-legged creature quite as destructive as an armoured man. Whoever he was, he would not hear her coming, for she took care to walk in his footsteps, where the squashed snow mixed with mud made little sound beneath her much lighter feet.

When she could hear the stream gurgling ahead, Rossa took to the trees, climbing the trunk of one before taking her boots off to use the branches as her barefoot highway. A whisper of magic added strength to branches that would not normally take her weight, as she slipped through to a gap in the trees.

There, she found a tiny waterfall, where the stream skipped down a line of rocks before tumbling into a pool a couple of yards below. The tree canopy here was so thick, no snow lay on the ground yet, though that would surely change as winter came. Instead, the pool's banks were carpeted in green.

Rossa wanted to laugh out loud. If she were

a deer, whose food had been suddenly covered by snow, she'd be headed here, too. So she settled down to wait.

Sal's bread was half gone – Rossa hadn't dared risk crunching into an apple – when she finally spied movement. Down went the loaf, up went her bow, though she didn't reach for an arrow yet.

The buck entered the clearing first, ducking a little so his enormous rack of antlers didn't snag on the tree branches. Perhaps a dozen red deer followed him – a mix of does and juveniles. As they spread out along the stream, Rossa took her time assessing her options.

If she shot one of the smaller juveniles, she could probably dress the carcass and carry it home easily. But some of the juveniles came close to rivalling the buck for size, and the buck would be a prize for any hunter. She knew the buck's harem would winter just fine without him, likely finding another protector before the spring snow had melted. Still, she'd likely need to use magic to carry his carcass, for he was far too big for her. Then again, if she used her magic, she might be able to carry two home…

The obvious first choice was the juvenile who'd been at the back of the herd, a young male who'd be fighting for his own harem next year, if he lived that long. Bringing him down would likely panic the others, so she'd be lucky to get a second shot off, and she'd direct it toward the big buck.

She drew an arrow from her quiver, and sighted along it. The young male moved toward the trees, almost as if he sensed something wrong, before dropping his head to nibble at the grass once more. If she felled him just right, he'd block the trail, buying her time to take down the buck before they found another way out of the clearing.

A roar erupted, louder than any deer she'd ever heard. Who was the buck challenging?

Her target bolted, as the rest of the herd panicked.

To blazes with it. Rossa sent her arrow

toward the antlered buck. It sank deep into the animal's eye, killing it, barely a moment before a massive paw broke the buck's neck.

Rossa reached for another arrow, aiming before she could truly process what she was seeing. It wasn't another deer that had roared, but a bear. A huge, white bear, which ripped her arrow out of the deer's eye and whirled to see where it had come from.

He spied her instantly, in her treetop perch. Her eyes met his, and she saw nothing but fury in them. Then he charged toward her.

Rossa didn't pause to think. She bolted.

Flying through the tree branches, leaping from one tree to another, until she reached the edge of the forest and was in sight of the castle gates. Still she ran, not stopping until she could bar the doors to the great hall and set her back against the impenetrable oak.

Sal came out of the kitchen to see what the noise was. She took in Rossa's dishevelled appearance and said, "Had a bit of a tumble, did you?"

Rossa shook her head, desperately trying to get enough breath in her lungs to force the words out. Finally, she managed to say, "There was a bear. In the forest."

Sal just smiled. "Oh, yes, we do get a few here. They come down from the mountains, to raid the orchards. They're quite partial to chestnuts and apples. They eat their fill and then go. Quite harmless, really, and nothing to fear, as long as you keep your distance and don't bother them. In spring, they sometimes bring the babies. Very cute to watch."

Rossa could only shake her head. There was nothing cute about that massive monster.

A monster she should have shot when she had the chance, she now realised, for a killer so huge, so close to the village was surely a danger to everyone here.

Instead, she'd run like a coward.

Anger fired her blood. Not at the bear, but at herself. How could she be so stupid?

"I'll be in the yard, chopping wood," Rossa managed to say, her hands shaking as she unbarred the door. She peered around the yard cautiously, making sure the bear hadn't followed her, before she dashed toward the axe and the chopping block.

If the bear did come here, this time, she'd be prepared.

Eighteen

Boris eyed the buck. The beast would be his dinner tonight, and perhaps on the morrow, too.

In the past, he might have brought it down with a well-placed arrow, but he hadn't thought to bring a bow when he left the capital, so he made do with what weapons he had. He leaped from his hiding place, fastening both arms around the beast's neck, and then he twisted until the bones snapped. Only then did he let the buck fall to the ground.

Boris blinked. There was an arrow in the buck's eye. An arrow that had certainly not been there a moment before.

He had no arrows, nor a bow, which meant…

Igor had found him again.

Boris scanned the trees, searching for his accursed squire. There, a flash of colour where it did not belong, and a terrified eye peering through the leaves. Boris roared in fury, and raced across the clearing.

The boy, more monkey than man, fled through the branches, faster than Boris could follow.

Boris sighed. He did not understand why the boy didn't just give up. After all, Boris let him go, much as he'd allowed the remaining Bisseni to flee into the mountains when the battle was done. Some things just weren't worth pursuing.

That deer, however, wasn't something he wanted to lose. He butchered it as best he could, and carried it back to his cave. Somewhere along the way, he'd acquired a flint and tinder, and while he knew he could eat the venison raw, he much preferred his meat cooked, which he could manage over the small fire he kept burning.

What he'd give to taste a proper hunter's stew, laced with pork and venison…one day, he promised himself. When he'd finally dissuaded the squire from hunting him.

Nineteen

It was a full week – and a month's worth of chopped firewood – before Rossa could bring herself to enter the forest again. Plenty of people who remembered her from when she was small had come to reassure her about the bears in the woods. They'd all advised her to bring a bag of apples with her if she went into the forest again, for all the local bears would completely ignore her for a bag of apples.

When she tried to explain what she'd seen,

no one believed her. The bear had only looked so big because she was frightened, they'd said. They preferred fruit to meat, though they occasionally ate carrion if they were starving at the end of a long winter. It must have been a very light brown, not white…

And so it went, on and on, until even Rossa was inclined to misbelieve her own senses.

But she knew she had seen the white monster bear kill a stag. The deer herd had panicked at the sight of it, too, so they'd known how dangerous it was.

Therefore, she had little choice but to venture into the forest, kill the monster, and bring back its body as proof. Then, she might persuade someone in the village to turn the beast's hide into a warm winter cloak that she intended to wear everywhere.

Even Father would have to take notice if she killed a monster. After all, wasn't that what his job entailed?

Today, she carried her bow and a new quiver of arrows – the old one was lost in the forest somewhere – twice as many daggers as before, and she'd found a leather breastplate with a matching helm in the armoury that seemed about her size. Likely they'd belonged to the squire of a crusading knight, centuries ago, but they were hers now. Sure, she could conjure a magical shield, but it didn't hurt to have a little mundane protection, too. Especially when she'd seen how easily the bear had broken the buck's neck.

She sent out a finding spell, the sort of thing Swanhild excelled at, and was not surprised to find the bear near the same clearing.

Of course he was.

There'd been no new snowfall, so what was left sat in patches beside the muddy trail, sometimes humped so high she'd wondered if what she saw was the bear, lying in wait.

But she didn't see him at all.

When she reached the clearing, she debated whether to walk right in, or climb a tree again. Then she cursed herself for a simpleton and scaled the nearest tree. She hoped her father never heard of her moment of stupidity. She was lucky it hadn't cost her her life.

Today, the clearing was empty, much as it had been a week ago. Though there should be some sign of what had happened. The buck's body, or at least what remained of it. Yet…there was nothing, not even any visible blood.

Her quiver sat in the tree she'd watched from before, leaning against the tree trunk like it was waiting for her. Cursing softly under her breath, Rossa wove her way through the branches to it. Better to have two quivers of arrows than one, especially when she still hadn't spotted the bear. She scanned the clearing, then turned to peer between the trees behind her, as well. Every snowdrift might be the bear hiding, plotting an ambush.

She snorted softly. Bears did not plot ambushes. They were creatures of instinct, without the kind of foresight and planning a man might possess. All a bear thought about was food and fighting and…ah, mating. She felt the heat rise in her cheeks. There were men back in Mirroten just like that, including her young nephew, Bruno.

Something moved in the snow. No…sparkled, as it caught the sunlight, filtering through the leaves, before the shaft of light vanished, then returned again.

Rossa moved closer, shifting from tree to tree until she stood over the object. It appeared to be a large brooch, with a dark stone that glittered red in the sun. It looked like one of the treasures Father brought home for Mother, when he came home from a mission. Except Rossa knew every item in Mother's jewellery chest, and this wasn't one of them.

She dropped from the tree to the ground, and reached for the brooch. The moment her fingers closed around it, the ground dropped out from under her. Rossa opened her mouth to scream, but then her head collided with something, and the world went dark.

Twenty

Boris peered into the pit trap, searching for the brooch he'd used as bait to lure Igor in. Blasted boy, he'd managed to drag it into the hole with him. Thankfully, Boris was much taller than the boy, so he hooked his legs around the nearest tree and lowered himself over the lip of the hole. He'd have to move Igor's unconscious body to the side to get to it, though.

Boris rolled the boy onto his side…only to

find it wasn't Igor at all, but some girl he'd never seen before.

He'd caught an innocent in his trap. Worse, she was bleeding from the blow to the head that had knocked her out.

Only one thing to do, then. Boris climbed down into the hole, grabbed the brooch and the girl, then laid them on the lip before hauling himself out, too.

What to do with her? He could hardly take her to the nearest healer – he had no idea who or where they might be, even if the healer didn't faint in terror at the sight of him.

He should take her to his cave, lay her down beside the fire, and wait for her to wake up.

And what if she didn't? He'd seen men take head wounds in war, from which they never recovered. Never woke…

No, she would wake, beside his fire, and he'd make sure she got home safely.

Somehow without letting her see him.

Boris sighed. What were her family thinking, letting this slip of a girl wander alone in the woods?

Twenty-One

The ghost of a headache haunted Rossa when she woke, stiff from a longer sleep than she would have liked on a bed that was most certainly not her own. Heavens above, had she fallen asleep in that hole?

No, she'd been knocked out, which is why her head still hurt, she told herself, touching the amulet she wore under her clothes at all times. She must have been bleeding, which activated the amulet's healing powers while she was unconscious. It must have been bad to still hurt, even a little, after so long.

She sat up, scanning her surroundings. A fire burned to her left, and stone walls – formed, not made – curved around her. She'd fallen into a cave, then, she mused, glancing up to see how far she'd fallen. Yet the stone stretched above her, too, smooth except for the spiky teeth she'd seen hang from cave ceilings in some of Father's books.

She hadn't fallen here, she'd been carried, and someone had lit that fire.

She wasn't alone. She reached out with her magic, sensing a second heartbeat in the cave with her, hidden in the shadows, deeper inside.

"Come out," she ordered. "I know you're there. There's no point hiding."

Whoever it was had not taken her knives from her, and her bow lay on the ground within easy reach, along with her quivers. Either he was so strong he didn't fear her, weapons or no, or he was stupid.

Whoever he was, she was going to make

him regret trapping her and then kidnapping her. By the time she was done with him, there would be nothing left for her father to cut off. Killing him would be a mercy.

Something moved in the dark, shuffling against the stone, but no one appeared.

"I'm going to count to three, and if you don't come out on your own, I'm going to light this cave up as bright as day, and then I'm coming in after you to drag you out." Rossa took a deep breath. "All right. One…two…"

Still he stayed in the dark. The man who'd made the path to the clearing, trudging through the snow, she decided, remembering the broken branches along the way. The size of his boot prints. He was huge, a giant even, but her magic was more than a match for any man, no matter how big.

"Three," she finished, and conjured a ball of light that she threw at him.

It splashed against the wall behind him, outlining him in blazing white for a moment before the magic sputtered out.

Rossa let out the breath she hadn't even realised she was holding. She was in a cave with…the bear.

Who was now moving toward her, stepping out of the shadows and into the flickering firelight. On two legs, like a man.

No, he was a bear, not a man.

"Where is your master? The man who brought me here?" she asked.

The bear shook his head.

"You don't know, or you can't tell me?" she pressed.

The bear stared at her, something like frustration burning in his eyes. Slowly, he brought a mighty paw up to his chest, over where his heart might be. Then he bowed, the way her father did to her mother.

"If you were a man, I'd imagine you mean to say something like, 'I am Sir Pompous Arse of Dead Deer Pond, at your service, my lady.'"

The bear made a strange sound in his throat, while his eyes appeared to crinkle.

"Yeah, I wouldn't like being called Sir

Pompous Arse, either. Snow White the Bear, then, until you tell me otherwise." Rossa rose to her feet and dropped a sort of curtsy, spreading the edges of her cloak in place of a skirt. "Lady Rossa of Mirroten. But you can call me Rossa. Everyone else does. Well, if you could, I mean."

She shook her head, which gave a twinge to remind her that she'd been hurt. "Look at me, talking to a bear. The monster bear which took down my deer a week ago. I know I hit my head but…"

The bear leaned down, picked something up off the ground, and held it out to her. It was the brooch.

Rossa sighed. "Yeah, if I'm going to dream up crazy things, of course I'd include jewellery worth a king's ransom. I don't know what things are like among bears, but you can't just give something so costly to a girl you barely know. Is it even yours?"

The bear touched its head, at almost the same spot where hers hurt most. Then it held the brooch out again, insistence in its eyes.

"Fine, I'll take it. In payment for the bump on the head, and for stealing my deer. That was my kill, not yours. It was already dead when you broke its neck."

If bears had eyebrows, his would have risen. Maybe he did have eyebrows, as white as the rest of his fur, and she just couldn't see them. He pointed at the antlers lying in the corner of the cave, then at her.

Antlers, but no other part of the deer. As if he'd butchered the carcass and buried it, like a man might.

"I suppose for someone the size of you, a whole deer wouldn't last you more than a week," Rossa said. A memory pricked at her mind, and she searched through her things until she found the sack Sal had given her. "Here, I brought you some apples. The castle cook, who is also the innkeeper in the village, said I should give them to you." Honesty made her add, "Actually, she said I should give them to you to distract you, so I could get away."

Surprise widened his eyes, before the bear bowed again, gesturing toward the cave entrance.

"If I didn't know better, I'd think you're telling me I'm free to go," Rossa said, eyeing the bear as her hand closed around the knife at her hip.

The bear inclined his head. Almost…regally.

She dropped the sack of apples at his feet. "Well, enjoy them. There's plenty more back home, though I suspect if I'm not quick, someone will turn them into cider. Maybe I should ask the cook to set aside a barrel or two, so I can bring you some, if I come to visit you again." She'd definitely hit her head, if she was talking about paying visits to bears. "Nice to meet you, I guess."

Her shoulders itched as she turned her back on the bear, and forced herself to stroll out of the cave, across the clearing, and all the way back to the castle, without pausing to look back.

Twenty-Two

Boris followed the girl through the forest, surprised to find the village – and the castle where she was headed – weren't at all far from his cave. Perhaps it wasn't so strange her family allowed her to wander through the woods, when she was so close to home.

She'd slipped the brooch into her pocket on her way home. Boris had wondered whether she'd wear it or sell it, until he saw the guards bow to her when she entered the castle. He'd known then that she wouldn't sell it, though he still wasn't sure whether she'd wear such a jewel. She lived in such an isolated castle, wearing men's clothes, instead of the silk gowns seen in court that befitted such a brooch.

Then, of course, he wondered what she'd look like in a wine-coloured gown, her dark curls tamed only by a crown of such splendour it cast the brooch into the shade…

In fact, he was certain he'd seen just such a crown in the sack he'd taken from the capital, encrusted with so many diamonds and rubies, you could scarcely see the silver metal beneath. So valuable it had been kept under lock and key in the capital, only being brought out to wear on the most momentous occasions.

Hardly the sort of thing you gave to a girl chance met in the woods. Then again, that brooch wasn't, either, and he'd handed it to her without a thought.

Silly bear with silly ideas. What had he been thinking?

He hadn't been thinking, which was the problem.

After swearing he would watch from the shadows, where she wouldn't see him when she woke, he'd definitely made a mess of things. Then again, he'd expected her to feel fear at the sight of him, and there'd been none whatsoever.

Ah, but she'd fired the arrow at the buck that day, hadn't she? It hadn't been Igor shooting at him at all.

A very strange girl, this Lady…Rose, is that what she'd said her name was? Whose eyes had glowed as red as the ruby brooch in the sun when she'd cast the spell which lit up the cave.

She was a witch, then, with powers beyond those of normal men. Boris had heard of such women, but he'd never met one, and he could not deny she intrigued him. For a slip of a girl to feel no fear in the presence of a monstrous bear, when she'd seen him kill…she must be a powerful witch indeed.

Perhaps she could break the spell that had

made him into a bear. Or, failing that, cast some sort of enchantment that would keep Igor away from him, and help him find his way back to court, where he would see Sviatopolk pay for his crimes.

If only he could ask her.

Twenty-Three

Rossa tossed and turned all night, debating what to do about the white bear. A day earlier, she'd been certain she should kill him, but now she wasn't sure. He'd pulled her out of that trap, lit a fire, buried a deer, bowed, given her a priceless gift, and maybe even laughed…in every respect, more like a man than a bear.

None of the villagers had seen him – they spoke only of brown bears, maybe as big as a man, and not a white one who stood head and shoulders above any man she'd ever met. Certainly not one who hunted deer.

No one from the village had mysteriously gone missing, either, or in such a way that the bear might be blamed.

That didn't mean anything, though. He might have only recently arrived in the area, so that he hadn't had the time to pose a danger to the village.

For a bear who could master fire was very dangerous indeed…

Which was why, as the first streaks of dawn lightened the sky, she stood at the mouth of the cave she'd woken up in yesterday. Inside, the bear was snoring beside a campfire that had burned down to glowing coals.

If he was a danger to her mother's people, she should slaughter him and be done with it. Yet even now she hesitated.

Was he a man or a beast?

She sent a whisper of magic through him, searching for the answer. He was a magical beast, with the heart and soul of the man he'd once been before someone had cast a spell on him. The magic was not his own, for if it were, it would course through his blood as it did hers, yet it was still a part of him, bonded to his bones, somehow. It was no mere enchantment or glamour, to be dispelled with a wave of her hand. No, to remove this spell might kill him.

While she'd been lost in thought, the snoring had stopped. The bear was awake.

Yet he did not move to attack her, and she did him the same courtesy.

"Did you want to be turned into a bear?" she said.

The bear sat up, then shook his head.

"Do you wish you were a man again?" she persisted.

The bear cocked his head to the side, thoughtful. As if he didn't have a ready answer to give her without words.

"Do you know if there is a way to break the curse? Did the witch tell you how you might become a man again?"

Another shake of his head.

Perhaps it was not possible. But animal transformations were usually curses, punishments for offending a witch in some way. It was dangerous to cast a curse that could not be broken. Usually the caster had to pay a high price, in her own blood, for her negligence. So either the witch had been playing a dangerous game…or the spell upon the bear was a blessing, not a curse, even if he had not asked for it.

"Did this…did this happen to you because someone was trying to help you?" Rossa asked.

His eyes regarded her, filled with yearning. Yearning for the words a bear could not say.

"Do you know the witch who did this to you?"

He shook his head.

Wonderful. So some witch had likely cast a spell on him as he slept. She was lucky he hadn't attacked her for waking him.

Rossa perched on a rock just inside the cave. "So now you're stuck as a bear, with no way of going back to the way you were."

He inclined his head.

She kept her eyes firmly fixed on his as she drawled, "Well, that's quite the problem, Snow. But I have a bigger one. Because I need to know if you're a danger to the people who live around here. My mother's people, in the village, and the monastery, and the castle. Are you going to hurt them, Snow?" With deliberate care, she conjured a fireball in her hand. The sort that gave off smoke and heat and definitely did damage when she threw it at someone. "Are you my enemy, Snow?"

His gaze never left hers as he shook his head slowly.

"Good." She turned the fireball into a ball of pure magic, then threw it at him.

When the ball hit his chest, it exploded into a shower of sparkles. He blinked, then raised those eye ridges that definitely supported his invisible eyebrows.

"If you meant to harm me, that spell would not have shattered harmlessly against you," she said.

He snorted, then held up his enormous paws, claws extended.

Rossa waved her hand, and a small shield encased his paws, so he could no longer move them. "Size doesn't matter as much when it comes to magic. My little magic hands are more than a match for your extra large ones, any day."

His eyes crinkled, just as they had yesterday, and the same sound came from his throat.

Laughter, Rossa realised.

Not the response she was used to. Her father would have given her one of his opaque looks, and told her that skill or quickness of mind mattered far more than size or power, before telling her to repeat the training exercise.

She pulled out the sack of food she'd taken from the kitchen. Bread, meat, cheese, fruit — even a handful of dried chestnuts that had been soaking in warm water overnight, and were now tender enough to eat.

"I'll need to get back to my training when it's light enough to see, but my father says the best warriors are ones who are well-fed. So, would you like to break your fast with me, Snow?"

The bear inclined his head, and for the first time in her life, Rossa found herself sharing a meal with a bear. The first of many, as it would turn out.

Twenty-Four

Boris began to look forward to Rose's visits, and not just because she brought him food. She wore boys' clothes because she came into the forest to train to fight and hunt, both of which she was particularly skilled at. She reminded him a little of the Bisseni raiders who could appear out of nowhere, attack, then melt into the mountains as if they'd never existed, except she left little trace of her presence.

More than once, he'd caught himself comparing her to Vica.

If Vica had been able to fight, and defend herself like Rose did, she might still be alive.

No, if he'd been a better protector and husband, Vica would never have needed to fight, and she'd still be alive, he corrected himself.

Vica would not have been able to wear a boy's tunic and hose, especially not after Lida was born. The tunic would have been too tight across her breasts, and the hose were too narrow for her generous hips.

Which was why comparisons between the two women were silly. Vica had been a wife and mother, while Rose was only a girl, unmarried without the responsibilities of running a household, even if she was the same age as Vica had been when she died.

And Rose was…unique, he decided, leaning back to watch her.

Now the snow lay thick on the ground, she'd put it to use, crafting little snowmen that she brought to life with magic. She'd made them dance like children's puppets at first, making him laugh, until she'd turned serious. Now the little figures darted around the clearing like angry demons while she hunted them. First with magic, then with real blades, thrown with such deadly accuracy that if they had been demons, they'd have been slaughtered for sure. Because they were her magical pets, though, the dismembered snowmen barely paused before the pieces got up and rejoined the hunt as smaller, more numerous targets.

She whirled and spun, leaped and shot, never missing, with an intensity of focus Boris had only seen in his best warriors. He began to wonder if he'd be any match for her in close combat. She was so fast…

Finally, Rose stopped to catch her breath, shooting a beaming smile that stabbed straight to his heart. God, she was beautiful.

"I need to spar with someone. Were you any good in the practice yard, Snow? We'll pick a spot where there's plenty of snow to cushion your fall, and I'll try not to hurt you." Rose sheathed her daggers, then beckoned. "Come on, fight me."

Boris looked her up and down – he was more than twice her size! One swipe of his paw and he'd send her flying.

She seemed to be able to read his mind. "I'm not stupid, Snow. Any man I fight is likely to be bigger than me. Confident in his size and strength. It doesn't matter. I need to be able to beat him."

Reluctantly, he lurched to his feet and took up a fighting stance. His hands itched to hold a sword again, but he knew his claws were deadly enough. Worse, he could not retract them, so each of his fingers was tipped with a wickedly curved dagger that could slice her open.

"Ready?" she asked.

He couldn't hit a woman. Not even this girl, with both her hands up and curled into fists, like she wanted to punch him.

Nevertheless, he nodded.

Her hands never moved, but somehow, her body twisted, and a blow to his gut knocked all the air out of his lungs. A second blow sent him face-first into a snowdrift.

"Snow? Are you all right?"

The gentle caress of her magic lifted him back onto his feet.

"Did I hurt you? Have you never fought before?" she asked, her eyes wide with concern.

Boris shook his head. The only part of him that she'd hurt was his pride, and heaven knew he had pride to spare. Cautiously, he mirrored her fighting stance, then inclined his head to tell her he was ready.

A moment later, when he came up, spitting out a fresh mouthful of snow, he knew he had not been ready at all.

A lifetime of war might not be enough to defend against the whirlwind that was Rose.

And yet…if the only good thing that came out of all this was that he helped one woman to fight, to not fall victim as Vica had, then Boris would know that his life had not been wasted. That Vica had not died in vain, and might even be smiling on him now.

Well, hopefully not now, with him arse-up in the snow and all.

He clambered to his feet, once more taking his stance.

This time, he would…

Wham.

…not drown in the icy pond.

Boris came up, gasping, then clawed his way over the bank and out of the water.

Rose looked worried. "I think that's enough fighting for today. I brought a jar of mulled wine and left it by the fire. It should be warm by now, and I think you need a hot drink in you after that dunking. Whoever you were before you became a bear, Snow, I don't think you were a warrior."

He wished he could argue, but her arm around his middle as she tried to help him inside sent a warm tingle through him that went straight to his heart.

And…maybe other parts, too.

Yes, a cup or two of mulled wine would likely send him straight to sleep, where he might dream of her, and what they might do, what he might tell her, if he was a man and not this clumsy beast. A dream that would make even a bear blush.

Twenty-Five

A particularly fat flock of pigeons had been found in the barn, gorging on the wheat waiting to be milled into flour. One of the miller's boys chased them off, while his brothers boarded up the barn so that they could not get in again, but not before Rossa had seen the fat birds in flight.

Pigeons roasted nicely over a fire, especially fat ones. She'd seen thieves hanged for stealing a bag of precious wheat, where most people could only afford chestnut flour for their bread. So a death sentence for the pigeons seemed fitting.

She set out into the forest to hunt them, hoping to find their roost, if not the pigeons themselves. If she could catch a couple, though, she might share them with Snow, for surely the bear hadn't eaten a fresh roasted pigeon in quite some time.

With a little help from her magic, she soon found where they'd flow off to, for the stupid birds had perched all together. Perhaps they were too fat to fly far.

Rossa strung her bow, nocked an arrow to the string, then selected her target – a particularly plump bird perched on a branch lower than the others.

She drew the arrow back, sighted along it, blew out a breath and…

The whole flock whirred into flight.

Cursing, Rossa fired at the nearest bird. It might not be the choicest, but she was damned if she was leaving here empty handed.

A squawk told her she'd hit her target, before it whumped heavily to earth.

Yet when the cloud of feathers cleared, she was surprised to see she'd hit a boy, not a bird at all. He must have climbed the tree to try and catch a bird, and he'd fallen out when she shot him. The arrow stuck out of his side, where it might have missed most of his important organs, but he'd bleed plenty if she tried to pull it out.

She'd need to find some yarrow to staunch the bleeding first, then.

Luckily, he'd knocked himself out in his fall from the tree, so he was likely going to lie there while she found what she needed.

Thanking Swanhild for teaching her this particular spell, she searched the forest for the nearest patch of yarrow. It wasn't far off, but it did involve some scrambling over rocks to reach it. Plucking handfuls of the feathery leaves that she then stuffed into a pocket in her cloak, she headed back to the injured boy.

The innocent she'd shot.

If her father knew…

Grimly, she pressed her lips together and knelt beside the unconscious boy. His tunic was so thin and threadbare, it was a wonder he hadn't frozen to death out here. Even his cloak had more holes than cloth. Whoever he was, he could not have come from the village — Mother and the monastery would never have allowed one of their neighbours to live in such poverty. Perhaps he was a pilgrim, who'd gotten lost on the way to the monastery.

Whatever or whoever he was, she'd take him there once she'd finished healing him.

She lifted the hem of his tunic, pulling it up carefully so as not to disturb the arrow. He was painfully thin, this strange boy, his ribs sharply outlined beneath his skin. Definitely not from the village, where no one would be allowed to starve.

She took a deep breath when she reached the arrowhead, then peeled the cloth away from his skin with the utmost care. To her surprise, the arrow came away with the cloth, revealing no wound beneath.

She yanked the arrow out of his tunic, finding it had gone straight through both the front and back of the fabric. How it had missed him, she did not know. It should have grazed him, at the least, but there was no sign of blood or a wound on his body, and the dark brown of his tunic hid any bloodstains that might have been absorbed by the cloth.

Rossa sat back on her heels, not sure what to do. She should carry the unconscious boy back to town, where he might get a good meal and some clothes he wouldn't freeze to death in.

The boy chose that moment to wake up, his eyes growing wide as he scrambled backwards, away from her.

"You shot me!" he accused.

"I was shooting at the pigeons," Rossa hedged. "I must have missed and hit your tunic instead."

The boy looked down, and his eyes grew wider still. He stuck two fingers through the hole in his tunic and made an obscene gesture through it. "You tore a hole right through it! My last good shirt! You…stupid peasant! Can't even tell the difference between a pigeon and a person!"

Rossa almost laughed. If anyone was a peasant, it was this boy, in his rough rags. "Come back to the village with me, and I'll see that you get a new shirt," she offered. It was the least she could do.

He reared back in horror, his face curling with disdain that would not have looked out of place on Bruno's face. "Certainly not! I'm not going anywhere with a peasant girl who shoots people!"

He stood up, dusted himself off, and marched away into the forest. In the opposite direction to the village.

Rossa just shook her head. She could use magic to bring the boy back with her, but why bother with such a rude wretch? If he didn't want her help, he could go off and freeze in the forest, if that's what he wished.

Meanwhile, she'd have to go back to the castle to fetch some food to take to Snow, instead of the fresh pigeon she'd hoped to catch. Or go deeper into the forest in her pursuit of those thieving pigeons.

Sighing, Rossa set off.

Twenty-Six

The first day Rose didn't visit him, Boris wasn't worried. Something at the castle must have kept her, he told himself. While she might not be the lady of these lands — that title belonged to her mother, he'd come to understand — she would still have some responsibilities, even if she ran away from them and into the forest most days.

She would come to visit him when she could.

But then he almost ran into Igor on one of the game trails, managing to hide just in time. Yes, it was definitely his traitorous squire and not Rose in boys' garb. Boris did his best to avoid the boy, and not lead him to the cave where he kept the sack of jewels, but everywhere he went, the boy seemed to appear.

Why wouldn't the former squire leave him alone?

Fuming, Boris set a trap for the boy – a pit trap, like the one Rose had fallen into. He baited it with a particularly ugly jewel fashioned out of gold so blackened with age it no longer glittered like it was supposed to. Igor coveted this particular piece as much as any of the prettier ones, but it would not draw the eye of anyone else.

It didn't even draw Igor's eye for several days, during which Rose was conspicuously absent. Had Igor somehow driven her away?

Perhaps the boy had attacked her, and fear had kept her at home.

No. Rose the Red, powerful witch that she was, feared nothing and no one. If she didn't fear him, she definitely wouldn't be frightened by a boy smaller than she was.

Unless he'd somehow surprised her, and she was hurt…

Boris's heart constricted in his chest at the thought of her lying unconscious and wounded, as

she had by his fire that first day they'd met.

If Igor had hurt her, he'd kill the boy.

A shout, followed by the thump of something falling, told him his trap had finally ensnared the boy.

The trap would hold him while Boris went up to the castle to see if Rose was all right.

He had only to see her, to know she was safe, and he could return.

If she was injured…

Then the boy would be right here, stuck in the trap, to answer for his crimes.

Boris nodded, then headed up to the village.

Twenty-Seven

Rossa was in the practice yard, taking aim at the archery target, when the screams started. She was supposed to be in the kitchen, helping Sal prepare tomorrow's Yule feast, when the whole town would come to the great hall to celebrate Christmas, but after she'd managed to tip a whole pot of honey on the flagstones instead of on the roast boar, and set one of the puddings on fire…Sal had shooed her out, saying she had hands enough to help her with the feast preparations. Sal said she'd call her if she needed her, so not to go far.

Rossa had sighed, knowing there would be no such call. She'd promised Mother she'd stay until the end of the feast, for it was rare enough that they came to the castle, and her people needed to see her. To know she shared their celebration and their sorrows, as well as the bounty of her table.

Rossa hoped Sal didn't tell Mother she'd almost set the table on fire, too.

But that meant she was stuck in the castle grounds, unable to head into the forest to spend the day with Snow, or even continue her hunt for those pilfering pigeons.

Those bloody pigeons…

It was almost as bad as being stuck in a scarlet wool gown that swished everywhere she went. So much for being a silent hunter on swift feet.

But she could still shoot, and while her skirts might impede her movement, they were no obstacle to her magic, so when she heard screams coming from the bailey, she brought her bow and arrows with her.

So that she might aim them at...

She blinked.

Maids ran screaming, for with no guards at the gate, now the mountain passes were closed and no one could enter or leave the town from outside, he'd wandered straight in, with no one to stop him.

"Shoot it!" one of the maids shrieked as she ran past Rossa into the castle proper.

But Rossa could not even bring herself to lift her bow.

"Snow?" she asked uncertainly. Surely there could not be more than one monstrous white bear in the mountains, but with the maids screaming so... "What are you doing here?"

The bear turned – for he stood on his hind legs, taller than any man – and stared at her. Then he lifted one enormous paw and pointed at her.

"It's Christmas, Snow. I can't go into the woods today. I'm needed here," she said, knowing even as the words left her lips that they were a lie. She wasn't needed, here or anywhere. For all that this was her family's castle, she had no place here. In the forest, it was different, but here…

Snow inclined his head, as if he understood. Then he bowed deeply, making her wonder if he truly had been a knight before he'd been transformed, and turned to go.

Her heart twisted within her, somehow wringing what moisture there was in her mouth until it was almost too dry to speak. Yet she could not bear to see him go, not when he'd come here to see her. It was Yule, and he was here, and the one person she wanted to see most of anyone. "Come inside, Snow. I haven't had my midday meal yet. I'm sure there's food enough in the kitchens for us to share."

She crossed the bailey, then threw open the doors to the great hall. Gritting her teeth, she took the folds of her skirt in both hands and performed her best curtsy, the sort her Father insisted she know in case she ever had to go to court and meet royalty.

Snow inclined his head, the way she imagined a king might, and went inside.

Twenty-Eight

The hall was set up for a feast, with all the tables and benches set out in readiness for guests who were not yet here.

Rose seemed to be able to read his thoughts, for she said, "We are hosting a Christmas feast tomorrow. The whole village is invited, including the monks. It is Mother's gift to her people. It's empty now because everyone is in the kitchens. Well, except me, because…I can't cook." She tucked her hands into the folds of her voluminous skirts and stared at the floor, as if ashamed to admit she had shortcomings.

He wished he could tell her that it didn't matter whether a lady could cook, for it was her husband's job to provide servants for her, if that's what she wanted.

She took off her cloak, hanging it on a peg beside the massive fireplace. And then she turned around.

Boris couldn't take his eyes off her. All these weeks, he'd seen her in her hunting clothes, bundled up against the winter cold in shapeless tunics that hid everything, but the gown she wore today…made it hard to draw breath.

It was modest enough, leaving nothing but her face and hands bare as the skirt swept dangerously close to the floor, but the cloth clung to her as ardently as a lover. Caressing her breasts, curving around her hips, all the while highlighting her delicate blush under his scrutiny, her lips ruddy from being bitten…she was Rose the Red incarnate today, both as delicate and as brazen as a rose in full bloom.

If only he were a man and not a bear…

Rose cleared her throat. "I'll just head down to the kitchen for some food. You should…probably stay here, out of sight, so you don't scare anyone else. Maybe…warm yourself by the fire?"

At home, any fireplace this large would have hunting dogs lolling about in front of it. Yet here, he had the space to himself. One reason to prefer being a bear to a man was that he might stretch out before the hearth, without worrying about dignity, or whether he'd get soot on his clothes.

So he accepted Rose's invitation, and luxuriated in the warmth from a blaze much bigger than the tiny campfires he kept burning in his cave.

Until the imperious tap of footsteps that did not belong to Rose's hunter-trained feet entered the room. The woman who owned the footsteps, the feet and undoubtedly every stone in the floor beneath them made an irritable noise in her throat.

Boris raised his head to meet her gaze.

Ah, so this was the lady of the castle, Rose's mother. Though her hair was almost all white to Rose's dark curls, and wrinkles blurred the beauty that he didn't doubt had once rivalled Rose's own, the resemblance was too close to ignore.

Boris rose to his full height, before offering the lady his best courtly bow, as befit a guest accepting her generous hospitality.

If she chose to offer it. From the frown on her face, he wasn't sure whether she wanted to turn him out or summon guards to slaughter him.

"Rossa!" she called, her tone promising dire consequences if her daughter didn't appear immediately.

Rose...no, Rossa, he corrected himself...raced up the steps and bobbed a quick curtsy. "Yes, Mother?"

The woman stabbed a finger in Boris's direction. "The servants tell me you brought a bear into the house. Is that your bear?"

Rossa hunched her shoulders. "Um…yes? And no? He's…he's sort of his own bear. I brought him in here, but…"

"He bowed to me." She made it sound like a crime.

Rossa wrung her hands. "He's…well, he's not really a bear. All right, he is a bear, but…" She buried her face in her hands for moment, then met her mother's gaze again. She sighed. "Snow, this is my mother, Lady Sara of Mirroten, and we're in her home."

Boris bowed once more. Crime or not, it was the courteous thing to do.

"And Mother, this is…well, I don't know his real name, as bears can't really talk, but I call him Snow White, because his fur's white, and…he didn't like the other name I tried to call him."

What had that been? Oh, she'd called him Sir Pompous Arse when they'd first met. Boris much preferred Snow.

One   sharp   nod   was   all   the acknowledgement he got from Lady Sara.

"Why is he here?"

Rossa stared at her feet. "He's…he came to see me, and I invited him to dinner, because we usually share dinner when I'm in the woods, and because I have to stay here, I wanted…"

Understanding softened Lady Sara's gaze, though Rossa didn't see it. "Is he dangerous?" Lady Sara asked.

Boris bowed his head. Yes, he was.

When Rossa didn't answer, Sara added, "I mean, is he a danger to anyone here? Will he hurt the villagers, or the servants?"

No mention of Rossa or herself. Interesting. Did that mean Sara was a witch, too, as powerful as her daughter?

Sara continued, "I'm sure I don't need to remind you, but you are Lady Rossa, and you have a duty to protect your people as much as I do. So if this bear is a danger to them, a bear you brought into the castle among them, then it will be your responsibility to drive him out, or otherwise remove the danger to protect your people."

Rossa stared at him, anguish in her eyes. "I can't kill Snow, Mother. He won't harm anyone here – will you give your word, Snow? Please?"

If he'd been able to speak, Boris would have offered them both his heartfelt promise to respect the laws of hospitality, in thanks for allowing him into their home. Instead, he placed a hand on his heart and dropped to one knee, bowing his head.

Lady Sara's mouth twitched, almost as if she were trying to hide a smile. "I've seen many things in my life, but that's the first time I've ever seen a bear swear fealty to someone, let alone me. Fine, your magic bear can stay for one night, as long as he confines himself to the great hall, but he must be gone in the morning. With the whole village coming for the feast…he cannot stay any longer than that. And as he's your guest, you'll have to come up with a Yule gift for him. I have enough to do."

She marched off.

Rossa blew out a relieved breath. "I can't believe she let you stay. If my father were here, he would not have permitted it."

Boris nodded. He would have killed a bear that came within ten yards of Vica or Lida.

"Especially if he found out you were once a knight. Father does not like knights," Rossa explained.

What manner of man did not like knights? They fought for the king, or their liege lord, and as Rossa's father and Lady Sara's husband, the man was surely a nobleman himself.

"Don't worry about Father. He's…off doing something for the Emperor. He won't be home before spring," Rossa said, patting his arm. "Now, the food should be ready, so I'll just go down to the kitchen to fetch it, because none of the maids will dare come in here while there's a bear in the hall."

And again she departed, but this time Boris took a seat at one of the tables. He might have the strength and appearance of a bear, but he had the heart and soul of a prince, and he owed these ladies his best behaviour.

And a Yule gift, he realised, his heart sinking. That would present a problem.

Twenty-Nine

Even after spending half the night in the great hall with Snow, talking and drinking far more mead than was good for her, Rossa woke at dawn. Only to discover she'd never left the great hall – she'd slept on the hearth, wrapped in her cloak and a blanket someone must have brought from somewhere.

But Snow…was nowhere to be seen.

She raced outside, hoping to catch him before he departed, but the bailey was empty.

Cursing, she headed back inside for some warmer clothes, so she might follow him back to the forest.

Only to run into Mother at the bottom of the stairs. Whose grave gaze told her she wasn't going anywhere until the feast was over.

"Is your magical bear gone?" Mother asked.

He wasn't hers. He was…tears threatened to spill from her eyes. Tears Rossa blinked ruthlessly away as she nodded, not trusting her voice.

"He left you a gift."

It took Rossa a moment before she followed her mother's pointing finger to the table where they'd eaten dinner yesterday. The plates, cups and jugs were gone, replaced by four fat fish, each as long as her arm, arranged in a square on the tabletop. All bearing the unmistakeable marks of a bear's claws about their gills.

He'd hooked them out of the water with his bare hands, Rossa realised.

"And is that…mistletoe?"

Rossa blinked. Sure enough, her mother was right — a sprig of mistletoe sat at the head of each fish, marking the corners of the square. And inside it were charcoal scratchings, almost like writing, as if done by a child, or...

A bear's claw.

Rossa turned her head this way and that, trying to make sense of the words, if indeed they were words. Then she rounded the table, and they became clear.

"My thanks," she read. "A blessed Yule to you and yours from Prince Boris, the Snow White Bear."

Her legs wouldn't hold her anymore, so Rossa sat down heavily on the nearest bench. His name was Boris, and he'd given her fish for Christmas. And, best of all...

"Thank all the angels and saints, he's not a knight," she breathed.

"No matter what that bear may be, it doesn't change what day it is. You're needed here, at the Christmas feast, not haring off after some bear in the woods," Mother said.

Rossa nodded. She wanted to run off after him, to ask a thousand, nay, a million questions, but her thoughts whirled too fast for even her to follow right now. It would be better to wait, until she'd had time to reflect. She'd make more sense then.

"And you need to be at your best. You are their lady, and they expect you to look your part. Go upstairs and bathe – your feast day gown is in my chamber, and you're not to come down until you're dressed and your hair is properly arranged," Mother said.

Yes. Rossa had seen the silk gown her mother had laid out, and she'd never dare venture into the woods wearing that. The dress was a death trap, with lace and ruffles and the neckline was so low every time she looked down, she could see her own breasts.

She didn't want to go into the forest wearing it. She didn't want to step into the great hall wearing it. Every man in the room would stare at her, thinking lustful thoughts, and, when they'd drunk enough of her mother's ale, some of them would talk about them, loud enough for her to hear. And her mother would not let her throw even a single fireball at them for it. Most unfair.

Men and their urges were the bane of her existence. No wonder she preferred the company of a bear.

"Yes, Mother," Rossa said.

But Mother wasn't finished yet. "When the winter is over and your father returns, I'll insist he take you to court. Whichever one suits you best, though I'll leave the choice up to him. When I was your age, I had a town to take care of, an estate to manage, and then a young son to raise. You have…nothing to hold you here. You should see some of the world, and find your place in it, for you're so much like your father. He was not content in the town where he grew up, either. There is a place in the world for you, Rossa. I don't know if it involves bears or princes or…things I've never seen, but can only dream of, but your father will be the one who can show you some of the world's wonders while you find it." She managed a smile. "Consider it my Yule gift to you. When your father comes home from the Emperor's court, he will take you, or we shall have words."

And while the world feared her father, Rossa knew her mother ruled his heart, so it would be as she decreed.

"Thank you, Mother," she said, her heart much lighter as she raced up the stairs. The gown was there, as impractical as she remembered, but she'd have to get used to such things if she was to go with her father to court. She'd have to learn to fight despite what she was forced to wear, or use weapons that did not depend on her agility or speed.

Like magic…

Thirty

When all the feasting and celebration was over, and Rossa was free to venture into the forest again, she still hadn't decided what to give Snow…or Boris…for his Yule gift. He'd given her fish, so food seemed fitting, but she brought provisions from the castle every day. What she should get him was fresh meat.

A deer, like the one she'd shot that first day she saw him, or a brace of those pilfering pigeons that had managed to elude her.

Though she'd love to bring him venison, once she'd remembered the pigeons, her ire rekindled at justice not yet served. Those pigeons needed to die.

Therefore, she resolved to go hunting first, so she might bring her kill to Boris in the afternoon. She checked the roost where she'd first found them, but the birds had not returned, likely frightened away by the beggar boy. So, she ventured deeper into the forest, sending her magic out before her, seeking them out.

After a couple of hours of searching and finding nothing, she began to suspect they'd been preyed upon by some of the mountain eagles and hawks that circled high above, looking for their next meal. Time to head back by a different route, and hope she encountered something that would make a better Yule gift than those pestilential pigeons.

But it seemed her new path was cursed, too, for she had not gone halfway before she began to hear loud cursing, which had clearly driven away the wildlife for miles around. What manner of idiot was out in the woods today? She definitely intended to give them a stern talking-to when she found them. Why, she wasn't even sure what some of those curse words meant…

The swearing seemed to come from the centre of a snow-covered bramble bush which alternated between shaking violently and staying unnaturally still. Someone had evidently become trapped inside the brambles and couldn't get out.

"Hello, do you need some help there?" Rossa asked.

"No!" came the angry response, followed by a few seconds where the bush moved as though caught in a high wind, before the swearing resumed, louder and more vociferous than before.

She longed to leave whoever it was to their fate, but her mother would have waded in with an axe to cut them free, before lecturing them on their use of foul language, and Rossa would do no less.

Sighing, she didn't need an axe, for she used magic to gently part the branches of the bramble bush until she'd formed a path to the centre of the patch so that the bush's captive might walk free.

Of course, it couldn't be that simple. The parted branches revealed a familiar snarling face over the same stained tunic – it was the beggar boy, whose matted hair was now hopelessly entangled in the brambles. Several bloody hanks of hair had already been claimed by the bush as trophies of their battle, and it didn't look like the beggar boy would win, even with her holding the branches back.

She'd have to go in after him.

Rossa drew her dagger and waded into the bush.

The boy didn't even seem to notice her until she started hacking at his hair, freeing him from the bush. He flailed at her, hitting her once more out of luck than any skill, and she saw red.

"Be still, idiot, or I'll leave you here for the carrion birds!" she hissed, then bit down on her lip and spelled him into stillness, rather than risk being hit again for helping this wretch.

Finally, she'd freed his hair from the brambles, though she'd shorn off a considerable amount in the process. She backed out of the bush, then a few yards more, before she released the spell paralysing him in place.

"You horrible, butchering witch! Look what you've done to my hair! Now I look like a fever victim, or a monk! How dare you lay hands on me, and cut my hair! Why, I should have you whipped for assaulting me so!" he howled.

Rossa folded her arms across her chest. "This horrible witch has just about had enough of you. I saved you from those brambles, and in about three heartbeats, I'm going to let go of the branches my magic is holding back, and you'll be trapped again, just like before, but I won't help you again, you ungrateful wretch!"

The boy's mouth dropped open in horror, silent for a long moment, before he spotted something on the ground that had his eyes widening with greed. Whatever it was, he snatched it up, then bolted out of the bushes and away, faster than Rossa cared to follow him.

Not a word of thanks, or an apology for his insults.

Next time, she told herself, she'd leave the boy in the bushes, and to blazes with him.

Thirty-One

The nightmare came again, as it always did. Every time, the dream was the same, and yet every time it was different, because in his heart he knew it was no dream – it was his reality, one he couldn't wake up from. Boris raced through the woods, his former squire chasing him with all the unnatural energy of a berserker in battle. Over and over, Igor would shout at him to just hand over the crown jewels, so that he could go home, but Boris knew there was more to it than that. If Igor got close enough to him, he'd attack, and there was no predicting those frenzied blows.

So far, Boris had been lucky, for his fur was thick and Igor's knife blade was short, so the boy hadn't wounded him anywhere that mattered yet. But he knew the boy wanted his head along with the jewels, for he'd said so often enough, and the stubborn squire would never stop. Couldn't stop.

And now there was Rossa, his Rose Red witch. If Igor found her, he'd try to use her against him. Use her as bait, to draw him out…

Because Boris would do anything to keep her from being hurt by the nightmares he'd run from, while vengeance for Vica and Lida's death slipped away from him, a little more each day, until he feared he didn't know the way back, would never find his treacherous brother, and his family's death would go unavenged.

He could not save Vica or Lida, but he

could keep Igor away from Rossa, who deserved the protected castle life she was born to, with gorgeous gowns, glowing jewels, and blazing fires to keep her warm at night in soft beds befitting such a high lady.

Not life in a cave, or on the run, not knowing when Igor or Sviatopolk's soldiers might catch up to him, and kill him as well. Because he knew Igor could not survive out here on his own, so he must have help. At best, he was a clumsy scout, who reported back to better, more capable men, in such numbers that they could overwhelm a man on his own, like Boris was. He'd been hunting enough times to know claws were no match for well-forged steel held by well-trained hands.

So Boris didn't stop, didn't pause, didn't dare even return to the cave where he'd stashed the crown jewels, lest they catch him, or her...

The rush of a river ahead made him slow, then speed up again, bunching up his muscles so he might make the jump…

For a brief moment, Boris flew, before landing heavily on the snowy bank. He clawed his way up and over, running before he knew where he was, or where he was going.

Behind him, he heard Igor splash into the river, swearing at the chill in the icy waters, but Boris didn't dare stop. Not yet. Maybe not ever…

<h1 style="text-align:center">Thirty-Two</h1>

It was with considerable pride and triumph that Rossa carried two brace of pigeons to Boris's cave. Yes, she was late bringing his Yule gift, but she'd been so preoccupied with hunting the pigeons to punish them for what they'd stolen, that she'd forgotten one of her father's most repeated tenets: that it was easier to make a mark come to you than chase it across the country.

So she found the sack of wheat they'd

already ransacked, scattered it on the snow outside the barn, and waited. Within hours, she'd had a whole flock of pigeons to choose from, fattened on lowland wheat. She'd picked them off, one by one, until Sal promised her pigeon pie for supper, and she still had enough left over to take to Boris.

Yet the bear wasn't here, and hadn't been for some time. The ashes from his fire were cold, and there was no food left. The only thing remaining in his cave was a small pile of firewood and a lumpy sack she'd seen before, which she knew contained treasures like the brooch he'd given her on their first meeting, back in autumn. Old jewels she wished she could ask him about, for surely such treasures had a fascinating story behind them. As well as how they came to be here, in a cave in the mountains, guarded by a prince who'd been turned into a bear.

She waited and waited, but he didn't appear, and even when she sent her magic out questing for him, she found no bears at all. Perhaps he'd gone down to the river to catch some fish, for he was most skilled at that, if her Yule gift was anything to go by.

She'd never seen a bear fish. It would surely be fun to watch.

So Rossa left the pigeons in the cave and set out for the river. She found the river easily enough, but still she didn't see a bear. Rossa had hunted all her life, but she'd never bothered to catch fish, so she hadn't the slightest idea where a good fishing spot might be. She followed the river upstream a way, until the banks grew too high and impassable, before heading down, toward the lake. The river grew deeper as streams joined it, widening as the banks became easier to traverse.

She fancied she heard a cry for help, then dismissed it.

Wait, there it was again.

She barrelled along the river bank, praying she'd be in time.

Then stopped and swore when she realised

it was the beggar boy. This time, he was chest deep in the river, howling as something pulled him under, before he popped back up again, coughing and spluttering, before calling for help.

She knew she'd sworn not to help him, after the last time, but she could hardly leave a boy to drown, no matter how ungrateful he was. Swearing, she stripped off her cloak and boots and waded into the water. It only came to her waist, but she was numb within moments – the boy was surely freezing. It was a wonder he was even alive.

It wasn't until she stood beside him that she saw the problem. A monster of a fish, easily twice as long as she was tall, had taken hold of his belt, and wasn't letting go. Every time it gave a mighty tug, the boy slipped under the surface, and had to fight his way up for another breath before the beast dragged him under again.

She tried to unfasten his belt, but it had swollen in the water, and her numb fingers could scarcely feel the belt, let alone work the knot free. Rossa pulled out her knife, and began sawing at the boy's belt. He was too busy fighting to breathe to notice, until she managed to cut through the belt and it floated free, dragged away in the maw of the monstrous fish.

Only then did the boy look down and let out a wail: "You horrible witch! Now I have no belt to stop my tunic flapping in the wind…and you lost me my dinner! That fish would have fed me for a month!"

He spat in the water, then struggled to shore. When he climbed up the bank, he stopped long enough to make a rude gesture in her direction.

Rossa barely noticed, for the riverbed was slippery, and she struggled against the current on her numb feet. More than once, she slipped and landed face-first in the water, so she was soaking wet from head to toe by the time she reached the bank.

Only then did she realise that her cloak was

gone – likely taken by the beggar boy turned thief, who was now nowhere to be seen.

Swearing and shivering, she did the only thing she could – head back to the bear's cave, to light a fire and hope it would be enough to warm her up and dry her wet clothes.

Thirty-Three

He heard her voice on the wind, and he thought he'd imagined it at first. But when he heard her call his name, he listened in earnest.

"So cold, Snow. So cold in the cave…"

He didn't think – he just reacted, breaking into a run, then a gallop, as four paws were faster than two.

He didn't stop until he reached the clearing.

Only then did he realise he'd been tricked, because it wasn't Rossa he saw, but Igor, holding the sack of treasures.

The last rays of the sun glinted on the squire's dagger as he raised it, a mad grin on his face. "Now, all I need is your head and I'll be free!"

The boy berserker charged at him, slashing wildly.

For the first time in Boris's life, he let rage wash over him, until he felt almost as reckless as a berserker, too. How dare this boy try to trick him with Rossa's voice, that she was in danger. And stealing the crown jewels from him?

No. Boris was done running. This ended here and now.

He rose up to his full height. His first swipe sent the dagger spinning into the pond, to vanish beneath the icy waters. His second ripped out the boy's throat.

Gasping and choking, clutching at the bloody remains of his neck, the boy went down.

Boris dipped his paw in the pool to wash

off the blood, before snatching up the sack of treasures to take it back to his cave.

Only then did he hear her voice again: "So cold, Snow…"

She was here.

Lying on her side in the cave, her clothes soaking wet, curled up and shivering in front of his empty fire pit.

She blinked and managed a weary smile. "Snow…"

He wished he could ask her what had happened. How she'd ended up all wet, without a cloak, out here in the forest.

Once again, she seemed to read his mind. "So…silly. A boy…pulled into the river…"

Igor had done this to her. Boris would have his head for this.

He pointed at the few sticks left in the woodpile, then outside, in an effort to tell her he was getting wood for the fire to help her get warm.

Rossa nodded.

Boris had never gathered wood so fast in his

life. He pulverised two dead trees, then brought them, piece by piece, into the cave. He laid a fire in the fire pit, then looked for his flint. Had the boy stolen that, too?

Wishing he could curse aloud, Boris didn't know what to do. He had to get her warm, and without a fire…

Hesitantly, he lifted her in his arms, cradling her to his chest as he tried to wrap as much of his fur around her as possible.

"Why did you let the fire go out, Snow?" she asked sleepily.

She was too cold. If she slept…she might never wake.

Boris took her hand and stretched it toward the fire. He'd seen her throw balls of magic – could she do the same thing with fire?

"Silly bear," she said, then bit her lip. Fire spurted from her fingers, snaking around the branches in the firepit until they burst into flame.

Boris added more wood, willing it to burn.

"Cold. So cold and…draughty." She did

something with her hands, and a small sphere appeared, growing larger. It passed through him with barely a tingle, and still it grew until it pushed against the cave walls. "Shield. Warm and...safe," she said. She nuzzled against his chest.

Boris didn't dare move. He just held her, and watched the flames, as her breathing grew even and the cold cave started to grow comfortably warm.

He'd give almost anything to be a man again. To hold Rossa in his arms, just the two of them...

When he was certain she was asleep, he leaned back, and tried to get some sleep of his own.

Because to sleep was to dream, and in his dreams he could kiss her as he held her, caress her with hands instead of claws, and she looked at him as a woman does a man, instead of a beast who deserved this fate, because he'd let his family die.

Thirty-Four

Somewhere in that foggy limbo between waking and sleep, she dreamed Snow returned, his warm arms encircling her as they had on Christmas Eve, his fur so soft she wanted nothing more than to stroke it, stroke him, all night.

She knew she'd slipped into a dream when he began to stroke her, too, and kiss her, but she didn't want to open her eyes, for that would end the dream. He peeled off her wet clothes, so that she was naked in his arms, but he didn't stop stroking, didn't stop kissing, leaving fire trails across her skin where he touched her, even with the warm, soft fur at her back telling her this was only a dream.

And then he placed the softest kiss on her thigh, higher than anyone else had ever touched, and her eyes flew open in surprise.

A white head sat between her thighs, her legs lifted over his shoulders, and then he kissed her again, higher still, before his fingers stroked her and she cried out, "Snow!"

He lifted his head and grinned at her, those same eyes in a human face, beneath hair so fair she'd thought it was white. "My sweet, sweet Rose. My true name is Boris, and you don't know how long I've dreamed of hearing your voice say it." His fingers stroked her again, slipping inside her.

A white bearskin cloak lay beneath her, as the man who'd worn it did the most delicious things with his hands and his tongue. She wanted this, more than anything she'd ever wanted in her life.

She wet her lips. "Boris." A spark of something shot deep inside her from where he touched her, setting her nerves afire, and she arched her back in pleasure. "Oh, Boris! My prince."

Dark soulful eyes regarded her, as his fingers never stopped moving, accompanied by the occasional kiss. Pleasure built and built, until it overflowed in an explosion of light.

"You don't know how long I've dreamed of you, like this," he said, his fingers already stroking her again.

Rossa did not want to admit it, but she'd dreamed of him, too, though she'd never been able to see his face. Now...

She tangled her hands in his hair – human hair, not fur – and dared to ask, "Was it this good in your dreams?"

He laughed softly, kissing her thigh again. "Nothing could compare to the wonder that is you, right here and now."

And as she screamed his name, she found

herself without the breath to tell him she felt the same. But from the look in his eyes, she suspected he knew.

<h1 style="text-align:center">Thirty-Five</h1>

When the ache in his own loins proved almost too much to bear, Boris had to force himself to release her. If he pleasured her any more, he'd surely surrender to his own desires, and Rossa was a maiden still. Though whoever she married would be a very lucky man indeed.

He reached for her tunic. "This should be dry enough to wear now." He didn't dare meet her eyes as he handed it over. Couldn't even bring himself to watch her dress, though the image of her naked body, writing with pleasure, would be one of his most treasured memories.

Rossa dressed silently, while he busied himself stoking the fire. He didn't want her getting cold again. He had to tell her, could not waste this opportunity when he had no idea how long he'd remain a man. The last time he'd been himself was the day Vica and Lida died.

"I was once a prince. My father's favourite son, though I had many brothers and sisters, and when he grew too old to defend our borders, he sent me out at the head of our army instead to fight back the raiders who invaded our villages. Then my father died, and my brother..."

He told her everything. How Vica and Lida had died, the potion he'd drunk, before taking the crown jewels. How he'd woken up in a cave, chased by the squire who'd betrayed him...

"I don't deserve any of what I lost, not any

more. My family, the throne…even the crown now gathering dust in that bag of things. But I am a man, if only for a night, and I dream of what I do not deserve. A beautiful lady, who permitted me to save her, if only a little, and to love her, as much as I am able, but I am…nothing now. A usurper sits upon the throne that should have been mine, and instead of seeking vengeance for my family, for my father, I fled with the crown jewels, becoming the beast you called Snow. And though I might look like a man now, I am a beast still."

She frowned, then laid her hand on his arm and closed her eyes. Magic tingled at her touch, or maybe it was just because it was her, and then it was gone.

"The spell is still there. I feel it. I…" Her cheeks reddened, and she withdrew her hand.

Ah, she felt guilt for the intimacy they'd shared. Boris knew he should feel it, too, but if anything, he was already damned, so steeped in guilt he barely felt it any more.

"Forgive me. It was my passion, the heat of it that overwhelmed us both. The fault is mine," he said. If he could take her sins from her, he would. Heaven knew a few more wouldn't hurt him.

"No, it's…all through your tale, you kept talking about your squire. The squire who is always watching you, hunting you. Did he see us…?" Her cheeks flamed as red as her name.

Boris shook his head. "No, he could not have seen us. Here, I'll show you." He held out his hand to help her to his feet, then wrapped his white bear skin cloak about her shoulders. He could not allow her to catch a chill. Only when she was properly dressed for the cold did he lead the way outside.

The moon sat high in the sky, casting its light down on the traitorous squire. The body lay beside the pool, but some night-time scavenger had dragged the boy's head several yards away, almost into the bushes.

"He will not bother you again," Boris tried to say, but no words came out. The only sound he could make was a growl.

He'd turned back into a bear.

Rossa stared in horror, her eyes darting from him to Igor and back to Igor again. "You did this? Slaughtered a starving boy I risked my life to save? He was a child – just a child! How could you, Boris? I trusted you – let you into my home, when all the while it was only a matter of time before you killed someone? You're wrong, you know. You're not a beast. A mindless beast, a creature of instinct, only kills for food, for survival. This…is the work of a monster, with the mind of a man. A monster who is not welcome in my mother's lands. If you are still here on the morrow, I give you fair warning, I will hunt you down and slaughter you like the monster you are. And then I will burn your body, for you do not even deserve a decent burial. Goodbye, Boris."

She turned on her heel and marched off into the dark night.

Boris raised a paw, wishing he could beg her to come back, but he no longer had the words.

Even if he were a man again, he suspected there were no words he could say that would make her forgive him for what he had done. Even if he'd done it for her.

He wished he could weep, for what he had lost tonight. He'd touched heaven, only to be thrown into the pit for it. But even tears were denied him. It was what he deserved.

Thirty-Six

When Rossa woke the next morning, she was still simmering over the prince. He didn't even deserve a name, for he was no one to her. That she'd very nearly given him her maidenhead last night…was a kind of foolishness she didn't dare contemplate now in the light of the morning.

He was a monster who deserved to die. And, without her father here to dispatch him, she would do the deed. With relish.

Thick, woollen hose encased her legs, rough against her skin, in contrast to his soft caresses. A thick linen tunic, topped by one of wool, before she buckled a leather breastplate over the breasts she'd let him kiss last night. Never again.

Her warmest cloak had vanished from the riverbank yesterday, likely stolen by the boy he'd slaughtered, but in its place hung a far superior one in unblemished, snowy white. She reached out to stroke the fur – as soft as she remembered it last night, for he'd laid her down upon it before making love to her. As a man, and not a bear, yet he'd been a bear again in the clearing with the body, so this fur had not been taken from him.

Maybe she should skin his corpse, and make a cloak from it, if only to remind herself of how close she'd come to disaster...

Or keep this one, so finely made, with fur on one side and thick lambswool on the other, for it would remind her of last night as well.

She would wear it while she hunted him,

and while she killed him, so that she would remember his end as well as why he deserved it, she told herself, as she fastened the fur with the ruby brooch he'd given her on the day they first met.

The thick leather belt she slung around her hips would not cut as easily as the one she'd sliced off that poor beggar boy...was it only yesterday? Better for him to have drowned than the violent end he'd met at the end of Boris's claws.

Bloody bear. She'd seen him kill, but she'd wilfully forgotten how brutal he could be when he was with her. When he'd sat at her hearth, in her home. All so he could lull her into a false sense of security so...what? He could seduce her? She'd been so stupid...

But she'd found wisdom at last, even if it was too late for that boy. It was a lesson the bear would pay for with his lifeblood, she swore.

She pulled on her heavy boots, so that he would hear her coming and know he could not avoid her. That she would bring him down, place her boot on his neck, and list his crimes before delivering his death blow. Justice.

Her sword and her bow she left behind. If she found she needed them, magic would take the place of blade or arrow. She was a witch, born of a line of powerful magic users who were more than a match for any monster, magical or otherwise.

She dragged a comb through her hair, braiding it back tightly before coiling it on the back of her head. There would be no free curls for him to wrap around his finger as he kissed her, looking for all the world like he loved her, telling her she was the most beautiful woman he'd ever seen...

Enough! She screamed it silently at herself, for the traitorous thoughts invading her own head. Yes, the prince had made a tolerable lover for a night. That didn't change the fact that he was a murderer, and that he deserved to die.

She marched down the spiral stair, ignoring

the grumble of her belly as the aroma of baking bread wafted up from the kitchens. She could break her fast when the deed was done, and not before. Lest she vomit up her breakfast on the snow, beside the bear's severed head.

Out the side door, through the gates, out to the...

Oh.

Outside the castle gate stood the monstrous white bear, carrying the corpse, the boy's head cradled in its lap.

He threw the body at her feet, then knelt down beside it to seize the head. He set it on top of the corpse's neck, as if the body were a puzzle that would come back to life, if he but pieced it together correctly.

"Have you come to turn yourself in? To confess your crime, so that my mother's guards will execute you, instead of me?" she demanded. Her heart ached as she hardened it against him, but she had no choice. She would not let him kill anyone else.

The bear shook its head violently, pointing at the corpse.

"Bringing him for a decent burial is the least you could do. They will not be lenient because of it. I shall see to that," she said. "You will still hang for – "

That's when she felt it. A whisper of magic, like the slightest breath of a breeze, between them. It wasn't the bear, and it wasn't her, which meant it had to come from the boy.

No. Corpses couldn't cast spells.

And yet…

She'd seen the ruin where the boy's throat had been last night. A dark hole, black in the moonlight, that appeared whole and healed now. If his head hadn't been severed, she might think…

The boy blinked. Then blinked again.

No. She'd imagined it. Surely.

"Where are the jewels? Give them back!" the boy demanded, staring at the bear. He tried to scramble to his feet, arms and legs flailing in the snow as the bear shoved him down with one massive paw, pinning him in place.

How…

Boris met her gaze and nodded, pleading for her to understand.

But what kind of monster didn't die when a bear decapitated it?

Absently, she sent a paralysis spell at the boy, like she had in the brambles, so he'd stay still without distracting her. If he was a boy, which she doubted.

Rossa closed her eyes, delving deep into the well of memories that weren't her own. Generations of spellcasters, all adding to the great store of knowledge she could access if she looked hard enough. Someone must have seen such a monster, put a name to it…

Djinn. This…thing…was a djinn, a magic user who had betrayed their king, and been sentenced to serve as a slave until the debt of disobedience was paid. Trapped in the form in which they were enslaved, unable to die, until their king released them from bondage.

She stared into the boy's furious eyes. How

had she missed the magic in his blood, for only a spellcaster could be punished so? Yet as she searched his body, she found no magic at all, in his blood or bones or anywhere except for the djinn curse that lay thick upon him like armour.

Boris had not cast this curse. No wonder he'd been running from this deathless thing, which could not be killed, relentless…

Nor had he slaughtered an innocent, defenceless child.

Her mouth suddenly dry, Rossa didn't know what to say. Boris deserved an apology, if her memories were correct, but she had to be sure…

"Take him to the barn. We'll question him there," she ordered.

Boris bowed, scooped up the boy, and followed her to the now pigeon-proof barn.

Thirty-Seven

Rossa issued orders like an army commander, and Boris could not do anything but obey. Within moments, she had Igor tied to a post in the barn, with a magical shield crackling around the walls so that no one would hear or see what went on inside. She cast a spell on Igor, too, telling him if he lied, his tongue would catch fire, so he had better tell her the truth.

Even Boris gaped a little at that. Surely the

girl who condemned him for killing the boy would not torture him so.

Would she?

Then she enthroned herself on a sack of grain and began to question the squire.

Why was he hunting this bear?

What was the bear's real name?

Why did he betray the man he'd served?

Why did he poison him?

Igor's answers could have come from Boris's own lips, for the story matched his own. More than once, he found Rossa nodding, and relief began to trickle through his veins. If she believed him, maybe she'd forgive him. Maybe...

"I didn't poison him!" Igor shouted, straining at his bonds.

Rossa rose. "You gave him the drugged drink at the feast."

"Yes, but only because I was ordered to serve him that ale. I tried to warn him, tell him not to drink so much!"

She glanced at Boris, who nodded. The boy

spoke the truth. If only he'd been more forthcoming at that long-ago feast, told him about the sleeping potion in his ale…

"Why didn't you tell him what was in it?" she asked.

"I couldn't!"

"Why?"

But he clamped his mouth closed and shook his head. He would not – or could not – say.

"Did you know what the potion you gave him later would do?"

"No! Only that it was supposed to help him!"

Boris nodded again. So the boy had said, but he had not believed him then. Now…well, Igor's mouth was not ablaze, so he was telling the truth about his words then, but that didn't make those words true. He wished with all his might that he could be a man again, so that he could question the boy himself.

"Did you know the ale was drugged?" she asked.

The boy nodded.

"Why didn't you tell him? Your prince, the man you served, who you owed your loyalty to…why?"

"I couldn't!

"Why not?"

"Because the witch told me if I ever breathed a word about the potion she put in the ale, it would be the last breath I ever took!" Igor exploded.

Then he began to wheeze, trying to suck in air that would not come. His face turned red, then blue, before he hung limp from the ropes that held him.

Rossa's mouth dropped open, and she darted forward to place her fingers on the boy's neck. "He's dead!"

Boris shook his head, but Rossa did not seem to notice, for she was too busy cursing.

She pointed at him. "You – stay here with him. I'm going to…I'll…I will return. Stay hidden. No one must know you are here." She marched out of the barn, sealing the door and the shield behind her, so he could not leave, even if he wanted to.

Sealed behind a shield, with Igor dead, and Rossa no longer out for his blood, Boris was safe for the moment. This time, he felt himself change.

He flexed his hands as Igor began to stir.

This time, Boris seated himself on Rossa's throne, where the boy's gaze landed the moment his eyes opened, before they widened with horror.

"How?" Igor managed to say.

Boris picked up a knife Rossa had left behind, and began to twirl it around his finger. "I'll ask the questions, boy. And if I don't like the answers…" He threw the knife into the air, and caught it, point down.

Igor swallowed. "What do you want to know?"

Thirty-Eight

By the time Rossa returned, Boris and Igor had reached an accord, though the boy was currently hanging limp for the third time, looking for all the world like the corpse he'd been out in the clearing. Except with his head still attached, of course. Rossa would not like it if he turned her barn into a slaughterhouse.

"I brought some breakfast. I thought you might be hungry," she said, her eyes on the tray in her hands. When she glanced up, she nearly dropped it. "You're…not a bear!"

Boris grinned. "No. I'm not sure how it happened. Perhaps it's something about being inside your shield, but I feel…more like myself."

Rossa hurriedly set the tray down and laid her hand on his arm again. She shook her head. "Yet I can still feel the spell inside you. The bear isn't gone, only…sleeping, or something. As if waiting for the opportunity to emerge…"

Boris might not be a witch, but he'd come to a similar conclusion. "Oh, there's a purpose for it, all right. I will need its strength to drag that usurper off my father's throne and make him pay for the lives he's taken. After he's freed Igor from his curse, of course, which is why he's going to help me."

Rossa shot a sceptical glance at the lifeless boy. "You'll need to resurrect him, and get a few decent meals into him first. He's hardly in any shape to attack a king at the very heart of his power. Why, there'd be guards, knights, courtiers…he'd have no chance. Not even with your help. One bear against a company of guardsmen…I've never been to court, but even I know that is suicide."

"Come with me." Even as the words left his lips, he wished they hadn't. He'd lost the woman he loved once to Sviatopolk. He wouldn't put Rossa in danger as well.

A wry smile curved her lips. "A bear, a beggar boy and a maiden with a bow. Oh, the bards will make ballads about us, filling every court in the land with gales of laughter that anyone could do something so stupid." She took a deep breath. "And yet…you will need me, I think. But even then, we might not be enough. If you want the king to listen, without killing us on sight, you'll need someone else. What we need is my father. He'll know what to do."

Boris opened his mouth to ask what some country baron could do against a king, but Igor took that moment to suck in an enormous, gasping breath, drawing Rossa's eyes to him.

"Is it true? Will you swear to serve Prince Boris again, as you did before, and help him right the wrongs that were done to him? Even if it means killing the king?" Rossa demanded.

Igor wet his lips. "I will."

"Will you swear not to harm Prince Boris, or anyone else unless I order you to do so? Will you promise not to run away if I untie you?"

"To all of it, I swear, my lady," Igor said.

She snapped her fingers, and the ropes around the boy slithered away to coil themselves up like a nest of snakes in the corner.

"And if I ordered you to go get a meal and a bath and clean clothes, as befitting your station as Prince Boris's squire, would you obey?"

"Gladly, my lady." Igor bowed low.

Boris hadn't noticed, but the sulkiness that had annoyed him so much before was gone from Igor's voice and expression now. How long had it been? Had he been running for years?

Boris glanced down at his clothes. He hadn't seen this tunic since the day Lida and Vica died, and it still bore traces of their blood. "Lady Rossa, might I trouble you for a bath and a change of clothing, too?"

She eyed him thoughtfully. "I'll see what I can find. We don't see many princes here in the mountains, so it may not be as fine as you are used to. At least until the passes open in spring, and my father will return."

That was at least a month away, maybe two! Boris swallowed. As a bear, he might attempt to traverse snowy mountain passes, but as a man, he'd likely die in the attempt. Even Bisseni berserkers weren't crazy enough to cross the mountains in winter.

After so long as a bear, he felt somehow diminished to stand before her as a man. Yet he bowed as low as he had dozens of times before. "I will be most grateful for whatever hospitality you offer, my lady."

When he straightened, he found Rossa blinking at him in bemusement. "Yes, I'll have to find you a bed, too, I suppose." And with that, she led the way out of the barn, gesturing for them both to follow.

Thirty-Nine

When Rossa rounded the corner and reached the kitchen gardens, she knew something was wrong. Too many people bustled about, fetching and carrying with a feverish intensity that told Rossa they feared the consequences if they failed in their task.

"What is it? What has happened?" she demanded of the nearest man.

"The master has arrived! Everything must be made ready!" He excused himself and hurried off.

The master? The only master Rossa knew was her father, in his role as Master Assassin. But he couldn't possibly be here — the passes were still blocked by snow, and would be for months yet.

Mother would know. Whoever was here, they would not have arrived without her knowledge. And at this hour, as she was usually to be found in the solar they used for a dining chamber instead of the draughty great hall, that's where Rossa headed.

Sure enough, Mother wasn't alone — a man and a woman stood before her, cloaked against the cold, for the fire had only recently been lit.

The man's grey cloak seemed to blend in with the wall behind him, so that her eye was drawn away from him, dismissing him, but the woman's cloak of regal purple was as vibrant as flowers in the spring. A member of the Emperor's family, perhaps? For surely only royalty could afford such costly dye.

"Rossa, I was just about to send someone to

summon you," Mother said.

The pair turned, and the grey man pushed his hood off his head.

"Father!" she exclaimed, rushing to hug him. It wasn't until she pulled away from him that she felt the purple woman's eyes on her.

Amethyst eyes, like nothing Rossa had ever seen before. Drawing her in, as if with a powerful enchantment she could not resist…

Father coughed, and the spell was broken, if indeed it was a spell. "Rossa, you won't believe where I found your fairy godmother. We got to talking about you, and the more we talked, the more we agreed that it was time she paid you a visit, so she cast a portal, and here we are." He spread his hands wide. "Lady Zuleika, your god-daughter, Rossa. And Rossa, this is Zuleika. My niece."

Lady Zuleika managed a nervous smile and ducked her head. "I'm still new to this. My mother Zoraida – Master Zoticus's sister – died only recently, and I am still learning the full extent of her duties as fairy godmother.

I'm sorry I haven't come to help you yet, but you seemed to be doing all right, not in need of my help yet, until Uncle told me of his vision…"

Father waved her into silence, which only intrigued Rossa more. She knew Father had visions of the future, but she'd never heard him having one about her.

"Ah, I'm not the only one who brought an important guest. Prince Boris, have you come to see the holy relics?" Father asked, striding past Rossa.

How could she have forgotten Boris and Igor?

Boris's eyes darted about, as if seeking an escape — not an uncommon response for someone meeting her father for the first time, as his reputation often preceded him — before he decided to hold his ground and offer a nervous smile to Father. "Forgive me, sir, but I do not recall where we met before today."

Father's smile was genuine, as he shook his head. "No, forgive me, Your Highness. It's just that you are so like your likeness in the cathedral, I recognised you instantly. A man with your reputation would surely have come here to pray over the holy relics my wife's ancestors brought back from their most holy crusade. The relics of the Holy Innocents, no less! It is no wonder you sought them out."

"I..." Boris seemed as lost for words as Rossa herself.

"You must stay here in the castle, with us, if Lady Sara does not object. Only our best guest chamber is good enough for such a prince!" Father said.

Mother moved to stand at Father's side, repeating his offer. Before Rossa could object, Mother whisked Zuleika, Boris and Igor off to show them their chambers.

Leaving her alone with Father. Whose gaze remained fixed on her, as he smiled, waiting for her to ask the questions that burned her tongue.

"Do you...Father, how do you know Boris?" she asked.

His smile widened. "Oh, his reputation is well-known. As a warrior, as a leader, and there are those who say he is a saint. Quite a remarkable man. I have always wondered…and now I have seen him with my own eyes. A remarkable man indeed."

A man she'd called a monster. Which she still hadn't apologised for…

Rossa ducked her head, not wanting to meet her father's eyes. Gah, she'd been so stupid. It was a good thing Father had left her at home.

"With your godmother's help, we will leave for court on the morrow. With Prince Boris, for I have an inkling he might want to leave earlier than the spring," Father said. He patted her shoulder. "If you have any suitable court clothes, you'll want to bring them, so you'd best go upstairs and pack."

"Yes, Father." Rossa was halfway up the stairs to her tower before she thought to question how Father knew all the things he did. Yet she didn't dare return downstairs to ask, lest he reconsider letting her go with him.

Finally, Father believed she was ready, though Rossa herself felt far from it.

Forty

What Father had meant, Rossa discovered the next morning, was that she would need to dress for court before leaving the castle, for Zuleika could cast magic portals that allowed her, and those accompanying her, to travel instantly from one place to another. Having nothing better than the red gown she'd worn at Christmas, Rossa had put that on, which Father had insisted on ornamenting with a ruby necklace that weighed more than the belt she'd sheathed her daggers in only yesterday. Father had brought her a new cloak from Byzas, in a deep wine red that rivalled Zuleika's for its brightness. She'd fastened it with the brooch Boris had given her, though she dreaded what her father might say when he saw it.

Boris and Igor wore clothes Mother must have found for them, all of which were very fine, yet Boris had chosen to wear his white bear skin cloak, and a crown she knew had come from the sack of treasures he'd kept in the cave. She hadn't looked too closely at it before, but now it sat in his pale hair, woven strands wrapping around his head, with a single sparkling stone in the middle of his forehead. A diamond, surely, though it was as clear as water and drank the light, sending out rainbows when the sun hit it. He looked every inch a prince.

Father chose grey, as always, but she recognised his grey finery as distinct from the grey travelling clothes he'd worn yesterday.

The only jewels he wore were on his weapons, and even they were few. The king might have made him a lord in name when he married her mother, but Father himself had not changed a bit because of it.

Zuleika had refused to wear any but her own clothes, and, to Rossa's surprise, Father had simply nodded and left it at that. Zuleika was younger than Rossa, Rossa had discovered, but the ease with which she created the portal to take them to the court in Buda demonstrated that she was a far more powerful enchantress than Rossa would ever be.

Zuleika's portal had barely faded before she said, "This is where I leave you, for I am needed at another court today. It is a small matter, regarding a ball and some shoes that shall be lost, but it is nevertheless of the utmost importance. Should you have need of me, I believe my other god-daughter will no longer need my services after midnight, so I shall return then." Before any of them could say a word, she cast another portal and was gone.

Rossa looked askance at Father, who merely shrugged and said, "My mother and my sister were forever flitting about the world, seeing to the affairs of their various godchildren. My sister fought a dragon for her godson once. To hear her tell the tale, it was more of a skirmish than a battle, which did not last long, but I have it on good authority that everyone else who fought the dragon died, right up until the day someone finally slayed the dragon. As she says, if we need her, she'll be here after midnight. I'm sure we'll survive a day without her." Father offered his arm, and Rossa took it. "Let's go see the king."

Forty-One

"This is not Prislav," Boris said, surveying the city walls. "I have never seen this city before."

Master Zoticus, as Rossa's father had insisted he was called, shrugged. "You have been away some time, Your Highness. The new king felt a new capital would be best, and he now rules from here in Buda. While we are here, you must allow me to show you your likeness in the cathedral. Beautiful work, though you will have to tell me if it does your brother David justice."

Boris closed his eyes. David. How long had it been since he'd thought of him? David deserved justice as much as Vica and Lida, and still Boris had not delivered it. His family deserved better. He clenched his fingers around the hilt of the sword he'd borrowed from the castle armoury. Lady Sara had said the blade had belonged to one of her ancestors who'd gone on a holy crusade to free the Holy Land, and that the man's spirit would surely be happy to see it in his hand.

In truth, it felt foreign to hold a blade again, when his claws had been his weapon of choice for so long. The bear roared within him, like a creature with its own mind, eager to be unleashed on Sviatopolk.

Rossa and her father led the way to the throne room, but when they reached the doors, Zoticus stopped to speak to the herald, while Boris did not stop. He would no longer endure a usurper on his father's throne.

"Prince Boris of Rostov, with Lord Zoticus

and his daughter, Lady Rossa," the herald announced.

The people parted, bowing as they cleared the way for Boris. He saw fear in their eyes, and so they should fear him. They'd supported a false king, a murderer, who did not deserve the throne.

He did not stop until he reached the foot of the dais where the king sat. Guards stood on either side of him, hands on their spears in readiness to defend the king, but Boris would not let them stop him. He'd broken larger branches than those spears with a single swipe of his paw.

He planted his feet, widening his stance, knowing the moment he beheld his brother's face, rage would take over and he would become a bear again, but this time, he was ready for it. He prayed that Zoticus would shield Rossa's eyes from the carnage.

Only then did he raise his eyes to meet the king's.

"You're not Sviatopolk!" Boris blurted out.

Forty-Two

"You're not Sviatopolk!"

For a moment, the king looked surprised, before he burst out laughing. The rest of the court followed his example. Father remained silent, and Rossa did the same. This was politics, which her father knew far better than she ever would.

"I thank heaven I am not Sviatopolk the Cursed every day, and I'm sure my subjects do, too!" the king said.

Boris just stood there, shocked, and Rossa's heart went out to him. Her father had evidently brought them to the wrong court. He should step forward and say something, instead of leaving Boris to bear the ridicule for his mistake.

It was almost as though Father had read her thoughts, for he strolled forward, keeping her hand firmly on his arm until a few steps before the dais. Only then did he let go, offering the king a courtly bow before he said, "Your Majesty, Prince Boris here has spent many years in search of the missing crown jewels, stolen by Sviatopolk the Cursed. I believe he has finally found news of them, which we would like to share with you, in private."

The king regarded Father for a long moment. Finally, he said, "If you have indeed found the lost crown jewels, then I would be greatly in your debt, Lord Zoticus."

Father winced. No, he did not like that title. The king only grinned, as if he knew this all too well.

"This audience is over. We shall resume on the morrow. See that refreshments are brought for our guests," the king said.

He led the way behind the throne, to a smaller, more intimate audience chamber. One where there were chairs clustered around a table, none more ornate than the others, though the king took the one at the head of the table.

"Lady Rossa, you must come and sit beside me. If I had known Lord Zoticus had such a beautiful daughter, I would have summoned him to court sooner." Desire burned in the king's eyes.

This old man was as bad as the boys of Mirroten. Rossa regretted that he wasn't the traitor Boris wanted to kill, for her fingers itched to send a fireball at him. Or maybe a gust of wind so icy, it froze off certain parts he surely no longer needed…

"She's an enchantress, Bela, and you'd be playing with fire you cannot begin to imagine," Father drawled as he took the seat at the king's left hand.

Rossa felt her cheeks grow hot. Even with her father there, the king was still staring at her.

"But she's your daughter. Any heirs she gave me would be the most well-guarded children in the world. No one would dare harm them…" the king breathed. "Give me an heir, Lady Rossa, and I will give you a crown, and name you Queen Regent upon my death."

Give him an heir? Have sex with this old man? Rossa wished she hadn't eaten breakfast, because she was about to vomit it up all over the king's costly carpet. Boris was the only man she'd ever considered allowing into her bed, and to share herself with anyone else…

"He may not be Sviatopolk, but say the word, Lady Rossa, and I will defend your honour with my blade. If you desire a crown, you have only to ask and I will give it to you," Boris said. He glared at the king. "Freely, for I ask nothing in return." He took the seat at the foot of the table, opposite the king.

Rossa swallowed, then slid into the seat between her father and Boris.

"I believe you would benefit more by talking about crowns with Boris, instead of my daughter, Bela. That's why I brought him," Father said, his tone edged with irritation.

"Fine," the king sighed. "Tell me, Boris, what do you know of Sviatopolk the Cursed, and the treasures he stole?"

"Sviatopolk was my bastard brother. He stole my wife and daughter from me, ordering them to be murdered, and I suspect he killed my father and my brother, David, too. He did not deserve the crown he stole from my father. So after he took everything from me…I took everything from him," Boris said. He lifted his sack of treasures onto the table, but he did not spill the contents. Instead, he seemed to be fixated on the king. "You're wearing my brother's crown."

King Bela touched the plain gold coronet on his head. "This was forged for King Yaroslav the Wise, after he and his army drove

Sviatopolk out of the capital. It has been passed down through my family for generations."

Boris shook his head. "No. My brother Yarik was given that crown on the day our father sent him to govern the north, while I was sent south to deal with the Bisseni raiders. He was Prince Yaroslav, then, my half brother. I suppose with my brother dead, me gone, and Sviatopolk a murderer and a traitor, the next in line for the throne would be Yarik, but…where is he now? He would have sent men out to find me, he said he supported me as the next king…" Boris trailed off. "How long have I been gone?"

Father winced. "Maybe we should have gone to the cathedral first. The likeness is quite remarkable. I imagine the artist must have known Prince Boris very well."

The king's jaw dropped. "Do you mean to say…this is Saint Boris? And he somehow miraculously preserved the crown jewels, so that he might return what his brother stole?"

He stared at Boris in wonder.

The men kept talking, but Rossa's mind would not stop whirling. She'd known Boris's story sounded familiar, but she'd never considered it might be the tale of a two hundred years dead saint. And yet…

The clang of metal on the table dragged Rossa out of her reverie. Crowns, jewels…the sack of treasure just sat there in an undignified jumble. Tarnished from age, kept in a sack for two centuries…

"My grandfather said the treasures had likely been melted down and sold, to pay for the civil war that erupted when Yaroslav died. For he might have been a wise king, but his sons fought like rabid dogs, killing each other off until none remained. My grandfather was descended from one of Yaroslav's daughters, who married a foreign prince. She attended her father as his nurse in his final days, and she wrote an interesting account of that time. His mind was so far gone that he imagined he and not Sviatopolk the Cursed had commanded that his father and brothers and their heirs be killed, and he had only framed Sviatopolk in order to claim the throne for himself. Perhaps it is true. I do know it was he who petitioned for Boris and David to be proclaimed saints, their bodies buried in the cathedral he built in their honour. I have seen the tombs myself."

"Has anyone ever opened them?" Father asked. "Because I would wager Boris's tomb is empty, or contains someone other than the saint."

The king scratched his chin. "What would you be willing to wager?"

"How long?" Boris demanded.

Both men stared at him.

"How long ago did your two saints die?"

Neither man seemed inclined to answer, so it fell to Rossa. "Two hundred years," she whispered.

"No! I swore I would bring them justice. That I would execute the man who ordered them killed. He can't be dead. He can't!" Boris rose so quickly, he knocked his chair over, but he did not stop to right it before he stormed out of the room.

Rossa rose to follow him.

Father put a restraining hand on her arm. "Let him go. It's a lot for any man to take in."

Rossa shook him off. "You knew, or at least you suspected. You should have told him, instead of letting him find out like this. And you." She pointed a damning finger at the king. "You laughed at him, before the whole court. A court that should be his, not yours, stolen by your ancestor's treachery. That man is our rightful king, and I will not just let him go!" She marched out the door, across the throne room, and out into the main square.

She had to find him. She had to.

Forty-Three

The cathedral was so grand, it rivalled the palace. Inside, it was even more ornate. Mosaics covered the walls, floors and even the ceiling, showing scenes he remembered hearing about in the much smaller church in Prislav, when he'd been a boy.

The altar at the far end stood amid the most brightly coloured pictures, but in the wings on either side of it were the Virgin's altar…and the one that was usually dedicated to the church's patron saint. The saint's altar was what drew Boris, for what he both hoped and dreaded he would find there.

Two stone coffins flanked him, each bearing a carved likeness of a man on top. Boris could not bear to look. He found himself on his knees, the mosaic floor rising up to meet him until his forehead kissed the cold tiles.

And he wept.

For two hundred years wasted. That Vica had not had a better husband, or Lida a better father. That Sviatopolk had won, and it had fallen to Yarik to avenge them. That they'd made him a saint, when he wasn't fit to scrub the floors in this church, let alone enter heaven.

Light footsteps padded on the tiles behind him. He wanted to snarl at the priest or whoever it was to leave him. Boris felt the bear rise within him, ready to vent his fury on anyone who helped to maintain this mockery.

"Do you want me to open the coffins?" Rossa asked, her voice quiet and calm to the storm raging inside him.

No, he did not want to see David's face in death. He, at least, deserved sainthood, so his remains would be incorruptible. But to look upon his face, to have to admit his failure…no, Boris did not have the strength for it.

But he also didn't dare admit that to Rossa. She'd come here to help him fight for justice for David, and he could not bear for her to think him a coward. And yet…that's what he was. He'd been running for nigh on two hundred years, instead of delivering the justice he'd promised.

"Well, I'm not waiting any longer. I want to see what's inside. So if you won't do it, I will."

The scream of stone scraping against stone set his teeth on edge, until a final clunk told him she'd set the coffin lid down.

"Looks like the artist carved him from life. The statue on top is holding a book, and so is he. Huh. I'd heard saints' bodies don't decay, but it's strange to see it. I would have thought he'd be a skeleton by now, but…Boris, is this your brother?"

Boris swallowed. Of course Rossa had the courage to look upon David's dead body. And if a maiden could do it, what did that make him?

He rose. Never had three steps seemed so far before, but he forced himself to take each one, until he could clutch the lip of David's tomb. He took a deep breath, and looked down.

The boy he'd remembered had become a man, and a monk, too, judging by the robes he'd been buried in. His hands were clasped together as if in prayer, over a book of psalms that had once belonged to their mother.

Boris's mouth went dry. He would have given anything to prevent David's death, but looking at his brother now, so peaceful, Boris didn't begrudge him his place in heaven. Though Boris had broken his oath to avenge his brother, he had the feeling the man who had briefly lived in this body would forgive him for it.

"I'm sorry, David," he whispered.

"What for? You didn't kill him. Didn't even know he was in danger, or surely you would have warned him. Or dealt with the danger. Why should you be sorry?"

Her words felt right, somehow, and yet he could not accept them. "I'm sorry I didn't deliver justice to his killer."

Rossa blew out a breath. "If it's any consolation, it seems the killer met a sticky end, anyway. Sviatopolk the Cursed did not keep his crown for long, and he did not live long after he lost it. If I remember my history rightly, a company of the Varangian Guard caught up with him and slaughtered him slowly, over several days. Father said he's been asked to do something similar on occasion, when his target deserves a slow death. He said he usually suggests they hire an executioner instead."

Boris closed his eyes. Sir Cyril would have taken command, and hunted him down. For him. Because they believed he was dead…

He scrubbed at his eyes. Cyril and his men were long dead, much like everyone he'd ever known. But to do such a thing for him…he could never repay them. Where he had failed, Cyril had succeeded. Of course he had.

"So, ready to open the other box, to see what's inside?" Rossa asked. She bit her lip, then stared at David's final resting place. The lid slid back into place, sealing his remains inside.

Would Boris ever be ready? He feared the answer was no, but he could not say it. Thank the heavens Rossa had the strength to open them when he could not.

He bowed to David's memory, before turning to face his own grave. At least when a man looked upon his own mortality, he was supposed to feel some apprehension. Even Rossa wouldn't judge him for suppressing a shiver.

"Right, here goes," she said. This time, she lifted the lid clean off, and set it against the wall. "Oh, that's…most unnerving. No wonder the mosaic likeness is so much like you."

Boris dared to open his eyes. Unnerving was an understatement – he found himself staring at his own sleeping form, or so it seemed. "How is this possible?" he breathed.

Rossa frowned. "There's magic here. A spell, so light I can barely sense it. It feels like…a glamour, for that uses hardly any power at all. I should be able to remove it, if you just give me a moment…there!"

The Boris in the box vanished, to be replaced by a vision he'd never thought to see again. Vica lay there in his stead, holding Lida to her breast, as if they'd both fallen asleep only a moment ago. Not as though, two hundred years into the past, they'd been sent screaming into a death they hadn't deserved. While he did nothing, like the illusion someone had laid over them.

"Was she…your wife?" Rossa asked, her tone almost timid.

Boris nodded. "Princess Slavica, though I called her Vica, and our daughter, Lida. They look like they might wake at any moment." But they wouldn't, he knew. And he did not want them to, for if they did wake, they would condemn him for letting them die, and rightly so.

"They're both so beautiful, though little Lida looks more like you, I think. You must miss them very much. I'm so sorry." Rossa wiped away a tear, then laid her hand on top of his.

It was on the tip of his tongue to ask her what she was sorry for, as she certainly hadn't killed them. Hadn't even been born while they lived and breathed. And while his heart still ached with loss as he looked at his family, it wasn't the same stabbing sensation it had once been. He'd said his farewells, and he knew Vica would never look at him with love again. That if he reached down to touch them, they would be as cold as the stone bed their bodies now occupied. Instead, he was becoming increasingly distracted by the warm hand on his. The living, breathing woman at his side, who knew his past, and all his failings, and still she stood beside him.

She wasn't looking down into the past, at the family he'd lost. No, she gazed upward, at the ceiling. "Whoever made this did a masterful job. Your brother's staring up at heaven, but you're watching over your family. As if the artist knew who truly lay in this coffin, though he's made your face exactly as it looked in the illusion…"

For the first time, Boris dared to look up, and what he saw had fury erupting in his chest. "I'm not some benevolent saint, watching over anyone. Whoever made that didn't know me at all. When it came down to it, when they really needed me, I could not protect them. Could not…" He buried his face in his hands and wept.

There. Now she would see him as he truly was, and leave him to his misery. He should have used that dagger the day they died, instead of dishonouring them by running…

Rossa's arms came around him, pulling him into an embrace. For a girl half his size, she had surprising strength. "You saved me. Twice. I'm not sure I ever thanked you properly for that. I'm certain you would have saved them if you could, and that artist knew it, just as they knew you were not buried in that box with them. There are witches who see the future. My grandmother did. Perhaps the artist saw something that has not happened yet, and that's what's on the wall. Not what was, or what is…but what will be."

Boris shook his head. "No, it can't be. I failed her. Failed them. What woman could ever love me, knowing I could not protect her? Or our children?"

He felt her stiffen in his arms.

"Well, I…I…I think if you kept your promise to Igor, and helped to break the curse your brother had cast on him, you'd at least demonstrate that you can save a child. That…that would be something." She pulled away from him, then waved her hand to close the coffin.

The quiet clunk of the stone falling into

place over them sounded so final, Boris wanted to reach out and shove it open again. To see their faces again, just one last time…

"We should return to the castle," Rossa said, her tone cold.

Loss slid through his insides, leaving him empty. He'd lost Vica and Lida, but why did it feel like he'd lost Rossa, too?

Forty-Four

When Rossa and Boris returned to the audience chamber, it was like they'd never left. Father and the king had a jug of wine between them, as they laughed over something one of them had said.

"Where's Igor?" Rossa asked.

Both men shrugged, and the king sent a servant in search of the boy. When he arrived, flanked by two guards, they said they'd found him in the castle kitchens. He'd remained in the throne room after everyone else had left, and when the guards had tried to throw him out, he'd told them he was the squire to the prince currently meeting with the king, so they couldn't, and one of the serving maids took him to the kitchens, where he'd eaten enough for three men and was well on his way to finishing a fourth portion when they found him.

When Igor saw the king, he fell to his knees. "Please, Your Majesty. I brough him back, and the crown jewels, just like you told me to. Please lift the curse."

King Bela frowned at the boy. "That is not an order I recall giving."

"But it was you. You're all old now, and fat, but you're wearing the same crown and you're still the king," Igor persisted.

That's when Rossa knew that an old man's deathbed ramblings had not been ramblings at all, but a confession. Which meant all these years, Boris had blamed the wrong brother, and the one who'd been called wise had deserved to die more horribly than the one they'd called cursed.

"I can do it," Rossa blurted out. "I just need a drop of your blood, Your Majesty. To break the spell."

It would take his blood and some of hers, and possibly the crown, for djinn were enslaved to an object, and for Igor to recognise a crown after so many years…it fit, in a dark, twisted way. The crown that had belonged to the brother Boris had trusted, who had betrayed him and the rest of their family…

"And I need to touch your crown, if only for a moment."

The king's eyebrows rose. "Do you hear that, Zoticus? Your daughter asked me to give her a crown. I believe I win that wager." He took off the coronet and held it out to her.

She refused to take it. "Blood and your crown, King Bela. Your ancestor enslaved this boy for two centuries, after he stole the throne he passed down to you. This is not about you or me, but about righting wrongs that never should have happened."

Father drew his dagger, and held the blade out to the king. King Bela pricked his finger on the point, then let a dark drop fall onto the hammered gold. Then a second, and a third, before he stuck his finger in his mouth and sucked it. "Now will you show me some magic?" he mumbled around his finger.

Rossa fought down her laughter. "Yes."

Father held out his dagger to her, and she ran the back of her hand across the blade, until a line of blood beaded her skin. She swiped the bleeding cut across Bela's crown, blending the king's blood with her own. Now she held the crown, she could feel the magic threads that tied it to Igor. One by one, she severed them, until the boy was free.

Igor drew in one great, gasping breath. "I can't believe it! Is it really gone?"

"Igor, take out your dagger, and stab yourself in the arse," Rossa said.

"No!" Igor snapped.

Rossa tossed the crown back to the king. "It

is done. If the spell had not been broken, he would not have been able to refuse. Now, I believe the throne owes this boy a debt. Especially as he is partially responsible for restoring the crown jewels to you."

King Bela's frown deepened. "What would you ask of me, boy? What is it that you want?"

Igor stared at each of them for a long moment, before he turned to face the king. "All I ever wanted was to be a knight. I'd only just begun to be Prince Boris's squire. I thought I would only spend a few years as a squire, with some training, and then I'd be allowed to become a knight."

"Perhaps Prince Boris…" the king began.

"NO!" said Igor, Boris and Rossa, all at the same time.

"Your Majesty, Igor has spent two hundred years hunting Prince Boris so he could bring his head back to…your ancestor, and Boris has spent the same amount of time fighting him off. As Prince Boris is still firmly attached to his head, he might not be the best teacher for the boy. Perhaps another knight..." Rossa suggested.

King Bela nodded. "I believe I can find a suitable knight to train you." He turned to the guards, who hadn't yet left. "Take him to the barracks hall, where the other squires are quartered, and see that he has a bed."

Out they went, leaving only four of them in the room.

The king leaned forward, his eyes on Rossa. "What would I have to offer you, for you to give me an heir, Lady Rossa? Name it, and it shall be yours. Your father refuses to bargain on your behalf, even wagering that you will not agree. That a crown is not enough. So, assuming I will already give you a crown, what else could you possibly want?"

Rossa glanced at her father. He met her gaze, looked at Boris, then winked at her.

She hoped he hadn't wagered anything he didn't want to lose.

"A boon," she said finally. "If you would grant me the right to ask for anything at all, at any point in the future, and you must give it to me…then I shall give you your heir."

A smile flashed across Father's face for a moment, before it disappeared, as though it had never been. Certainly too fast for the king to see it, for he was fixated on her.

"You shall have it, Lady Rossa. And I shall commission a crown made just for you. Any jewel you wish, wrought in whatever shape you desire. Tonight, we shall have a feast to celebrate – "

"The announcement of your heir, Prince Boris," Rossa interrupted. "Say he is your son, or your nephew, for no one will believe that he is your many-times-great-uncle. You shall say he has only just returned from his successful quest to return the crown jewels that were stolen so long ago. A man proven in battle, trained to rule…of your own blood, as royal as you yourself…who was denied the throne because of your ancestor's treachery. For him to return when you are without an heir is fortuitous for you both – perhaps some might say it is fate, or even divine intervention. Invoke Saint Boris, if you wish. I give you the only rightful heir to your throne."

Father began to clap. "Well played, daughter. What say you, Bela?"

The king did not look pleased. "I had hoped…" He sighed. "Very well. I defer to the wisdom of Lady Rossa. Who would make a brilliant queen, though it is not to be." He rose. "What say you, Prince Boris? Though you are a saint, and my many-times-great uncle, though my ancestor betrayed you…would you agree to assume the throne, upon my death?"

Boris stared at the king for what seemed like forever. Finally, he said, "I came here, with my friends, to kill the man who sat on my father's throne. Now you're offering it to me upon your death. Perhaps this is why my father died, far sooner than any of us wished. Do you desire death, King Bela?"

Bela gave a wry smile. "No, I do not. I'd like to think I have at least a few years left to live. Maybe many more."

Boris dropped to one knee. "Then we are in agreement. I will agree to be your heir, as long as you mean to live many years yet."

Bela's gaze grew wistful. "I wish I had been blessed with a son like you. I'm sure your father would have been proud of the man you have become."

Boris inclined his head. "In everything, I strove to make my father proud, and I honour his memory now when I ask you, in proclaiming me as you heir, you also declare me to be your only son. A clear succession is the easiest way to avoid civil war. The kingdom I remember was a strong one, and I mean to help you keep it so."

"Then we should send word to the kitchens, that tonight there shall be a grand celebration feast for the whole court, and in the meantime, allow me to bring you up to date on the history you might have missed…"

Bela led Boris off to his private chambers, leaving only Rossa and her father in the room.

Rossa swallowed. Her quest was at an end —

she'd helped free Igor, and win Boris back his father's throne. She should feel victorious, happy, triumphant…but all she felt was emptiness inside.

"Shall we go home, Father?" she asked.

Father shook his head. "No, we'll be expected to sit at the high table for the feast. Bela likes to pretend I am his pet assassin, to frighten any enemies he might have, and I lost a wager today, so I must pay him what is owed. You…should enjoy the feast. There will be food and wine and dancing, and more courtiers than you can count, at least after you've had a few cups of wine. Perhaps one of them might catch your eye, or it may be that you develop a taste for court life, and that you'd like a place here. Tonight will be your victory feast, and you should celebrate." He guided her out of the chamber, then waved for a servant. "Can you show us where we shall sleep tonight?" he asked.

The flustered maid dropped a deep curtsy as she stammered out, "I…do not know, my lord.

I shall find out directly." She hurried away.

"Oh, and your fairy godmother will return at midnight, after she's dealt with the shoes girl, or whatever it was. In case you need help with anything," Father said.

Forty-Five

Boris had attended many feasts, even sitting at the king's right hand, but he suspected this was the one he would least remember, for he had eyes only for Rossa in her red gown. He'd never thought he'd want another woman in his life after Vica, but now…he wanted nothing else. And he'd give up the throne and all the honours Bela wanted to heap on him, if only Rossa would smile at him again.

Of course, he could scarcely see her while

they both sat at opposite ends of the high table, and he'd lost count of the number of courtiers who'd come up to talk to him, hoping to earn a place in his favour early on. Much might have changed in two centuries, but the self-interest of the king's courtiers was ever constant.

Boris drank sparingly, waiting for the feast to end so he might seek out Rossa to speak with her. But King Bela had other ideas, commanding the musicians to play something they might dance to. Boris quickly realised he would only embarrass himself in attempting to join the complicated dances, for that much had changed since he'd last been at court. He glanced at Rossa, wondering if she knew these modern dances. Perhaps he could persuade her to teach him…

But her place was empty, as was her father's. Boris scanned the room, searching every face for the one he wanted most. It was her gown that caught his eye, a quick flash of red before she vanished through a side door.

Boris excused himself and followed.

The door led to a dark passage, then another, until he glimpsed light around the corner. He crept closer.

"I must apologise for my lateness. I promised I would stay at the ball until midnight, if she needed my help, but she did not. I waited until the very last moment, too. I hope she and her prince will be very happy. Even if she did lose her shoes…" he heard Zuleika say.

"Do your god-daughters usually marry princes? Are you supposed to act as matchmaker?" Rossa asked.

Zuleika sighed. "I'm supposed to help them when they have no other hope of happiness. Sometimes with little warning, too, so that I am forced to portal thousands of miles in a night in order to be in two places at once. I don't know how my mother managed it all, to be honest. But I infinitely prefer it to staying tied to one court, so there is that."

"I wish I could travel. This is the first time

Father has let me leave Mother's lands, but the more I see, the more I want to know. Like whether all courts are like this one, or if everyone eats the same dishes, or does the same dances, or even plays the same music. Or what the ocean tastes like. Or how desert sands would feel beneath my feet. Or…"

Zuleika laughed. "Sounds like you should do my job for a while, if only to see some of the world. Heaven knows I could do with the help. Ah, but then there is your prince to think about…"

"Boris is not my prince." Rossa's voice sounded so flat.

"That's not what it looked like when I arrived at your home. Unless you've had a disagreement…in which case, perhaps I can help?"

Rossa sighed. "No, there is no disagreement between us. I agreed to help him win back his father's throne. The king has named him his heir before all the court – he has his heart's desire. He no longer needs me, so I should go home. Yet I have this yearning not to…"

"You wish to stay here, then?"

"No! I want to see the world. One court is not enough."

"A pity, for your prince will be king one day, and he will need a queen, for that's how succession usually works."

"Could you see me as a queen?"

"Well, you certainly have the bearing for it. Not to mention the right gown and jewels to impress even this court. You'd need to wear a crown, though…what of this one?"

"Don't be silly!"

"I see nothing silly about it. It's quite stately, in my opinion."

Boris edged closer, hoping to catch a glimpse of Rossa in a crown, if her godmother succeeded in persuading her.

"Here, let me help you," Zuleika said, turning Rossa to face her. She lifted his mother's ruby and diamond crown high into the air and took several tries to settle it among Rossa's dark curls.

Boris swore he saw Zuleika wink at him before turning her attention back to Rossa.

"Now, Crown Princess Rossa, nay, Queen Rossa, for that's who would wear such a crown, you must sit on the throne," Zuleika said.

"That's going too far. What if someone sees us?"

"Then you should do it quickly, for what other opportunity will you have to know what it feels like to be a crowned queen, seated upon your throne?"

Fearless Rossa did not hesitate. She ascended the dais, and took her rightful place upon the throne, staring out across the throne room as if it were filled with courtiers and not shadows.

Boris's mouth went dry. He would dream of this sight. Of Rossa in all her glory. And wish...

"It suits you," Zuleika said.

"No, I..."

Boris stepped forward. "It does. That is

indeed the queen's crown, which was only worn a few times a year, at the most important events. Bela promised you a crown, and I think you should tell him you want that one."

Rossa shuddered and set the crown aside. "King Bela is an old man. He might be a wise and just king, but I could never marry him."

Boris's heart sank. "And I am so much older than him. If I were to ask…would you refuse me, too?" He had to know.

"I…"

Boris closed his eyes. He wanted to become the bear again, a creature who did not mourn or cry, but who might run forever.

Rossa swallowed. "I'm not ready to marry yet. I've seen so little of the world, and I want to see so much more. If my father would only allow me…"

"You are an adult, are you not? Mistress of your own fate? Your father cannot control you forever. Your fate is your own, and he has no choice in the matter."

Zuleika dropped a silent curtsy, cast a spell

that unleashed a blinding light, and when Boris managed to blink the bright blindness from his eyes, she had gone.

Rossa managed a smile. "Even my fairy godmother is afraid of my father. No one dares risk his ire, for his reputation precedes him."

Boris took her hands. "I'm not afraid of him. If you wish to travel the world, come with me. King Bela has named me Captain of the Varangian Guard, just as my father did, for the Emperor has dismissed them and sent them home. We will defend the borders, and protect our own people, going wherever we are needed. I've seen you fight. We would be honoured to have you with us, as you earn a name for yourself, separate from your father's."

"Truly?"

"Truly."

Rossa threw her arms around his neck and kissed him. What started as a chaste peck did not stay so for long. Boris drank deeply, as though her breath were wine, wishing he could never let her go. Like that night in the cave, when he'd first regained his manly form, thanks to her.

Her thoughts seemed to mirror his own. "Take me to bed, Snow."

"Are you sure, my Rose? I haven't asked you to marry me yet, let alone said the vows."

She met his gaze, unflinching. "One day, when the time is right, you will ask. And on that day, I will say yes."

"And one day, you will sit on that throne beside me, with the queen's crown on your head."

"Yes."

"Can I persuade you to wear it to bed? Just the crown and nothing else?"

Rossa laughed. "Perhaps."

He set the crown upon her head, then swept her up in his arms. "My bedchamber, or yours?"

"Whichever one has the bigger bed."

Down the in the great hall, the festivities

went on, while Rossa and Boris barred the door of his bedchamber. Court clothes slid to the floor, no longer necessary for two people who only wanted each other. Maiden she might be, but Rossa was as ready for Boris as he was for her, and she did not hesitate. A blissful gasp was the only sound she made as their bodies became one, and Boris swore nothing and no one would ever part them again.

Cross:
Three Billy Goats Gruff Retold

DEMELZA CARLTON

A tale in the Romance a Medieval Fairy Tale series

One

No one should have been abroad with such a storm raging outside, but the man who entered Father's great hall, drenching the flagstones with every step, feared far more than just the storm.

"The sea wall has been swept away. The last of the harvest is lost," he gasped out.

"What of the village?" Father asked.

The man hung his head. "The villagers have already sought high ground, and we will not know how much they have to return to until morning. But with so much water coming through, and the size of the waves…they will need sanctuary for more than a night, while the village is rebuilt."

Father nodded gravely. "On better ground this time, I hope." He clapped his hands. "Summon my men. See to it that every man who can help with the evacuation and rebuilding is on hand, first thing tomorrow morning."

All Romein's brothers rose as one. "Yes, Father." They filed out of the hall, leaving Romein alone at the table.

He got to his feet. "Father, I am almost a man. Please, let me help the relief effort." Younger boys than he served as pages at court, he knew, but Father kept him here at home instead. Likely because the nearest court was ruled over by the Bishop of Maastricht, the mortal enemy of Father, his family and all those who swore allegiance to Father as Count of Gelderland.

Father regarded Romein. "Do you have your sword?"

"It is upstairs, in the chest by my bed," Romein replied. Swords were not worn to dinner, his mother had said so many times he and his brothers knew it was as good as law.

"See that you wear it when you ride out tomorrow. While the others are seeing to the evacuation, you will guard the bridge to Elst. Your job will be to warn anyone who attempts to cross it of the terrible fate that awaits anyone who reaches Elst, or the Bishop's lands at Veluwe."

Romein wet his lips. "What kind of fate?"

"Last time floods swept away the village, many of our people sought shelter in Saint Martin's Church, in Elst. When the Bishop heard, he had them arrested, as thieves and trespassers, and punished accordingly, before I or your grandfather could intervene."

Romein's mouth dropped open in horror. "But it's sacrilege to violate the sanctuary of a church! How could the Bishop get away with it, and not be excommunicated?"

Father shook his head. "The Bishop is the priest's superior, and he denied them sanctuary, seeing as they were already trespassers on his land. They never reached the church. And they cannot be allowed to cross the bridge now, for once they set foot on the Bishop's lands, he may do with them as he pleases. So you must stand firm, and guard the way."

"I will go now, Father," Romein said. Better that he go without sleep than see any of his father's people punished for trying to flee the floodwaters.

"No, you will ride at dawn, and no earlier," Father said. "No one should be out in such a storm."

Romein sank down onto the bench, pushing his plate aside. He had no appetite now. "Yes, Father."

Little did he know that the storm and the flood would be the least of his worries on the morrow.

Two

"The horses have been saddled and packed for an hour or more. Should we not leave?" Julia asked, gazing from William to Thibault and back again.

"We should have been in Elst yesterday, instead of passing the night in some common inn," William said, glaring at Thibault.

Thibault's gaze did not waver from the fighting pit. He flapped a hand vaguely in their direction. "One more round. I have placed a large wager on this bird, and I am certain he shall be victorious."

William seized his arm. "We need to go now, Thibault, before the floodwaters rise any further. If the bridge is washed out, it could be weeks until we reach Veluwe!"

"All the more reason to focus on the cockfight, then, if we are to stay a little longer. The better I know the birds, the more I can win when I bet upon the winner!"

The more he would lose, more like, Julia thought but did not say, for she'd learned quickly that Thibault was quick to anger, and not above cuffing her. Oh, William would chide him and Thibault would shrug it off, saying it was nothing, while Julia was too busy rubbing her jaw or trying to quiet the ringing in her head to argue.

It didn't help that she was dressed like a pageboy, so none of the Count of Gelderland's men would know a prize like the future Lady of Veluwe rode among them, with only two men to guard her. Well, William was a man, though she suspected Thibault was more of a beast. He reminded her of the mean alley cat back home, howling and yowling all night, and attacking any creature that approached him, in between rutting with any female cat he could find.

She'd heard one of the maids calling him the Prince of Cats – the alley cat, not Thibault – for he must be royalty, to lie with so many queens. The other maids had giggled, and a prince the cat had become, though he had but one ear, one eye and no crown.

"William," Julia began.

He hushed her. "You go on ahead, cross the bridge to Elst. Make your way to Saint Martin's Church, and wait for us there. If we have not arrived by dark, tell the priest your true identity, and ask for lodgings for the night. I will make him come."

If only Thibault were not such a large man, much bigger than William by far, she might have believed him. As it was, she knew William would likely have to use the weight of his words to get Thibault to move. And words were something Thibault rarely listened to, unless they came out of his own mouth.

But if she made it to Elst, she wouldn't have to pretend to be a page any more. She wouldn't need to bind her breasts or wear hose that chafed around her hips when she rode. Or fetch food and drink for William and Thibault, like she really was their servant.

"Fine," she said, and marched off. Her palfrey – and it was hers, for the mare did not permit Thibault or William to touch her, let alone sit atop her back – shivered as Julia mounted, as though the horse was just as eager to reach their destination as Julia herself. Julia only had to touch her knees to the mare's flanks and she was off and running.

The inn was soon far behind them, and the river loomed larger. Why, the waters were swirling around the bridge supports, the waves licking hungrily at the bridge itself. She urged her horse to move faster.

Only at the last moment, the palfrey balked

at the bridge, prancing about on the river bank as though she'd seen a snake. Julia swore and slid down, wrapping the reins around her hand so that she might walk the frightened creature across the bridge.

Unless the horse was right, and the bridge was more dangerous than staying on the bank…

Julia bit her lip, tasting blood, then sent her magic into the swirling waters, questing, asking. She'd heard that the other elements — fire, earth, air — were not as capricious, and could be commanded. But commanding water was like trying to stop it from flowing through your fingers. You could not force it – only ask.

Today, she asked if the river meant to sweep the bridge away, or if it would hold.

Water never answered in words, but the response was still clear, as the waves calmed, showing her the layers of moss the bridge had collected beneath it over the centuries, proof that it had withstood many floods, and likely would still stand for many more.

Julia inclined her head in thanks, and stepped onto the stones, following the high arch to its peak, before running down the other side, the palfrey's hooves clattering after her.

Until she found her way barred by a naked sword.

"Halt!"

Three

Romein stood guard on the bridge until noon, when the sun vanished behind the clouds. Not a soul had even attempted to cross the bridge. He sighed as he sat down. Father had sent him on a fool's errand again. Well, not precisely a fool's errand, but one where even a fool would be capable of carrying out Father's wishes, without finding himself in the least whiff of danger.

His brothers were likely rescuing people and

their belongings from floodwaters, carrying them to safety and beginning to build a new, better village, on higher ground than the first. While he was sitting on an empty bridge, wondering whether the tree that was wedged against the bridge supports would work its way free and continue its journey downstream, or if someone would haul it out of the river to chop into firewood for the winter, when the floodwaters died down.

If he had a pole, like the riverboat men used, he might tip the tree into an angle in the current, so that it could right itself and flow through the bridge and away. Alas, he had no pole, and his sword was too short to reach. A jouster's lance or a spear would do the job. If only Father had given him a spear to carry instead of a sword…

The clatter of a horse's hooves on stone sent him leaping to his feet, drawing his scorned sword. A foot soldier was no match for an armed knight, he knew. He should have remained on his horse, instead of letting her graze in a nearby field while he did guard duty. He should have…

"Halt!" Romein hoped the man running toward him wouldn't hear the tremble in his voice. At least he was leading his horse, instead of riding it.

The man skidded to a stop as the bridge levelled out, and Romein found he wasn't facing a man at all, but a wide-eyed boy, at least half a head shorter than himself. His fine clothes and hacked-off, shoulder length hair marked him as someone's page, for he was surely too young to be a squire yet. Besides, the horse he was leading surely belonged to some great knight, for the mare pawed the ground, eyeing Romein with disdain like a trained warhorse that wanted to trample him into the dust.

Romein lifted his chin. He was more than a match for this page. "You cannot pass. If you wish to cross the bridge to Elst, know that you will pay a terrible toll."

The page frowned. "What sort of toll?"

Romein swallowed. His father had spared him the details, but he knew that the Baron of Maastricht's justice involved frequent use of the lash, and it was rumoured that he was fond of the wheel. The lucky ones were those who were executed after, but he'd heard stories…

"A terrible one," Romein repeated. "The cost will be so great, few survive."

The page looked thoughtful for a moment, then drew his dagger and held it out, hilt-first, to Romein. "I do not have much, but this is the most valuable thing I possess. If I give it to you, will you permit me to pass across the bridge and on to Elst?"

The dagger was beautiful, with waves carved into the hilt, shining silver like the sea in the sun. Whoever this page was, he came from a wealthy family, to own such an ornate eating knife. But a costly dagger would not defend this boy from the Bishop of Maastricht.

"Keep your knife. You have more need of it than I do." Romein waved his sword, before sheathing it. How to explain the Bishop's evil to this boy without frightening him? "There is a monster…"

"Like a troll? My mother told me stories of trolls who guard bridges," the page began eagerly.

Romein found himself nodding. Better that the boy believe in mythical monsters, than men who looked like anyone else, but behaved like monsters. "Yes, just like that. If you cross this bridge, he will take such a terrible toll, it will take more than a lifetime to repay." Romein couldn't suppress a shudder. The worst stories were of men broken on the wheel, crippled for life, forced to labour for the Bishop until he deemed they had repaid him for their crimes.

The page paled. "In that case…thank you, sir, for the warning. My knife will certainly not be enough, but my brothers are coming. They will surely have the means to pay the troll. If you will but let me past, I must reach the priest at the church of Saint Martin before nightfall."

Romein hesitated. If it was up to him, he'd happily let the boy go to church, but the

Bishop was another matter. "You'll never reach the church. If the monster knows you have crossed the bridge…"

The page patted his horse's neck. "Epona is swifter than any monster. She will carry me as surely as the wind itself. And no monster would dare set foot in such a holy place as Saint Martin's church, not with the relics of Saint Martin himself beneath the altar. My brothers will see to the monster, you may be sure of it."

Romein shook his head. "You do not understand. No man is a match for the evil Bishop of Maastricht. He is a monster the likes of which would give the devil himself pause."

"Did you hear that, Billy? Not only did that wretched bird lose the fight and all my money, but now we're expected to listen to insults from some troll who looks like he crawled out from under a bridge." Two men on horseback crested the top of the bridge, then dismounted on either side of the page. Almost like they meant to defend the boy against Romein.

"No, he came to warn me about the troll, and the toll for crossing the bridge. A terrible one, by all accounts," the page began, looking from one man to the other. "You must deal with the monster, for is that not why you have come?"

"The only monster I see is some bully telling scary stories to frighten you, and offering mortal insults to his betters," the larger of the two men taunted, stepping up to stand directly before Romein. "What did you say about the Bishop, troll? I dare you to say it again." He seized Romein by the collar and lifted him off his feet.

Romein swallowed. Even if he could draw his sword, the man was too close for him to properly defend himself with it. He should have accepted the page's dagger. "The Bishop of Maastricht is an evil monster, and any man in Gelderland will tell you so!"

The man slammed Romein against the side of the bridge, knocking the wind out of him, then held him out over the roiling waters. "Beg the Bishop's pardon, and I shall let you live."

Romein's arms and legs flailed wildly, looking for purchase, but the man's reach was simply too long. Then he accidentally managed to kick the man in the head.

Fury blazed in the man's eyes for a moment, and then he let go.

Romein screamed as he fell, before he landed hard. Pain exploded and everything went black.

Four

"No, Thibault, don't!" Julia cried, reaching for her cousin.

Her brother William was frozen in horror. No help at all.

They were both too late. Thibault let go, and Julia would remember his terrified eyes and flailing limbs forever, until he hit the tree floating beneath the bridge with an ominous crack and lay still.

"You've killed him!" she screamed at

Thibault. "He came to warn us!"

Thibault just shrugged and pushed past her, on his way back to his horse. "You should be thanking me for defending your honour, and your father's," he said, mounting up. "Your father would have had his tongue torn out first for spouting such lies. I did him a mercy." He dug his knees into his gelding's sides, and headed off.

"Come on, we should get going. Thibault wasted enough time. We'll have to spend the night in Elst, before heading on to Veluwe. And pray that there is nothing to gamble on in Elst, or the journey will take even longer." William peered over the side of the bridge and shook his head. "Thibault was right about one thing. Your father never would have tolerated such an insult." He headed for his horse.

Julia could not just leave him lying there. Whoever he was, whatever he'd said…the boy had not deserved to die. She bit her lip, and asked of the water, "Does he live?"

The sound of the boy's heartbeat drifted up

to her, magnified by the water.

She dared to breathe again. "Will you please carry him to where he will be safe, and he may receive healing?"

A wave rolled down the river, rebounded off the bank, then lifted one end of the log the boy had landed on. A second wave turned the tree so that it faced downriver, instead of pointing toward the banks. For a moment, it bobbed in the water, before another wave swept it under the bridge, speeding it downstream.

"Protect him," she whispered, biting her lip one last time so the river might taste her magic, and know how much she wanted it to help her.

Another wave crested, carrying the log and its precious cargo around the bend, and out of sight.

Julia peered after it, wanting one last glimpse. Or at least an answer that he would be protected…

"Come on! No wonder this journey takes so

long. Just get back on your horse and forget about him. That's what your father would do," Thibault shouted.

Julia sighed. She was not her father, and she would not forget about the boy. He hadn't been wrong – Father's justice was swift and brutal, for she'd seen the evidence of that herself, back home. If the people here had experienced it for themselves, no wonder they said such things about him. But these were her lands now, as they had once been her mother's. Things would be different now she was Lady of Veluwe, she swore.

But she had to get there first. So she slid into Epona's saddle, patting and praising the horse for coming across the bridge, even though it had scared her, and rode into Elst.

Five

Romein woke to an unholy screech, a sound that had chased him through his dreams until he'd fallen and hurt his leg, for it was pain which had awoken him.

"Good, you're awake."

Romein did not agree. He couldn't remember ever hurting so much – his leg felt like it was on fire. "What happened?" For even on the edge of sleep, he knew that a man could not be injured in a dream, only to wake with the same wounds.

"A miracle, I'm certain of it. When I went down to the river to fetch water for the horses, I found you, lying on a log, floating in my millpond. I dragged you ashore, thinking only to give you a suitable burial, but when I touched you, you cried out, for you were not dead. That was this morning, and I've been waiting all day for you to wake. I wanted to send for a physician, but it's only me here, and I have work to do, so I can hardly leave, especially with a sick man in my house…"

"Send for the Count of Gelderland. Tell him to send his physician for me. For…Romein."

"Romein, is it? Well, I am Vermeulen, though most just call me Len. I must finish grinding this batch of wheat, and then I can send the horses out into the field, and set off for Valkhof." Vermeulen nodded. "I shall leave you some supper, and I will return by morning." He left.

The unholy screeching sound resumed. Romein's mind might be fogged by pain, but now he knew the man's name, and that he worked a horse-powered mill, he could repay the man for his kindness. For such screeching should not be borne.

"Tell the Count to bring butter. A whole crock of butter," Romein said. He tried to rise, but pain shot through his leg and blackness swooped in to claim him again.

Six

William insisted on riding into the bailey before Julia, with Thibault grumbling in the rear. On the outside, Veluwe looked like any timber castle, with a sheer ring wall broken only by the open gate, beckoning them to enter. But when she accepted her new home's invitation, Julia could not help but gasp. This was no ordinary castle.

The walls were thicker than she expected, and it wasn't until she stood in the middle of the bailey that she saw why. They weren't just fortifications, but actually parts of the house, enclosed rooms that went right the way around the bailey, until they merged into the main keep, a structure that towered over her.

Julia was vaguely aware of William explaining why they were there to the hastily assembled staff, but she did not want to wait.

"Show me everything," she said to the grey-haired woman, whose hands clutched at the ring of keys tied to her girdle, marking her as the castle chatelaine.

The woman looked startled, then bobbed a quick curtsey. "Yes, milady."

Julia dismounted, and a boy darted forward to take her horse from her. Julia felt a twinge of guilt at not taking care of the mare herself – while pretending to be William's page, she'd had to tend to the horses for much of the journey, a duty she had not minded – but things would be different now. Things would be expected of her, as the Lady of Veluwe.

"What's your name?" she asked the woman.

"Mistress Amma is the housekeeper, Julia," William said. "I'm sure she has other duties. Perhaps one of the maids…"

Father had often said that one must begin as one meant to continue. Usually, that meant harsh treatment of those who crossed him, but even Julia could see that he was right about making a good first impression – once they'd seen Father's justice, none believed they would ever see mercy from the man.

And Julia was the ruler here, not William. "Mistress Amma, please show me everything," she commanded. "This castle is to be my home now, and I wish to see the extent of my domain."

Amma ducked her head, but not before Julia glimpsed a proud smile. "Yes, milady. The best view is from the top of the keep…" She led the way inside.

Julia puffed a little as she reached the top of the stairs, but the housekeeper showed no signs of distress. She crossed the chamber at the top and flung open the door. "Behold, my lady. The lands of Veluwe."

Julia stepped out onto a balcony that ran right the way around the keep. From here, she could see for miles…why, she'd had no idea the sea was so close!

But from here, she could see far more water than land, reflecting the clouds as clearly as a mirror. "This is not how my mother described it. She said the lands where she grew up were green, green as far as the eye could see…"

Amma bowed her head. "And so it was when Lady Lia lived here, but the floods have swept away everything. When the waters recede, perhaps the fields will be fertile again. But that is not your concern, my lady, but a matter for the Count. The lands of Veluwe are above the floodwaters, and it is only Gelderland under the water." She leaned over the railing and pointed. "Those are the fields of Veluwe, all harvested and ready for whatever snows the winter might bring. Your flocks are grazing among the stubble, before they return to their usual pastures. Veluwe is the richest part of the lowlands, and the Count of Gelderland surely rues the day your mother refused him, and married your father instead."

Mother must have had her reasons, or perhaps her father had. That was all so long ago.

"But we must hold these lands against the Count, or so my father says. Can we hold?" Julia asked.

Amma hesitated. "As long as the Count keeps to his borders, and we keep to ours, there has been peace. But should one of his men…or worse, one of ours, trespass…all our men are loyal to your father, milady, and the Count's men, misguided as they are, cleave to him, so when the twain meet, there have been…hostilities…"

"She means fights, cousin," Thibault said, striding out onto the balcony. "One of the village cockfights was between the Count and the Bishop, or at least that's what they called the birds, and it had the largest prize purse of all the bouts put together. Some of the villagers said it was like putting a Bishop's man and a Gelderlander into the ring together — none could predict the outcome, but they would fight to the death for their lord's honour. Of course, they had never seen me fight, or they would know your father's man would win, every time." He flexed his sword arm, making the muscles stand out.

Julia shuddered at the sight of such unsightly bulges. She wished she could order the men not to fight so, but men were hotheaded creatures, driven by their passions far more than reason, and they would fight from when they drew their first breath until they gasped their last, Thibault included.

Thank the heavens Father had chosen to send her here to rule Mother's lands instead of marrying her off to some sword-waving bull of a man with nothing between his ears but an echo of her father's orders.

"Enough talk of men. I wish to see the rest of the castle, Mistress Amma," Julia said.

"And I wish to find the bottom of a wine

jug. I think I'll go find the kitchens, or maybe a wine cellar, and leave you women to your housekeeping," Thibault said, disappearing down the steps as quickly as he'd arrived.

"Will your cousin be staying at Veluwe long, my lady?" Amma asked.

Julia shuddered. "God, I hope not. If I have to put up with him another week, I'll push him into the river myself."

Amma made no effort to hide her smile. "Very good, my lady. I have several stout sons who would only be too happy to be of assistance."

Julia couldn't help it. She burst out laughing. She suspected she was really going to like living in Veluwe.

Seven

"His leg is broken."

"Will he ever walk again?"

"Here, drink this, it will numb the pain a little."

"Nothing is certain, but it does not look good."

"What will he do, if he cannot walk?"

"Perhaps the Queen…"

Words washed over Romein, like the waves on the river. Occasionally, just like swimming in the waves, he'd get a mouthful of something foul, but when a voice coaxed him to swallow the bitter brew instead of spitting it out, he did, and the voices dimmed for a time.

Until the voices were replaced by the clattering of wheels on cobblestones.

"Ah, you're awake. The physician said I should keep dosing you all the way to the capital, but he's gone back to Valkhof and it's just us now, so I thought you might want a say in how much of the journey you remember."

Romein blinked, and the blurry face above him became the visage of Benvolio, his cousin. "Did you bring the butter?"

Benvolio laughed. "I did, though the poor miller was mystified as to why. Luckily, you kept asking for it, so I put it into your hands, and even with your eyes closed, you tried to tell me what to do with it. The miller greased his gears and axles and everything else in the mill, for you would not rest until the screeching stopped. Though now we're gone, I have no doubt he'll wash and scrub everything so it's squeaky clean. How he lives with the din, I don't know." Benvolio shook his head. "Now I've answered your question, I have one of my own. How did you come to break your leg?"

Well, that explained the pain. Romein struggled to sit up. With Benvolio's help, he managed it. His leg was encased in a wooden box full of wool, in the middle of a wagon loaded with sacks of the stuff. It did make for a well-cushioned ride. But where…and how…and why? He opened his mouth to ask all this and more, only to see Benvolio's expression. He would receive no more answers until he gave one in return.

Romein closed his eyes. His father had set him one task, and he had failed at it. "A pack of the Bishop's men tried to cross the bridge. I called them to halt, cautioning them against going further. They took insult at this, and set upon me. One of them hurled me over the side of the bridge, into the river below. I thought I had fallen to my death, only to wake when I heard the screeching of the mill. By some miracle, the river carried me into his millpond."

Benvolio looked thoughtful. "Would this lackey of the Bishop's happen to have worn a scarlet cape, as if he thought he was Hugh Capet himself, swishing it about as he boasted about the score of men he'd beaten on the bridge, until one of my party bit his thumb at him, and the fool was forced to find out the mettle of real Montague men of Gelderland? I broke his nose myself, but between us, we also slashed that pretty cloak to ribbons. I have never seen a man run away so fast!"

Romein cast his memory back. He had not seen the man for but a moment before he set upon him, but now he thought about it... "Yes, the man wore a cloak, but it was faded and dusty, more like rust or old blood than true scarlet. He wore a fleur-de-lis pin, though, made of silver."

Benvolio grinned, and delved about in his pocket for a moment. "Did it look like this?"

He held up a silver cloak pin, though the pin itself was bent almost in half.

Romein lay back, satisfied. Whoever the Bishop's man was, Benvolio had most certainly avenged him. "Indeed it did."

"Now, do not tell your father, but I suspect the Bishop's man actually did you a favour, unwittingly and all. While you were missing, a letter arrived from Isaak."

"Who is Isaak?" Romein knew all of his father's men, and he prided himself on remembering their names. He knew of no one called Isaak.

"Our cousin, Isaak. Aunt Maja's son, by Baron Abraham of Rumpelstiltskin. Uncle Chase sent word that Isaak was to serve at court, as the Queen's own ward. You were only a baby then, too young to remember. Actually, you are probably of an age with Isaak. We shall find out when you meet him."

"If he's coming here, why are we in a wagon full of wool?" Romein asked.

Benvolio stared at him. "Why would you

think Isaak would come here? He serves the Queen, I said, and he sent a letter. A letter with a note from the Queen herself, offering an apprenticeship for any boy who has an aptitude for all things mechanical with her own artificer." Benvolio coughed. "We have heard rumours that the Queen is collecting scholars at court. Some say she is searching for the secret of eternal life, and only the most skilled alchemists need apply, but others say it is children she wants most, younger sons from noble families, to become apprentices to her scholars and alchemists. Isaak's letter seems to confirm the stories…"

"But why are we going? Am I dying?" Romein prayed it was not so.

Benvolio laughed. "No, the physician says you will live, though he could not say whether or not you shall walk. But if the Queen has collected the finest scholars in the world in her court, looking for the secret to eternal life, then she must also have the best physician. So I convinced your father that he should send you to court, officially to answer Isaak's call for an apprentice, but even if the Queen does not choose you, it is your best chance to walk again." He frowned. "Now, the physician said I am to put a pinch of this powder into a cup of wine, and see that you drink it whenever you wake, so that you will not be in pain for the journey. Or we could not bother with the powder, share the wine, and swap tales all the way to the capital!"

"So your dull tales will put me to sleep, but I shall have nothing for the pain?" Romein teased, though his smile was forced. His leg ached abominably, and every jolt of the wagon only hurt worse. If the physician's magic powder would see that he felt nothing, and slept through the journey, he would welcome its embrace. "I shall moan and groan all the way to the capital, and not have breath to tell you any amusing stories."

"You do not know any amusing stories, for you have not been on any adventures yet," Benvolio said. "Once you've been at court a few months, I wager that will change. Perhaps you will not want come home. Or perhaps you will become the Queen's favourite and the Queen herself, or one of her lovely daughters, will fall in love with you and you will spend the rest of your life at court, and never think of us at Valkhof again." He poured a cup of wine. "So we are to obey the physician, then?" At Romein's nod, he added the pinch of powder, swirling the wine about in the cup until it dissolved. "Drink, and sleep. Perhaps when you wake, we will have already arrived."

Romein drank, and darkness descended. He did not resist it this time.

Eight

For weeks, all Romein saw of court was the four walls of his chamber. Isaak, a boy his own age, was a frequent visitor, and even if he hadn't brought books with him, Romein could not help but like him. They were cousins, after all, and Isaak was full of stories about the wondrous machines he'd worked on with the Queen's artificer, Master Zimmerman.

Looking at diagrams of these machines, either in the books Isaak brought him or drawn by his own hand, was not enough. Romein longed to see them, to understand their workings. So when the Queen's physician fitted his leg with a sort of walking box and gave him a stick to help support his weight, the first place Romein hobbled to was Master Zimmerman's workshop.

He found Isaak in the middle of a small crowd of people, all staring at an enormous wheel that sloshed water from the river into a narrow canal in the city walls.

"By my calculations, the canals should be full within the week, and we should have running water in every town square," a woman said. "Perhaps if we even channelled the rain from the rooftops directly into the canals, opening them up…"

"Nay, if you open the canals, instead of leaving them closed, they will be filled with refuse within a day. They will be open cesspools, and not fit to drink or wash clothes in. Let the rain run to the river as it always has. Or, if you wished to dig cisterns, perhaps…"

The man took a piece of charcoal and began to sketch a system of pipes and pits.

Romein leaned forward, fascinated. If an entire city's rainwater could be trained to flow only into such a system, built big enough to hold all the water that came down, the city would never be flooded. If they could build a system of canals back home, forcing the water to flow only where it was wanted, and not allowing it to flood the fields…

"Hey, Isaak, why don't we have such a system back home, so there isn't any flooding?" Romein asked.

Isaak's eyes widened. "I did not expect to see you up and about so soon! And what is this talk of flooding? There's a flood? We must help!"

"The waters have likely gone down since I left, but it floods almost every year back home. It was especially bad this year, for the sea broke down the banks and surged across the fields." Flooding all of Gelderland except Veluwe. The Bishop had surely done some sort of deal with the devil to ensure that his lands were untouched.

"The Queen will know how to help. Could Romein build such canals back home, to stop the flooding?" Isaak asked the woman.

She frowned. "Only if the water has somewhere to go. It naturally flows to the lowest lying land. If Romein is from the lowlands, then there is nowhere for it to go, and it would take a great amount of work to make it move somewhere else."

"But if we dug deeper in some parts, so they are lower than the rest, surely they could hold some of the water, and drain the surrounding lands," Romein said eagerly. "Not cisterns, but maybe lakes."

The woman pondered for a moment, then said, "Perhaps. You would still need to find a way to make the water move, but as you can see, once you get a waterwheel going, it practically drives itself." She gestured toward the wheel that had occupied everyone's attention only a few moments ago.

A girl perhaps a year or two younger than Romein came running into the square. "Mother, the boys are making Father Tristan tell them all the gory stories in the bible again, and it is time for my lessons. If you do not make them stop, I will miss my lessons again, or I will finish too late to go riding this afternoon. It's not fair!"

The woman frowned. "Your brothers know they only spend the morning with their tutor, and he is yours for the afternoon. You tell them they are to be in Master Zimmerman's workshop the moment they finish their noon meal, and not a second later. I shall be up directly, and if they are still in my bower when I arrive…"

The girl beamed. "Thank you, Mother!" She raced off.

The woman sighed. "Zimmerman, can you examine the new boy while I sort out some domestic matters? If his grasp of water mechanics is as good as it sounds, perhaps he can join Isaak on this project."

Zimmerman bowed. "Of course, Your Majesty."

Romein's jaw dropped, and by the time he'd managed to close his mouth, the Queen had marched off in the direction of the castle. "That was…that was…?"

Isaak grinned. "That was Queen Molina, and her favourite daughter, Princess Rosaline. She means to bring running water to every home in the city, like the legends say the ancients did, but we still have a long way to go yet. The hardest part was bringing the water inside the city. Now that is done… maybe this will actually work."

Water running through every house? The Queen was trying to bring about a miracle. Then again, it would be a miracle if they could stop Gelderland from flooding. Cisterns and pipes and canals and wheels…the cogs began turning in Romein's head, and once they did, they had no intention of stopping.

Nine

Thibault stayed for three days. Father allowed William to stay for almost three years, before summoning him home, too.

"I hope she is as lovely a girl as you could wish for, and you love her from the moment you lay eyes on her," Julia said as she bade William farewell.

William made a rude noise. "Father picked her out, so her only virtues are likely her dowry and the influence her family has, and what they

501

can do for Father. It isn't like I need to even bed her – Aran has a wife and several children. Plenty of heirs to keep Father happy. But it is not me you should be worried about. Once I am married, his eye will fall upon you again, and he'll pick a husband for you next, so you have children you can pass Veluwe onto. I shall do my best to convince him to give you someone nice, for I don't imagine there are many men who deserve you. Few women could manage lands as well as you do Veluwe."

William only thought that because he had not seen Veluwe before the floods. Only half the fields had yielded a decent harvest this year, with the rest still full of salt. And the salt encroached more every year, turning fertile fields into desert.

"I do what I can," Julia said. Lately, that meant supplementing their stores with fish caught from the little sailing boat she ventured out in every morning. William did not know about that, either.

She waved to him from the gate, then

ascended the tower and watched him until he was too far away to see. It would be four years more before another member of her family arrived in Veluwe and sought to interfere in her life, but after seven years as the Lady of Veluwe, she knew her people as well as they knew her, and they would stand firm to hold the land they fought the sea for, every day of their lives. Gone was the girl who'd dressed as a page for her journey here, and, while some days she might long for the silks she'd worn in her father's house, most days she preferred her woollen gowns, which could withstand the salt that blew in off the North Sea.

As it was now, for she could see another storm brewing. She clattered down the steps, calling for Amma to make sure everything was secured before the arrival of the coming storm.

Ten

"Good morrow, cousin."

Romein recognised Isaak's cheerful voice, but he did not let up. Parry, thrust, and parry again…if he was a better swordsman, perhaps she would reconsider, look upon him kindly, instead of…

"How goes your suit with Rosaline?"

Romein growled, and overreached. Mercutio stumbled back to avoid Romein's sword and landed flat on his back, with a sword at his throat.

Until a blade crossed his, and he was forced to contend with Isaak instead.

"I asked you how you fared with Rosaline," Isaak repeated.

"Out of her favour, where I am in love," Romein said, lunging at Isaak.

Isaak was the better fighter, and he had not Romein's lame leg to contend with, so he danced back, sword at the ready, with a grin still on his face. "Alas, that love, which I had thought so gentle, should be so tyrannous and rough in proof!"

"He would not be so rough with Princess Rosaline!" Mercutio said, clambering to his feet. He winced, for several of Romein's blows would likely bruise on the morrow.

"But Princess Rosaline will not have him, for she has her heart set on a political marriage, where she will be a queen like her mother. One such as she will never marry some country lord, whose first love is waterwheels, with which he means to save his country!" Isaak's grin never wavered. "You should forget her, cousin, and go home as you planned. You have learned much from the Queen and from Master Zimmerman. You must now take your knowledge home, and use it to save your people from the floods, as the Queen intended. Meanwhile, Rosaline will likely be married off to some old man who needs heirs, and when she is done labouring for him, she will hear tidings of your triumph, and regret the poor choice she made today. Because you, the hero of your people, will have your choice of ladies falling at your feet."

Romein dropped his guard, holding his free hand up in surrender. "I might save my people from the floods, but if you think I can love another as deeply as I have loved Rosaline, you are mistaken. She is one woman my heart can never forget."

Isaak sheathed his sword. "Ah, but we are both about to set out on impossible quests. You mean to save your people, a far harder task than winning one woman's heart, if it belonged to anyone but flint-hearted Rosaline, and I am supposed to find and save the Queen's eldest daughter, before my family's curse claims me, as it has all my predecessors. Yet you do not waver. I believe you truly will save your people, and I…the Queen is certain that I will save her daughter, though we both know I am no match for the formidable witch who stole her as a baby." He shook his head. "You speak of impossible quests, and yet…"

Romein sighed. Isaak's story was a pitiful one, with little chance of happiness before its end. "Forgive me, cousin. You are right, of course. The Queen has given me a task that may take a lifetime, but at least I know I shall have that. If you carry your father's curse, you will die young, like all the Rumpelstiltskin men. I pray that you may have your miracle, and that you shall find this girl, who your father believed could break the curse, so that you may live a long dend happy life at your family estates, which the Queen will return to you after you find her lost princess. Perhaps one day I shall look forward to a visit from you, so that you can show your new bride my miraculous waterwheels, for surely the princess cannot help but fall in love with the man who saves her from the witch…"

Isaak's smile was sad now. "If that is so, then we will both have our miracles. I will introduce my bride to yours, as you show me the lands you have saved. Do we have an accord?"

Romein shook Isaak's hand, not wanting to let go, for he knew this might be the last time he saw his cousin. The Rumpelstiltskin curse had claimed every man in his line but him, and he had precious little time left before it would take him, too.

"Farewell, and may God go with you. For without Rosaline, I travel alone," Romein said.

"But not, I think, for long," Isaak said.

Romein could only shake his head. He could walk the world thrice over, and never find Rosaline's equal. But let Isaak believe what airy fantasies he would, for he had a far darker path to tread.

Eleven

Perhaps William had taken her luck with him. Or perhaps Veluwe was cursed. The salt waters which had left Veluwe untouched for so long were now claiming the land for her own. Four years of increasingly poor harvests, losing field after field to salt. There was not even enough fodder for the dairy cows. If Julia did not go out fishing every day, she might have no meat at all for her table.

She did not keep a fine table, not like her

Father did, but even she had seen the stores in the cellar dwindle, never quite replaced by the next year's harvest.

Men who had worked the fields at Veluwe all their lives, like their fathers and grandfathers before them, melted away, likely to seek work with the Count of Gelderland, and Julia could not blame them. They had families to feed, and she had little to spare.

It wasn't until she headed to the orchard to oversee the apple harvest that she saw just how bad things had become. Instead of apples, the trees sported a coat of salt crystals, turning the leaves to brown parchment and the branches to sticks only suitable for kindling. She wanted to weep, for the fertile lands lost, but she knew her people looked to her, so instead she stood strong and ordered the dairy herd reduced to salt beef, for she could see no other way to survive the winter.

Today, standing atop the tower, she could see nothing but desolation. There was no sign of the rolling green fields her mother had loved. The only things rolling now were storm clouds, mirroring the waves below, as the first winter storm brought what could only be a new spate of flooding to her already ravaged lands.

A sob caught in Julia's throat. She had failed. Failed her people, failed her land, failed her mother. Now, her only hope was to head home to her father's house, and beg for his help to restore her mother's lands. For without a miracle, she was about to lose Veluwe to the sea.

She allowed herself time only to pack her things, before saddling Epona and heading back across the bridge.

Twelve

Romein kicked the waterwheel and swore. There was nothing wrong with it. He'd constructed it just like the ones he'd made in Zimmerman's workshop, and connected it to the mill exactly as the designs said he should. Yet the wheel scarcely moved, and if the wheel did not move, then it could not draw water from the flooded field into the channel like he wanted it to do.

It could not be the wheel. It must be the

river, which lacked the great snowmelt fuelled currents in the river that ran beside the capital. The Maas was scarcely a river at all, for it was as lazy as a lake. There was water aplenty, but no power in it which he could harness. Now, if he could harness the ever-present wind, that might work…

A small, one-man sailboat plied the waters, far off into the distance. Its sails harnessed the wind well enough. If he could only attach sails to the wheel, and make it turn…

Romein ducked inside the mill for some paper and charcoal, and began to draw.

Thirteen

A sound somewhere between a screech and a creak began to sound in Julia's ears. It was like no bird she'd ever heard before, but a bird it must be, or a whole flock of them, for no door could keep creaking for so long.

Epona flicked her ears irritably. She heard the sound, too, and she did not approve of it. It took all of Julia's stubbornness to make her keep moving forward, for Epona evidently wanted to turn around and head back to

Veluwe as much as her mistress did.

The sound grew louder, the closer they got to the bridge. But it wasn't until they reached the top of the stone arch that Julia saw it was no bird at all.

A giant wheel, like something that belonged on a cart the size of a house, sat beside the riverbank, turning slowly in the current. What made the wheel more remarkable still were the enormous sails sticking out the side of the structure – and the whole thing creaked in protest as it turned.

The storm was fast approaching, bringing with it strong winds that filled the sails, making the contraption groan even louder…until one of the sails suddenly snapped off, and took flight.

Epona whinnied in fright as the sail headed straight for them on the bridge, and bolted.

Julia, too distracted by the curious sight, was a moment too slow reaching for the horse's reins, so that when the horse moved, she found herself flying backward, toward the edge of the bridge and the river below.

She bit her lip, sending out a desperate plea to the water to protect her, before she landed on the river's surface, which felt as hard as any rock. Her breath blew out as pain exploded in her chest, and she wasn't even sure if her cry for help left her lips before blackness claimed her.

Fourteen

The page blurred before him, and Romein let his mind wander into a daydream. In it, the north wind deposited a sailboat at his door, begging him to board, before sending the boat soaring up into the air, blowing it all the way back to the capital, where he could see crowds forming to celebrate a wedding. Princess Rosaline stood before the cathedral, in a gown tossed by the wind, but there was no sign of her husband. For a moment, Romein dared to hope, and his boat skimmed across the stones in the square, before being whipped up, higher than the highest tower, as the wind changed, sending his boat tumbling back the way it had come, and he helpless to stop it. The stars in the sky hung low, peering at him as though to mock him for daring to look so high, until he feared for his life, for if he was to drift on the high air currents for the rest of his days, then he should surely die, and die alone.

His heart filled with lead, he offered up a prayer to God or fate or whatever other power in the universe had steerage of his course, that it would direct his sail true.

But the answer he received was not the one he wanted.

Romein heard the ominous crack and he raced outside, just in time to see a sail break off and flap toward the river. He swore. This was his second attempt at making a sail wheel, and it was an even bigger failure than the first. The Queen and Zimmerman would know what he'd done wrong and how to fix it…but he had no idea where to start. There must be some better way to make the sails and fasten them to the wheel so they did not snap off and go sailing away on their own.

He sighed and sat down to write a letter to the Queen. He told them everything he had tried, even drawing diagrams of his failed sail wheels, then sealed the letter and asked one of the men toiling away in the salt works to take it to the capital and put it into the hands of Master Zimmerman.

He only hoped he would receive an answer soon, and a better one than fate had offered him.

Meanwhile, he'd best try to retrieve the sail that had taken flight, to see if he could fasten it back on the waterwheel.

Romein set off along the riverbank, dodging the reeds as he searched for his lost sail. He walked for more than a mile before he decided the stupid thing must have sunk, and headed home.

Only to find the sail had made its way into

the millpond instead, just as he had on the day Vermeulen found him. Only Vermeulen was gone now, and Romein was responsible for the mill, which also meant fishing out debris from the millpond. He reached out with his billhook, catching the spar the sail was wound around, and dragged it toward shore.

It wasn't until he tried to lift the sail out of the water that he realised it had gained some cargo during its journey – a woman's body. She must have drowned recently, for she hardly looked dead at all. An angel, fallen to earth.

A dove consigned to the crows, called too soon. Beauty too rich for use, for earth too dear. Had his heart ever known love before this moment? He swore it could not, for he had never seen true beauty until now. He dared not profane this angel with his rude hand, and yet, he longed to touch...just her hand, perhaps...

Then she coughed, and groaned. Startled out of his reverie, Romein waded into the pond to save her. The chilly water set his teeth chattering, so he could scarcely imagine how cold she must be. He carried her inside to the warmest place he had, his box bed, then built up the fire, hoping to have a pot of soup ready for when she woke.

He hung her things before the fire, so that they might dry, for he had no other women's clothes for her to wear when she awoke. Her gown was made of fine, heavy wool – like Queen Molina might have worn while working outside. Whoever this woman was, she was no commoner.

But it was her girdle that interested him most – for sheathed at her waist, she'd carried a curiously ornate eating knife. He'd seen such silver waves before, but it took him some time to remember when. The last time he'd seen a knife like this one, it had been in the hands of a boy who rode with two of the Bishop's men – men who had thrown him into the river, and turned him into a cripple.

Surely there could not be two such knives. If this was the same blade, though, that meant this woman was…what? The boy's wife? For the boy was likely a man now. One of the Bishop's men…

A man who would come looking for her, for they could not have been wed long. And what little he'd seen of her as he bundled her out of her clothes and into his bed, he knew had been fair indeed.

Romein sighed. He'd be wise to send her on her way the moment she awoke, or better yet, as soon as her clothes dried. If the Bishop's men knew the Count of Gelderland's son had undressed one of their wives and put her into his bed…Romein would have a fight on his hands, and he knew the Bishop's men did not fight fair. No, they would make sure they outnumbered him, and no amount of sparring with Isaak over the last seven years would prepare him for the beating they'd give him.

As if to remind him, rain began drumming on the roof above. The first of the winter storms was here.

He closed his eyes. Beating or no, he could

not send a woman out into the storm. The Bishop's men might be cruel enough to do so, but his own father had raised him better than that.

A broken sail, a waterwheel that wouldn't work, and a woman who belonged to the enemy asleep in his bed. And a storm raging outside, that would likely do so for some days yet. Romein wasn't sure whether to laugh or cry at such a run of bad luck.

So he settled down in the chair by the fire, to wait for whatever his abominable luck would bring next.

Until a distressed whinny from outside reminded him that the mill ponies were not yet in the stable for the night, and he headed out to take care of them, too.

Fifteen

The sound of rain woke Julia, for it sounded much louder than the patter of raindrops on the thatched roof of the keep. This was an incessant drumming that seemed to echo through the room, if a room it was. A place so dark must surely be a cellar.

But not one of Veluwe's cellars, for she knew those intimately. She reached out, and her fingers grazed wood almost instantly. The ceiling wasn't far above her head, either, as though someone had stuffed her into a large chest and closed the lid. At least they'd given her blankets and a mattress, though it seemed they'd taken her clothes in exchange.

She tried to raise the lid, but no matter how hard she pushed, it did not seem to want to budge. Swearing, she set her back against the wall and tried pushing with her legs instead.

Only, it wasn't the roof that moved, but the wall behind her, pitching her out onto a cold floor. She snatched up the nearest blanket and wrapped it around her before anyone could see her nakedness, only to discover she was alone in a circular room, and what she'd taken for a chest was actually a box bed, which took up most of the room.

But there was a chest, and it contained an assortment of men's clothing. Better than nothing, she decided, as she found a tunic and hose that fit well enough. It was almost like pretending to be a page again, as she had on the journey to Veluwe, though those clothes no longer fit her. She'd given them to one of

Amma's grandsons.

Dressed, she ventured down the stairs. On the level below, a fire burned in the hearth, while her clothing was draped across the table and benches. Hmm, almost dry. She must have slept for a while if someone had had the time to wash and dry her gown and her underthings.

The smell of something delicious drew her back to the fire. Ah, there was a soup pot on the hearth, keeping warm. It was a rich, meaty stew, judging by the smell, so whoever lived here was not poor.

They probably ate better than she had these last few months, for all that she was the Lady of Veluwe. She sighed. Stealing their dinner was beneath her, though she couldn't deny she was tempted. She had coin to pay for it in her saddlebags, but those were on Epona's back and she…

Now Julia remembered. Epona taking fright at the flying sail, bucking her off, and she'd landed in the river. Well, that explained why she'd been naked – her clothes had likely been soaked. That still didn't explain the searing pain in her side that made it hard to breathe, though.

Another glance around the circular room, bigger than the bedchamber above, gave her the clue she needed to orient herself. This was the mill she'd seen beside the wheel in the water. So the miller had likely been the one to pull her from the river. That explained the rich stew, too, for most millers were not poor – she'd paid enough for flour these last three years to know that. She would have to thank the miller's wife for washing her clothes while she slept.

A door slammed somewhere, and the sound of heavy footsteps tromped up the stairs. The man dropped his heavy bags on the floor beside the fire, then stared at her for a long moment, before he exclaimed, "The boy from the bridge!"

Julia blinked. The boy from the bridge? She hadn't thought about him for years. And yet, now that she looked at this man, it had to be…

"You!"

Sixteen

There was a fine horse in the field among the ponies, prancing about with saddlebags strapped to her back. A familiar horse, though he could not remember where he'd seen it before. This was the lady's horse, which had likely thrown her, Romein decided. Perhaps he'd seen her out riding in Valkhof. Well, the lady was not going anywhere tonight, and her horse would need shelter as much as the mill ponies, so he led the way into the stable, gave them their feed, and closed the door.

Only when the mare had her nose deep in the feed trough did he dare approach to remove the lady's bags. The horse eyed him warily, as though she was considering trampling him to death for daring to approach her, before deciding that the apple in the trough was far more worthy of her attention.

Romein threw the bags over his shoulder and headed back to the mill. He hung his wet cloak up just inside the door, so that it wouldn't drip anywhere else, and headed upstairs to check on the woman.

Only to find her awake and in his kitchen, wearing a set of Vermeulen's clothes. Romein's breath caught in his throat. Instead of an angel, now she looked like a boy. Then there was the knife, and that horse…

"You're the boy from the bridge," he blurted out, then bit his tongue. She was not a boy at all, but on that day, he'd thought she was.

She stared at him a moment, before

recognition kindled in her eyes. "You!" Then she ducked her head, shaking it sorrowfully. "I feared you'd died. That Thibault had killed you, and I had not been able to stop him."

So Thibault was the oaf's name, was it? "I fear neither of us were a match for him that day," Romein said.

"I am sorry. And now, you have saved me, when I could not save you?"

He shrugged. "I did not do much saving. You washed up in my millpond, on a raft of sorts. A sail that had come off my waterwheel. I was looking for the sail, and I found you. I brought you inside…oh, and your horse is in the stable, with the mill ponies. I brought your things." He gestured at the bags lying beside his feet.

"I thank you."

He expected her to grab the bags and go upstairs to change into more appropriate clothing, but she just stood there, perfectly comfortable in the dead miller's tunic. By all that was holy, he could see her legs! Sure, they were covered in hose, but the woollen hose clung to every curve, showing just how shapely they were. He'd tried not to look as he undressed her, but now he could not seem to tear his eyes away from her.

"I can pay you for your hospitality. And a hot meal, if you have enough to share."

By God, he'd forgotten about the soup. Thank all the saints he'd at least taken it off the fire so it wasn't burned to ashes now.

"More than enough for us both, and a fresh loaf of bread, too. The baker in the village, one of his sons is employed in my salt works, and he is kind enough to bring fresh bread every morning. My family see to it that I never run out of butter…" It was a standing joke among them that when he'd been rescued by the miller all those years ago, he'd asked for butter, and Benvolio never let him forget it. The mill never screeched like it had for Vermeulen, either, though, so he was glad of it.

Her eyebrows shot up. "Butter? Oh, it has been too long since we had butter at Veluwe.

When we lost the best pastures to salt..."
Then she pressed her lips together and shook
her head, as though she'd said too much.

So she was in some way beholden to the
Bishop. He'd heard stories from some of the
salt workers, who claimed to have left Veluwe,
but that didn't sound like the Bishop's usual
tactics. He insisted on loyalty until death – the
Bishop would never allow even the lowliest of
his servants to leave him and take up with the
Count of Gelderland. "So it is true, then, that
the jewel of the lowlands does not sparkle as
brightly as it once did?" Romein asked
carefully.

She hung her head. "I only wish I knew
why. The floods are all I can think of, but the
water never touched Veluwe, yet the salt crept
up into the fields like some malicious imp had
sown it there in place of seeds. I fear I may
have to desert Veluwe entirely. Only a few
trusted servants remain."

If she weren't a woman, Romein would
have suspected he was speaking to the Bishop

himself. Unless she was the Bishop's wife...the men had said a lady ruled at Veluwe, but the Bishop would never let a woman rule in his stead. Why, even his own father would not trust a woman to rule. And while Queen Molina was capable enough, she was still only Queen Consort to her husband, King Lubos.

"And what does your husband say about it?" Romein asked.

The girl burst out laughing. "Oh, I have no husband, nor am I likely to ever find one, if we lose Veluwe."

Relief rushed through him. She wasn't the Bishop's wife, then. Good.

"Shall we eat? I have a bottle of mead I'd been meaning to save until Yule, but tonight seems a good enough night to share it. It will go well with the stew, and chase off any chill you took from your dip in the river. I could bring up some butter, too."

"I would be most grateful," she said.

Things were fetched, the table was set, mead was poured...and for the first time in his life,

Romein found himself sharing a meal with an enemy. She might look like an angel, but if his suspicions proved true, she might be the devil's own spawn. Worse, when he glimpsed her pretty smile, beneath those laughing eyes, he feared he did not dislike it as much as he should. In fact, he did not dislike her at all.

Seventeen

By the time they'd finished their meal, the rain had slowed to a drizzle, which the miller declared was fine enough weather to return to fixing his waterwheel.

Julia sighed. The miller was a very pleasant sort of man, and she wanted to know more about his waterwheel and salt works, and why he'd given the wheel sails, but she knew she couldn't stay. She needed to ride home to Father, to tell him about the sorry state Veluwe had fallen into, and ask for his help to fix it.

She rose, smoothing down the sides of her tunic. That was another thing she owed the miller – for reminding her how she ought to travel.

"I thank you for your kind hospitality, and for the loan of these clothes. I'd be happy to pay you for them, as I do not know when I will come this way again, and I truly must be off."

He stared at her for a long moment. "It is not often I am blessed to have such a charming dinner companion. Please, take the clothes as a gift, and your company is payment enough. I wish you well on your journey, though I admit I am curious."

"Yes?" she prompted.

"Why do you travel as a man? When you first arrived here seven years ago, and again now?"

As a man himself, the miller had likely never had to consider such things before.

"It is not safe for a woman to travel alone. There are men who might do her harm." If the

Count of Gelderland caught wind that the Bishop of Maastricht's only daughter was travelling alone on the road, he would send men to capture her for sure, before forcing her to relinquish Veluwe to him. Father had said so enough times. "My father felt it safer for me to travel in disguise then, and I doubt the world has changed so much that it is any safer now. Especially as I do not have the travel companions I did then." Not that Thibault had been much protection. The number of times they'd gotten into trouble because of him.

But if William were here…

"You must miss your brothers," the miller said, as if reading her mind.

She did miss them. Both William and Aran had been protective, as older brothers always were, but their protectiveness had always been founded in their love for her. But both were likely married now, with children of their own to protect. If she wanted a protector, she'd have to hire one. Or find a husband, which was probably what her father would expect.

Her father probably already had some poor sod picked out, waiting to woo her, as soon as he could spare the man to send him to Veluwe. So Julia would be doing her father and her future husband a favour, then, in coming home.

She shivered. She should wear her cloak as she rode, to keep the cold and the rain off her. The rest of her now dry clothes, she shoved into her saddlebags with her other possessions. Then she headed outside to find her horse.

Epona allowed Julia to lead her out of the stable amiably enough, and stood still to be saddled. Julia would miss being able to do things for herself, as she had for so long out here. At home, Father would expect her to let the servants do the work, while she stood by and looked useless. Worse, she'd feel useless, too, for there would be nothing for her to do but sewing and embroidery. If Father found out how well she could sail, or how swiftly she could gut a fish, he'd probably expire in horror.

Funny, she'd rather catch and gut a thousand fish, and sail straight through a storm, than head home to Father right now to confess her failure. But duty called her, and Julia had always been a dutiful daughter.

She set one booted foot in the stirrup, and swung up onto Epona's back. Or at least she tried to. Pain lanced her side, stealing her breath and threatening to steal her sight, too.

Strong arms caught her, easing her down onto the ground again as Julia struggled to breathe. Just inhaling left her sobbing.

"Easy, easy. You must have broken your ribs. You can't ride with broken ribs. You must stay here and rest until they are healed."

She couldn't stay. She had to go to Father. To tell him…

"What would you know? You're a miller, not a physician. Why, you can't even make sails properly," she snapped, though her voice was not as strong as she wished it to be. "Your sail broke off and spooked my horse, or she would not have thrown me. Any injuries she has done me, I can surely lay the fault for them at your feet."

He chuckled softly. "Ah, but I've fallen and broken my ribs, too, thanks to the ministrations of your brother. I know exactly what that feels like."

Oh, by all that was holy…her pain now was penance for not stopping Thibault all those years ago. "Cousin. Thibault is not my brother, he's my cousin, and a bastard cousin, at that."

"Ah, I could have told you he was a bastard on the day I met him. But it's funny. I know your cousin's name, for you have mentioned it before, but I do not yet know yours." He rose, then bowed in such a practiced fashion, Julia swore he must have spent time at court. "I am Romein, the current owner of this establishment, which I hope to greatly improve."

Yes. With sails and strange wheels. Julia would not have believed it, if she had not seen his contraptions with her own eyes. She sighed. What did it matter if the miller knew her name? It was likely a common enough name for girls in these parts, for it had been her mother's and her mother's before her. "I'm Julia."

He took her hand in his and kissed it. "I am honoured to have met you, Julia, and I look forward to listening to many a lecture from you on my shortcomings in sailmaking, until you are fit to continue your journey."

Stay…here? With him? Julia blinked. Well, if she could not sit upon a horse, nor ride home to Father, of course it followed that she could not head back to Veluwe.

"Thank you." While the words fell from her lips unbidden, she was grateful. For deep in her heart, she did not want to leave.

Eighteen

She stood and watched while he climbed atop the waterwheel and took down the sails, working in haste to finish the job before the lull in the storm passed and the wind picked up.

Julia could not do much to help, except pluck the sails from the river when he dropped them, snagging them with his billhook before pulling them to shore.

"The river current was not enough to push

the wheel, so I thought if I used the wind as well, it might help. There was a small sailboat in the distance, and so I thought of using sails," Romein explained, letting another sail fall into the water.

She waded in up to her knees and hooked it, dragging the sail out of the river. She wondered if it was her sailboat he'd seen, for most fisherman took their boats to sea, where they might net a finer catch than a few river fish. She had only her own supper to catch, while they had whole families to feed.

"But as you say, I must be doing something wrong. I have never seen a sailboat torn asunder like these were." Romein frowned at the last sail, before tucking it under his arm to wade ashore.

"That is because few fishermen are foolish enough to take their sailboats out in a gale, and if they do, they reef their sails, not run before the wind. A sail must move, to catch the wind as it changes..." Julia shook her head. It had been seven years since she'd learned to sail, and she did most things by instinct now, for the old fisherman who'd taught her had not been a man of many words. She could not talk the miller into being a fisherman, any more than her words could wish a new sail into existence.

Romein reached her side, then turned to regard the water wheel. "So what you're saying is that I must look more closely at a sailing boat, and rig the sails to the wheel accordingly..."

"No! If you want a wheel to turn in the wind, then you make a wheel that catches the wind, like the one the ponies turn in the mill yard, and then somehow make that turn the other wheel that you want..." Oh, this was even worse. Now she was trying to teach milling to a miller, for heaven's sake, when she scarcely understood how one wheel could move another, even when she watched them in action.

Romein's mouth dropped open. "Oh my God, you truly are an angel. A saint sent from heaven itself. Of course. We use sails, but we also use wheels and cogs, axles and gears. Then get those to turn the waterwheel and..." He seized her shoulders and kissed her.

Julia's heart stopped. An eternity passed, though it was but a moment, before he released her, and she dared to breathe again.

"Forgive me, dear angel, for such a passionate kiss of peace, but I was overcome with gratitude. Tonight, I shall attempt to draw what your divine inspiration has made appear in my head, and you shall tell me if it will sink or sail."

She might be able to breathe, but her voice had not yet returned, so Julia only nodded as Romein gathered up the sails to take them inside, where they would be safe from the storm. But the storm brewing within her breast, sparked by that kiss, would prove far more dangerous.

Nineteen

Julia wasn't sure how she ended up sewing the sails for Romein's new wind wheel, or whatever it was he was calling it today, but it kept her busy inside the mill while Romein banged away in a corner of the stable, fastening together the spokes of the wheel, the spars that would hold the sails.

She reasoned that she could sew as well, if not better than any man, and though she would not call herself a sailmaker, nor had she ever made her own sails, the sails had never come off her boat, so she had to be better at sailmaking than Romein.

The sound of hammering floated up from downstairs. Had Romein decided to move his wheel inside the mill? Surely not.

No, the sound was coming from outside the door.

Whoever was knocking did not content himself with merely hammering at the door. No, he began to shout in between blows.

"Romein! Madman! Lover!"

And again:

"Romein! Madman! Lover!"

A pause, then:

"I conjure thee! I conjure thee by Rosaline's bright eyes,

By her high forehead and her scarlet lip,

By her fine foot, straight leg and quivering thigh!"

Some swearing, followed by:

"Curse you, Romein, in the Queen's name I come, in answer to your missive!"

More swearing, then a final:

"Then I shall leave the Queen's gift here, but I shall go, for this field-bed is too cold for me to sleep." Something thumped against the door, and the sounds ceased.

Julia set down her sewing and made her way down the stairs. When she threw open the door, there was no sign of the Queen's messenger, except for a leather bag of papers left on the doorstep. The first was a folded letter bearing the royal seal.

Why would the Queen send a gift to a miller, so far from court?

The rain began anew, sheeting in sideways, and Julia was forced to close the door before the whole lower levels became awash. She set the Queen's gift on the kitchen table, and when she heard Romein come inside for the night, she pointed to the bag and said, "This arrived for you. From the Queen, he said, though he also said some scandalous things about a lady named Rosaline."

Romein grinned. "Then it must have been

Mercutio! Where is he?"

"When you didn't come in answer to his shouting, he left. He was already gone when I reached the door, but he left this." She lifted the bag and let it thump onto the table.

His eyes lit up. "The Queen sent an answer!" He ripped through the royal seal as though it was nothing, his eyes scanning the letter before he threw it down and began pulling papers out of the bag. "We were on the right track with the wind wheel. She has sent drawings of wind wheels…nay, wind mills…crusaders found in the Holy Land, and accounts of how one of the southern cities, built actually on the water, if you can believe that, has reclaimed the sea bed to build houses upon, and grow orchards, by pumping out the water and using the salt…it is called Rialto, she says, and they have been doing this for more than a hundred years…"

Julia could scarcely believe it. "You know how to turn salt-sown lands into gardens? Orchards?"

Romein ducked his head. "Well, not yet, but I knew it was possible, and when I have read all of this, that is what we shall do here. And when we are successful, we will repeat the process throughout the lowlands, until the whole country is a garden, as green as you please, and we never need fear the sea or salt water again!"

"And Veluwe? Would it work there, too?" She held her breath, wishing it could be true, yet knowing what she asked was impossible. Salt-scarred land had never been saved before. Never. Unless this Rialto was real…

"I can't see why not. Though the first step would be getting this windmill working, and we are a long way from that…"

"But how will people feed themselves, while their land is still tainted by salt? If nothing will grow…"

Romein grinned. "Ah, but you forget how valuable salt is. We have more here than we could ever need, a veritable mine of the stuff. And those who live inland pay handsomely for it, to preserve meat through the winter. When I sell the salt from my salt works, I make enough coin to pay men to work it for me, and keep meat in the pot for every day. And that is just one small field. If we were to work the whole lowlands...just imagine."

Julia could imagine. If her father heard of it, he would insist she start work at Veluwe immediately, before the Count found out and began to reclaim Gelderland from the sea, too.

"I'd better get back to my sewing, then," she said.

Twenty

Finally, the rain stopped, and a day dawned that was cold and clear, when the sun sent watery rays of light to tempt Julia to step outside. She intended to visit the stables, to see what progress Romein had made with his new wheel, but one of the men from the salt works called, "Lady Julia!"

In a moment, they were all calling greetings and exclaiming over her return, for they'd heard word from Veluwe that she had gone home to her father.

"Do you mean to mine the salt, as Master Romein is here, Lady Julia?" one of the men asked.

She racked her brain for his name. Henk, wasn't it? Or was it Jan? No, because Jan, the stouter of the two brothers, stood beside Henk, holding a shovel.

"I would like to. Is harvesting salt harder than harvesting crops?" she asked.

The men laughed.

"Yes, and no, my lady," Henk said. "The harvest is more work, for salt is heavier than wheat, but there is no need to sow or plough the field. If you mean to mine the salt at Veluwe, me and my brothers are ready to come home the moment you give the word. Now, if you wish it, for Master Romein has offered us three weeks' holiday for Yule, and a sack of salt to carry home to our families, as reward for our good work this year."

That was kind of him. She had always given the families of Veluwe gifts of food at Yule, but this year she had precious little to give. Even she lived off Romein's kindness, for he refused to accept any payment for her board and lodging. The saints be praised he hadn't stopped her from sewing the sails for him, or she would be even more deeply in his debt.

But the weight of Henk's words began to sink in. "You mean…you could start turning Veluwe's salt-scarred fields fertile again, so that we could plant crops in the spring?"

The men laughed again. It wasn't malicious – most of them had known her since she'd first arrived at Veluwe, a wide-eyed girl asking questions about everything, for the more she understood, the better she could manage the estate. If anything, they seemed only too happy to help her understand.

"As soon as the ground freezes, there will be nothing simpler, Lady Julia. Master Romein has had the mill ponies working a pump to shift the water from the field, but when the ground freezes, so does the water, and we only have to lift the ice onto barrows and cart it to the river. Once the ice is gone, there is only salt left. With enough men, we could clear several fields before year's end, and if Master Romein will spare us until the spring…perhaps we could even clear the salt from the orchards, too, so you shall have apples again come the autumn."

Julia felt her cheeks flush. These men knew her too well. Amma must have told them how fond she was of apples, for surely no one had seen how she wept at how pitiful this year's harvest was. Scarcely enough to make a single pie or tart, let alone last them the winter. Just the thought of celebrating the new year without any kind of apple cake had been the last straw that sent her scurrying home to her father. Only now, here she was at the mill with Romein, and still there wasn't an apple in sight.

But if she knew next year would be better…

She would take that wager. "Yes. As soon as you are finished working for Master Romein, please get started on the fields at Veluwe. And any salt you mine before year's end is yours to keep."

"You truly are a saint, Lady Julia," Henk said, as the other men nodded their agreement.

She managed a smile at the compliment, but if they knew she was gambling her future and theirs for the hope of an apple cake, they would be more likely to compare her to Eve in the Garden of Eden than any angel or saint.

Twenty-One

It was a week before Christmas when the supply boat finally arrived. Two weeks late, and Romein had begun to fear that he would be forced to spend the entire Yule season at the mill instead of at home with his family. So when he heard the sailors' shouts from the river as they tied up, he dropped his tools and raced outside to see for himself.

The men from the salt works pitched in to help unload, and they were soon trooping in and out of the mill, carrying sacks and barrels enough to see him through the winter. Julia stood just outside the door, staring, but then one of the men ducked his head and said something to her, and she answered him with a smile.

Curious, Romein moved closer.

Another man ducked his head as he stepped over the threshold with a sack over each shoulder. "Lady Julia," he said.

"Henk," she said.

These must be men from Veluwe, that she knew them by name. Yet they called her Lady Julia, not miss or mistress, as he would expect of anyone but the Bishop's wife, the lady of the estate herself. But Julia had said she had no husband, and he did not believe she had lied about that. So if she was not the Bishop's wife, then she must be his daughter. Romein had heard nothing about the Bishop having a daughter, only sons, but he'd also seen how she travelled as a man in company with her brothers, so it made sense that the Bishop wished to protect his only daughter as best he could. Sending her out to Veluwe, where no one would see her, until he meant to marry her off to cement some alliance or other.

That must be why she was headed home – answering a summons from her father, to obtain a husband she did not yet have.

His heart ached at the thought of Julia, handed over to some old man, like a Yule gift. Stuck in a loveless marriage, her brilliant mind confined to the great house of some lord as she was forced to lie with him, and bear his heirs. Just the thought of some stranger touching her…undressing her, caressing her, slaking his lust with her, when she deserved to be loved, and worshipped, and cherished…

God, what he would give to be allowed to do those things to her. For her, to her, with her willing consent, a joyous smile and…and…

At least Rosaline had chosen that fate. Julia had been exiled to Veluwe, and now she faced a worse punishment on her return. And for what crime? That of being born a woman, a daughter to that ruthless Bishop, instead of a son.

"I have strict instructions from your mother to stuff you into a barrel and carry you home, if you are not willing to leave the mill and your projects," the captain of the boat said.

Romein looked up, startled out of his dark thoughts about Julia. "What threats did my mother issue this time?"

Captain Balthasar grinned. "That I should eat nothing but apple cakes, washed down with cider, until spring. The apple harvest has been unusually bountiful this year, and we've eaten them until we were sick, and still the barrels are overflowing. If I am not mistaken, there will be plenty of apples among your supplies, too. The cider will not be ready until the new year, so the cider kegs will be ballast in the boat when I bring you home."

Romein rubbed his hands together. A jug of spiced cider in the evening was just how he liked to end a hard day's work. If he could share it with Julia…

But what to do with her, while he was gone? He could hardly leave her here alone in the mill for Yule. She might not be able to ride yet, which meant she could go neither home nor back to Veluwe, but there was no reason she could not come with him to Valkhof.

Well, other than the fact that she was the Bishop's daughter, and not exactly a welcome guest in the house of Count Montague of Gelderland.

Romein gritted his teeth. This feud be damned. The Bishop and his father could hate each other until their dying day, but Julia was his guest. By the laws of hospitality, he was bound to protect her from the moment they shared a meal together, and he would make sure his father did the same. Even if he had to serve Julia bread and wine with his own hands at his father's table, so that his father was bound by the same laws.

His mind made up, Romein marched up to Julia. "I'm going to spend Yule with my family in Valkhof, and closing up the mill. The men are going home to their families, too. Will you come with me, as my guest?"

For a moment, her eyes shone, before her face fell. "You forget that I cannot ride yet. My ribs are not yet healed."

Romein grinned. "Who said anything about riding? We shall be sailing, and I will need you as my guide to make sure we do not sail into any storms, or do anything else stupid."

She stared at him, the sort of look that measured his soul. "I think that if you set your heart on something, stupid or not, not all the angels and saints in heaven combined would be able to stop you, once your mind is made up. Any other man would have given up on this windmill long ago."

He leaned in. "And any other woman would have given me up for a fool even sooner, yet still you sew sails for me. I think you believe in this windmill as much as I do, and you wish to see it work, so that together we can free this land of the watery burden that has weighed it down for so long."

She opened her mouth, ready to retort in kind, then closed it again, as a delicate blush heated her cheeks. She swallowed instead. "I would do anything to save this land."

He believed her.

"But not during Yule, which is a time for feasting and family and I forget what else. So come with me. The windmill will be waiting here on our return, when we come back, refreshed." He held out his hand. "I have not spent Yule with my family for seven years. They will be so happy to see me, that any guest I bring with me will receive so warm a welcome, you will think they are your family, too." He fought to keep a straight face, for the thought of the Bishop's daughter as family to the Count...

But oh how he wished she could be...

Slowly, Julia gave a nod, and slipped her hand into his. "I hope I do not regret this."

So did Romein. For if his family found out who she was...

"If you wish to leave, you have only to seek out the good Captain Balthasar here, and he will take you home directly," Romein said. "Isn't that right, Captain Balthasar?"

For a moment, the captain hesitated, directing a searching look at Julia. When he did not appear to find what he looked for, he bowed. "It would be my pleasure to transport your lady anywhere she wishes."

Romein opened his mouth to admit Julia was not his, and might never be, but Balthasar would surely demand an explanation. An explanation he dared not give. Instead, he sighed. "We'd better pack some clothing, then, for they depart as soon as the salt is loaded, and the men are making quick work of that."

Julia nodded and led the way inside. Romein could do naught else but follow.

Twenty-Two

It had been seven years since Romein had seen Valkhof, but the city had changed irrevocably in that time. Great earthen walls had sprung up around the buildings, towering above the deep canals that now ringed it round. It took him a moment to recognise it as the embodiment of the plans he'd sent his father, the first year he'd been at Queen Molina's court. Then several more minutes, surveying the surrounding fields, before he was certain.

"It worked!" he crowed.

Captain Balthasar and his men took no notice, too busy sailing the boat, but Julia shot him a questioning glance.

"It was my first plan to drain the flooded fields, to keep the towns safe," he explained. "High earth walls to keep the water in or out, and deep channels carved into the earth to hold more water. You see…"

She nodded as he pointed out the details as he noticed them, her gaze following his finger here, there and everywhere. He knew her well enough to be sure she wasn't just feigning interest. He suspected it would only be a moment or two before she asked…

"Is that what you intend to do to the lands around Elst and Veluwe?"

Ah, her first question.

"It is, though the ground is lower there than here at Valkhof, so the salt has had longer to sink into the soil, and the water lingers for longer. It is around Veluwe that we must start to tame the waters, before it can spread to the rest of the country, but that will take years, so in the meantime, earth ramparts around the cities and towns are the best defence we have..."

They discussed how such walls might be used in Veluwe as the boat docked, and they walked through the winding streets up to Father's house. His family were at dinner when they arrived, so he had only a moment to stare at the sea of faces and mumble something along the lines of, "This is Julia. She's helping me convert the mill from horse power to wind," before he was pulled into the nearest pair of arms for a hug.

Julia, too, was subjected to the same treatment, passed from hand to hand until seats were found for them on a bench at the end of one of the tables. Loaded trenchers landed on the table before them, and they were expected to do little more than eat, drink, smile and nod, as the conversation continued around them.

Twenty-Three

Julia had never seen so many people in one place. Her father had never allowed her to attend a feast so full of people, and family meals were a quiet affair, attended only by her parents, her brothers, and herself. This was Romein's family – just his family, not their bannermen. His brothers and their wives, nieces and nephews, plus his parents. This great hall had no dais, for all the tables were equal…well, perhaps not the ones where the children sat, and there seemed to be a great number of those.

She'd half expected someone to ask her for details about Romein's windmill, for she had been introduced as his assistant in the enterprise, but no one seemed to care. Even Romein's explanations were cut off, still half-formed, as the only thing his relatives wanted to ask about was what life was like at court.

She listened, rapt, as Romein told them the story she had not had the courage to ask for.

He'd spent the last seven years serving Queen Molina at court, as a sort of apprentice to her artificer, Master Zimmerman. Where a normal queen had ladies in waiting, Queen Molina had only female apprentices, which Romein had evidently told his family about in his letters home. That explained why no one questioned her introduction as his assistant — they all thought her one of the Queen's ladies. Julia only wished it were true. To think, she might have been learning how to save Veluwe instead of watching it sink beneath the waters, unable to stop it.

But there were too many people around to allow Romein to monopolise the conversation long. The talk turned to this year's harvest, and how hard the winter might be, whether there would be flooding or snow, and when, and whether the talk of a new crusade would be endorsed by the Pope…her head spun by the time someone showed her to her chamber, where she found her things waiting for her, and she fell into bed, asleep almost before her head hit the pillow.

The next day, she was dragged off to help the other women decorate the house with pine boughs, holly and mistletoe, then to help the children make gifts for everyone for New Year's Day. This mostly involved having her hands sticky with honey, and flour dusting her gown, as the scents of spices and dried fruits made her mouth water.

Luckily, a maid carried away her soiled gowns every night, and returned with them, dry and fresh, several days later, without a word of admonishment. Amma would not be so forgiving, but then there seemed to be so many more people here than she'd ever seen at Veluwe.

At the New Year's Eve feast, a grander affair than any she'd attended yet, Julia was pulled aside by Lady Mona, Romein's mother, the one woman whose name she didn't dare forget.

"We have a tradition here, that I'm sure my son remembers, though he has been away from home for too long. Ever since he was old enough to join the feast, his favourite food has been the oil cakes the cook only makes for the new year. And because they are his favourite, and he was the youngest of all his brothers, the tradition is that he must have the first one, before anyone else."

Julia nodded. Her brothers had spoiled her, too, often bringing her choice morsels from the feasts her father had not allowed her to attend.

"The cook is making them now. I think the

best way to remind Romein of this tradition would be if you brought the first dish of cakes out, instead of one of the maids, and set it before him."

As though she were one of the maids? Is that what his family thought of her? Julia wasn't sure what to say. She knew her gowns were not the fashionable silks surely worn at court, but…

"New year is when we unite the old and the new. We celebrate the past, and look to the future. So for past traditions to be carried into the future by one who will be an important part of Romein's future…" Mona smiled. "My son cares a great deal for you. He would not have brought you here if he did not. It is true, then, that you and he have plans for the future together?"

Of course they did. Together, they would make a working windmill and lift the curse of flooding from the lowlands, Veluwe and Gelderland alike. "Yes…"

"Then please, go to the kitchen and bring

the platter of cakes that the cook will give you."

Julia tried to catch Romein's eye, but he was too busy talking to one of his brothers to notice. Sighing, she resolved to do as Lady Mona bade her. It was hardly the first time she'd been asked to pretend to be a servant. The whole journey to Veluwe, Thibault had insisted on her being his cupbearer. At least Romein would have the good manners to thank her, instead of spilling ale down her tunic.

Even in a house she did not know well, Julia only had to follow her nose to find the kitchen.

"You are young Romein's lady?"

Julia blinked.

The cook emerged from the shadows, her eyes intent on her. In her hand, she held a spoon so large it could have been used to stir a cauldron...or cudgel someone to death.

Swallowing, Julia said, "Lady Mona said I should come and fetch the oil cakes?"

The cook grinned. "First, you must taste them, and when you are married, you must send your cook to me, so that I can teach her how to make them. Some stuff them with raisins, but mine are always sweeter, for the secret is fresh made apple sauce."

Apple? Julia's mouth watered. It had been too long since she'd tasted one. To think they had enough here to make apple sauce…and use them in cakes…

"Or you could tell me how to make them, and I can write it down, and share that with my cook," Julia said. For there was no guarantee that she would ever marry, or come back…

The cook looked her up and down. "So you are a scholar, too, reading and writing like young Romein? No wonder he has taken such a fancy to you. Trust him to find the only pretty lady scholar in the world."

Julia was saved the need to answer, for the cook disappeared into the smoky darkness then, reappearing a long moment later bearing a bowl of steaming balls that smelled divine.

Cinnamon and apple and honey, oh…she nearly cried as she reached for the bowl.

The cook hugged the bowl to her breast. "They are too hot yet, mind. I shall set them on the table to cool a moment. Then you may have one without burning your tongue."

But leaving Julia alone with temptation itself was even worse. The cakes steamed, sending up tendrils of scent that begged her to take just a bite. Eve in Eden could not have resisted. Julia stretched out her hand…

Only to have it smacked away.

Twenty-Four

Curse it, he could smell apple and cinnamon. He knew the cook was making oil cakes, but his mother would not cease her chatter and allow him to go off in search of them. Yes, he might have been absent for seven years, and one of his nephews had likely taken his place as the first to eat the new year cakes, but he was home now, and by all that was holy, he would not yield this year.

Mother paused for breath, and Romein

blurted out, "Pray excuse me," before he bolted away, intent on reaching the kitchens.

And there they were, sitting on a table alone, calling his name.

Until a small hand reached out of the darkness to steal one.

Romein's fury knew no bounds. Who dared steal the first cake? Whoever's son this was, he deserved to be whipped.

Romein smacked the boy's hand away.

Only to hear a startled cry that belonged to no boy.

"Oh God, Julia, forgive me!" He seized her hand in his own, stroking the reddened skin he had dared to strike. "Please, permit me to smooth my rough touch with a tender kiss." He did not wait for permission, but pressed his lips to her hand. He should have stopped at one kiss, but he could not. Dared not, until he had covered her injured hand in kisses and still he begged for her forgiveness.

There was only one thing to do. He seized the nearest cake and held it out to her. "Every year, I have broken and eaten the first cake to bless the new year. I came to bring them to you, so that we might share it, and the new year's blessing might fall on our…fall on our…"

Her fingers grazed his as she took the cake, and bit it in half, then held out the other half to him. Then the taste must have hit her tongue, for she cast her eyes heavenward, as if in prayer.

One look at her parted lips, and it was not prayer or cake Romein thought of, though the taste of apple and cinnamon was still on her lips, and the sweetness of honey lingered on her tongue. Though he knew it was surely the greatest of sins, he leaned in to kiss this angel again.

Twenty-Five

The apple cake was everything the cook had said, and more. A bite of heaven, surely. Julia closed her eyes, savouring the taste. No wonder Romein had defended the cakes so fiercely. Having tasted, now she would fight with equal ferocity, should anyone threaten to take what was hers.

Warmth brushed her lips, and for a moment, she thought he meant to feed her another cake, but this smelled of spiced cider, far richer than any cake.

"Yes," she breathed, a moment before his lips touched hers, and he kissed her. This was no kiss of peace, over in a moment and forgotten a moment later. No, this was one stolen breath after another, a dance of lips and tongues and air that sent her head whirling and her heart drumming while pipes skirled in her belly and her legs turned to water that would scarcely hold her weight any more.

She gazed into his eyes, and for a moment, she saw forever. She would be lost forever if she did not go now.

So she fled, forcing her unwilling legs to carry her out of the kitchen, out of the house, and down to the river where Captain Balthasar and his boat would take her to safety.

Twenty-Six

His arms wanted to pull her closer, but when she resisted, he knew he had to let her go. And she flew into the night, as if borne by angels' wings. Angels saving her from him, for nothing good could come of Romein, son of Montague, kissing Julia Capet. For to ask for her hand would be to hand his own life over, in his foe's debt.

But for her, perhaps it would be worth the cost…

He longed to chase after her, to beg her forgiveness once more, but he dare not. His mother would come looking for him, and there were the damned cakes to break in the new year. Romein closed his eyes.

He would find Julia later, when his ardour had cooled, and apologise. He might blame the cider for heating his blood, but he knew it had nothing to do with the cider, and everything to do with her.

The rest of the night passed in a blur, until he could excuse himself to retire. It was noon before he rose, only to find no sign of Julia. Even her clothes were gone.

Evening was falling by the time he recovered his wits enough to head down to the dock, where he found Balthasar, tying up his boat.

"Have you seen her?" Romein begged.

"Your bird has flown home. The last I saw of her, she was crossing the bridge to Elst, headed for Veluwe," Balthasar said. "But I fear you will not catch her before she reaches the

Bishop's lands."

No, but he must follow her anyway. "Send word when you are ready to sail again, and take me with you," Romein said.

Balthasar laughed. "My men have sailed all night, and most of the day, too. We must rest, and eat, but when we sail, we shall not leave without you, for if I am not mistaken, she is still your lady love."

Romein prayed the captain was right.

Twenty-Seven

"Amma!" Julia shouted as she led Epona through the gates of Veluwe. "I am…can you…help me…" She could scarcely stand, after loading Epona with food from the mill. She'd left Romein the contents of her coin purse, which would more than pay for what she'd taken, and then walked all the way, leading Epona.

And now, she could not…could not…

The ground swooped up to meet her.

Twenty-Eight

Julia awoke in her own bed, with a chill in the air that berated her for not sending warning, so that a fire might be lit to chase away the chill before she arrived. She sighed.

She should not have kissed him. She should not have enjoyed it so. And, most of all, she should not have run away. No, a sensible woman would have slapped him for taking such liberties.

Never mind that she had liked those

liberties very much.

She shouldn't have…

Oh, no, she most certainly should not have fallen in love with the miller, for her father would never allow them to marry.

Unless…well, his family had certainly not been poor. He might be the youngest son, but he had the ear of the Queen. Perhaps…

She dressed and headed down to the kitchen, to see if there was any breakfast. There was no one but Amma, pulling a tray of steaming apple cakes out of the oven. Not quite as fragrant as the ones last night, for there was no cinnamon left, nor oil, but there were apples and honey and flour, and it would be enough.

"Trust you to bring a whole barrel of apples, but not enough flour to last the week," Amma said tartly.

Julia couldn't help but laugh. After lifting the barrel onto Epona's back, she was lucky to have managed to lift anything else at all. "We can ask the miller. He will sell us more."

"Which miller?" Amma asked.

"The one whose mill lies beside the river, across the bridge to Elst," Julia said. The one who kissed like an angel, who she very much wished to taste again.

"The miller there died some years ago, soon after you arrived," Amma said.

"There is a new one now, who recently took the place over," Julia said.

"You mean young Master Romein, the youngest son of Count Montague of Gelderland? He would sooner sell us to the devil than trade with us for flour."

Julia's heart turned to ice. "The son of who?"

"Montague. The son of your great enemy, the Count of Gelderland."

No. He could not be. The Count of Gelderland was…she couldn't have been…in the richest house in Valkhof, which could only belong to the Count…

Oh God.

She had fallen in love with the Count's son.

Her first and only love, sprung from the loins of the man her father hated most. If she had but known…yet now she knew, it was too late. Fate must truly be laughing at her, for falling in love with a loathed enemy.

Twenty-Nine

"Lady Julia, you have a visitor," Amma said as she set down a platter containing Julia's noon meal.

Her heart lifted at the thought that it must be Romein, for surely no one else could possibly be travelling on such a cold day. Then her heart plummeted just as rapidly as it had risen, as she realised Romein did not know she had returned to Veluwe, or that she lived here at all.

No one visited Veluwe, for fear of the Bishop's wrath.

So who, then, could her visitor be?

"Send the visitor in, then," Julia said.

"Are you sure?"

For Amma to question her was a strange enough occurrence to give Julia pause. Perhaps it was Romein, who had learned her whereabouts from Henk or one of the other men, who were even now digging the salt out of her orchards.

"Would you advise me to send him away, then?" Julia asked.

Amma wrinkled her nose. "It is not my place to advise you in such things. Nor do I think that you would be successful in sending him away. The man has arrived in full armour, with sword unsheathed, and none of my boys are much of a match for an armoured knight."

Not Romein, then, for he owned no such armour, and she had never seen him carry a sword, let alone wield one.

"Did he give his name?"

"Sir Paris, I think. It was difficult to be sure, as he has his visor down and his voice was much muffled by all that metal."

Julia sighed. A man who entered her home with his sword drawn did not mean to invoke the laws of hospitality. She'd be a fool to let him in at all. "So he is in the bailey now?"

"Yes, as all the doors are barred. He shouts your name, and demands to see you."

And likely had no intention of leaving until he had seen her. Very well, she would be seen. Julia rose from the table and headed up to the balcony. She glimpsed Henk and his brothers, hard at work, but didn't dare stop to watch them. Instead, she turned toward the bailey, and the noisy knight.

He strode about the bailey, muttering unintelligible things, and hammering on various doors that did not open. His nervous horse shied away from him, looking longingly out the gate, but the creature did not dare flee for freedom.

Julia allowed herself a small smile. Epona

would not be so timid. The mare would have lost patience with the man long since, and tried to trample him. How her hooves would fare against armoured plate, Julia wasn't sure, but Epona would have at least put some dents in such shiny armour before retiring from the fight.

"Who are you?" Julia called.

The knight stopped and looked around. When he didn't see her, he shouted something unintelligible and hammered on the tower door again.

Julia leaned over the balcony. "Take your helmet off, so that I might actually hear you. I asked for your name, knight."

Finally, the knight looked up and saw her.

It took him a moment, and many muttered words that were very likely unfit for a lady's ears, before he managed to wrench the helmet off. "For God's sake, Julia, let me in. I bring news from your father."

The man only had one eye. She stared at the patch that covered his deformity, then at the rest of his scarred face, before she finally recognised him. "Thibault?" she asked.

"Of course it's me, silly girl. Who else would your father send?"

William or Aran, for her brothers were surely more trustworthy than her bastard cousin. And…was he missing an ear, too? Now he truly resembled the tom cat back home, with his battle scars. Prince of Cats, indeed.

"But that is not the name you gave to my housekeeper just now."

"We are family, so you may call me by name. But a mere servant…" Thibault curled his lip in disgust. "They must address me as Sir Thibault of Paris, renowned tourney champion."

Well, that explained where he'd been for the last seven years, and the scars. "What are you doing here?"

"Your father sent me. The Count of Gelderland has grown wealthy of late, with rumours of a new salt mine in the lowlands.

Your father wishes a strong hand to hold Veluwe against whatever forces he might send against it. For there are plenty of knights for hire who would happily take his money, and more besides."

It took Julia a moment to work out how that involved Thibault. "So, you're here for my protection."

"Of course. As a renowned tourney champion, your father knew I was the best man for the job."

One knight against an army of mercenaries, or even a small company of knights with both their eyes…unless Thibault was a far better fighter than she remembered, he could not offer more protection than the walls of Veluwe. They had only to close the gates.

"Thibault…" She had to find the right words so that he would not see the facts as an insult.

"Sir Thibault. Though I suppose you may call me simply Thibault when we are alone together. We are to be married, after all."

"What?"

He puffed out his chest. "Your father will arrive in a week, with more men to defend you, but he expects us to be married by then. You must organise a feast, of course, for that is women's work, and I shall be too busy defending this place and taking stock of my new estate to bother with such unimportant things. I insist there must be suckling pig, and roast venison, and a fat goose, for it is hardly a wedding feast without them."

Julia's blood boiled. They did not have pigs or deer or geese anywhere in Veluwe, unless Thibault counted as a goose, for thinking she'd ever agree to marry him.

"What makes you think I would marry you?" she said.

"Your father, of course. He promised me your hand in marriage when you are old enough. Why else would I have escorted you all the way out here when you were a girl? You were too young for marriage then, your father said, and he said I must wait. But now...now he says you are ready, and you shall be mine, as you were always meant to be."

She hadn't eaten more than a bite of her midday meal, but now she wanted to vomit up everything in her belly at the prospect of allowing Thibault to touch her, let alone marry her. She swallowed back bile. This was no time to lose her head, or her breakfast, either. She had to think. "That is…glad tidings indeed. But surely my father would want to be present at the marriage of his only daughter, and feasts take time to prepare. I shall…send word to the priest at Saint Martin's church to await my father's arrival, for on that day, God willing, we shall be married."

She'd rather marry one of Romein's mill ponies than Thibault. This was madness. Her father could not possibly give his only daughter to a penniless bastard, with no honour to his name except a tourney title. Unless that was Father's intention — to buy Thibault's loyalty with her maidenhead, so the man would be more likely to do her father's bidding. Perhaps her father intended him to fight and die for Veluwe, while taking her home, far from the conflict, so that when she was widowed, he might marry to her to a more worthy man...

In a week, she would find out, for she could ask her father himself. In a week, she still might have to marry the man. Julia suppressed a shudder. She would have to formulate a plan to avoid such a fate, and she only had a few days to do so.

But in the meantime...

She sighed. "Fine. Take off your armour, and you can come inside. We can post guards at the gates, who will give us fair warning if any of the Count's men approach, so you have time to put it all on again."

Thibault beamed. "You shall make a fine wife, cousin. See that there is goose for dinner. If I am to be the lord of the manor, my table should reflect my station."

His table would be far more sparse than he expected, what with it being winter after a poor harvest and all. But there was some goose confit in the cellar, which might satisfy him for at least a little while. God forbid she have to feed him for more than a week.

Because if there was one thing she knew for certain, it was that she would rather die than become Thibault's wife.

Thirty

The pile of coins on Romein's kitchen table told him Julia had come to the mill, and taken supplies with her. Judging by the quantity of what was gone, she could not have travelled far – Veluwe, most likely, just as Captain Balthasar had surmised.

Father had been generous, loading the ship with enough food to see Romein well into spring, but Romein knew that was only a fraction of the value of the salt he had given his father during his time here. Which would multiply tenfold once he had the windmill working…

And for that, he needed Julia.

He would find her, apologise for his foolish, cider-fuelled kisses, and offer her anything and everything she could possibly want to come back to the mill and help him. Because only together could they save the lowlands.

He loaded up two of the mill ponies with some of the choicest foods Mother had sent, including a basket of oil cakes, left over from the new year feast, and set off across the bridge to Elst.

Thirty-One

Romein had never seen Veluwe before, but he'd imagined something more like his father's house in Valkhof. Not this strange wooden fort, walled in on all sides like a miniature city, with a tower rising up in the middle, overlooking the lands it ruled. There was only one gate, and it was closed.

So Romein strolled up to the gate and knocked.

"Who goes there?"

For a moment, Romein considered actually giving the guard his name, and his father's, too. For it was no secret – Julia surely knew the truth, for what reason would she have had to run from his father's house except finding out she'd been kissed by her enemy?

It could not have been the kiss itself, Romein told himself. It couldn't have. Or she would have pushed him away or frozen or something, other than kiss him back. And she had most definitely kissed him back.

Or maybe it was the kiss. Maybe he should have practiced more when he was at court, instead of mooning after Rosaline. Then, he might still be in Valkhof with Julia, sharing a cup of mulled cider in the warmth of his family's hall, as he worked up the courage to ask her for her hand.

Instead of standing outside the gates of her castle, praying that they would open. He glanced at the mill ponies, labouring under full loads. He had no intention of making them carry such weights home again. "I brought supplies. Delicacies for Lady Julia's table."

"What sort of delicacies?" The man peered over the palisade. His cloak pin caught the light, and Romein blinked in surprise.

Of course, he should not have been surprised at all to see the Bishop's family crest on the man, for Julia was a Capet, after all, and the fleur-de-lis her family's emblem. But he'd only seen such a cloak pin once, and the man who wore it had been the oaf who threw him in the river.

Romein squinted up at him. The young man he remembered must have been in many battles since then, to own a face so scarred. But his voice had not changed.

"I don't rightly know. My master told me to deliver the food to the castle for the lady, and I don't ask questions. Just do my job," Romein said, trying to slow down his speech to sound like one of the salt workers. "The miller said he'd give me an extra loaf of bread if I returned the ponies before nightfall, though, so if you'd be so kind, sir, and open the gate..."

The oaf waved to someone behind him, and the gates swung open.

No one helped him unload the horses, but Romein did not mind much. Everyone seemed to eye him with suspicion – first the oaf up on the battlements, and then the grey-haired woman in the kitchen. Julia's cook, he presumed.

Romein pressed the basket of oil cakes into the cook's hands. "For Lady Julia, with my best wishes for a prosperous new year," he said.

The cook's eyes narrowed. "And who might I tell her they are from?"

Romein bowed low. "From a friend, who wishes her every happiness, and hopes that this gift will at least make her smile."

The cook seized his hand. "If you are truly her friend, then perhaps you can help her. Come to the orchard after dark, for the lady surveys the progress on the salt works every evening from her balcony. If you would have her see you..."

Romein grinned. "I would love nothing more. Thank you, mistress."

He hurried to unload the rest of his cargo, before hustling the horses up to the village, where he knew Henk and his brothers lived.

When the sun set, and the men arrived home, they invited him to join them for dinner, but Romein declined, saying he had business up at the castle with Lady Julia.

The brothers exchanged glances, before Henk said, "The best way to reach Lady Julia, with that fool guarding the gates, is to take one of the ladders in the orchard, and set it upon one of the snowdrifts beside the walls. It might not quite reach the balcony, but it will get you close enough to exchange words with her, without the fool knowing anything about it."

Romein clapped him on the shoulder. "You are a good man, and loyal to Lady Julia. I'll make sure she knows it."

"Oh, she knows all right. We are her people, and no Count or Bishop will sway us from her, not while she still draws breath."

"Then you will not tell..." What was the oaf's name? He should remember it, but he could not...oh! "You will not tell Thibault who I am, or that we have spoken?"

Henk spat twice on the ground. "There's for Thibault and that's for his airs and graces. He's the Bishop's brother's bastard, and no better than the rest of us. It is only out of respect for Lady Julia that we do not run him right off her lands. The only time he deigns to look or speak to us is to complain about where we put the snow when we dig the salt from her fields. Thrice he has told us to stop, for he dislikes seeing bare earth where he thinks there should be white snow. But we are here on Lady Julia's orders, restoring her fields, and we will not stop unless the command comes from her lips alone."

Romein's heart dared to hope. "So she still wants to save the lowlands from the salt?" Perhaps she did not hate him, then, if she still shared his plans.

"She wants Veluwe to be green again, as it

was in her mother's day, just like the fields around the mill. She wants the trees to bear fruit, and for the cows to have fresh pasture and…is there a saint of growing things, Master Romein? For if there is not, then I am certain that when she takes her place in heaven, that saint will be her."

If not before she'd saved the lowlands, then definitely after, Romein reflected. But he merely bowed his thanks to the man, and headed back to the castle.

Thirty-Two

The wind was cold, so Julia shut the balcony doors. All right, the doors also muffled the sound of Thibault's voice as he shouted at someone in the bailey, so she didn't have to listen to him, but now the doors were shut, she did not want to open them again. Henk and the other men were making good progress on the orchard – she'd glimpsed the dark soil that lay hidden beneath the salt before she'd retreated inside.

Amma came up the stairs, carrying a basket. It was early for dinner, but Julia did not have much appetite these days anyway. "What is it today?" she asked.

Amma set the basket on the table. "A gift from the miller, who asks only that you venture out onto the balcony to see how work is going in the orchard, after the sun sets."

"Which miller?" Julia asked suspiciously. Surely she could not mean…

"The miller who knows it is death to him if he should set foot on your lands, yet he delivered the basket to me with his own hands, and begged me to give them to you."

Romein. It had to be Romein.

She pulled the cloth covering from the basket and nearly cried at the contents. The basket was full of oil cakes, no longer hot and crisp from the pan, but soft and richer smelling, almost as if the cinnamon had infused the dough since they were first baked.

Julia couldn't resist. She bit into one, and it tasted just as good as the first one Romein had given her.

"Did he say anything else?" For if he had come here, he knew who she was, as she knew who his family was.

"Only that he desires your happiness, and wishes you to smile."

Oh, what she would give for happiness, instead of a blighted future with Thibault as her husband. Try as she might, she had not been able to work out a way to avoid it.

But it would warm her heart to see Romein again, and know that he did not hate her.

"The sun has set, Lady Julia."

Julia jerked out of her reverie. "Thank you, Amma. I shall…retire early tonight, instead of coming down to supper. I will bolt the doors after you go."

Amma dropped a curtsey. "Very good, my lady. I will see that your guest has plenty of strong wine to drink, so that he sleeps well tonight."

Julia nodded. She waited for Amma to depart, then bolted her bedchamber door, before throwing open the door to the balcony.

It was cold and dark out there. She wrapped a cloak about her shoulders and reached for a lamp before she dared step through the door.

"Soft! What light through yonder window breaks? It is the east, and Julia is the sun!"

Julia whirled, to find him crouched in the shadows beside the door. "Romein?"

"It is, my lady."

"What are you doing here?"

"Admiring your beauty, for it has been several days since I last beheld it. Your eyes outshine two of the fairest stars in the heaven…"

"Oh, don't be silly. How did you get here?"

"With night's cloak to hide me, and love's light wings to fly over these walls, for no stony limits or your kinsman could keep me out."

She held her lantern out, looking toward the orchard. "You took one of the ladders, set it upon a snowdrift so that it leaned against the walls, and…you cannot be here. Thibault is here, and if he sees you, he will murder you, to finish the job he did not do all those years ago."

"I have not come for him, but for you." He rose and entered her chamber, for all the world like he had every right to be there. "Did you like my gift? Beneath the cakes, there is some parchment. I wrote down the recipe, for my mother's cook insisted I do so."

Julia closed her eyes. "Your mother, the Countess of Gelderland?"

Romein nodded, grinning around a mouthful of cake. "The wife of Count Montague of Gelderland, my father. As you are Lady Julia Capet, only daughter of the Bishop of Maastricht. Mortal enemies in name only, for I cannot hate you, and I believe you might have some fond feelings for me, if only because I bring you gifts. Including a barrel of strong wine that will see your new gate guard sleep soundly tonight, or so your cook promises me."

Her gate guard. Oh, if that was all he was. "My father means to make me marry him. He will be here within the week, to preside over my wedding to that man. He fears your father, and the mercenaries he might hire with his new-found wealth from his new salt mine."

"Your father would not be so cruel."

Their eyes met, full of knowing at that lie. The Bishop's cruelty knew no bounds. He would even sacrifice her, if he must.

"I will not allow it."

Julia laughed. "I don't see how you can stop him. I don't see how I can stop him, either, though I have spent every waking moment trying to work out how I might."

"Marry me instead."

Her heart soared. Oh, if only she could. "My father would never allow it."

"Then do not wait for his permission. We will go to Elst tonight, to the church of Saint Martin, and there, we will entreat Father Laurence to marry us. Those God has joined together, no man may separate."

"Romein…" She had never wished for anything more. Never wanted anything quite as much as she wanted this. And yet…

"Marry me, Julia. Be my wife, and together we shall build windmills and salt mines, and save the lowlands from floods."

She had to laugh. Only Romein could talk of windmills and marriage in the same sentence. "And what of love?"

"If you will permit me, I shall show you more love in one kiss, than in all the arranged marriages your father could devise. The moment my lips touch yours, you shall know the depth of my devotion is greater than the ocean, wider than the sea, more constant than the waves that pound the shore…" A faint flush coloured his cheeks. "Perhaps we should not speak of such things yet. At least not until we are married. If you will have me."

The Bishop's obedient daughter considered saying no, but Julia was more than one man's daughter. She was the Lady of Veluwe, chatelaine of these lands, responsible for its people, and the mistress of her own destiny.

"And if I have you, what of my father, when

he comes with his men to wrest Veluwe from us?" Us. The word seemed to whisper on the wind, of what might be, if she only dared.

"We shall do what he fears most, and hire mercenaries to defend your lands. For they are yours, as they were your mother's, and together we will protect them as no one else has."

"But he is my father. My family. I could not go to war against my own family!"

Romein took her hands in his. "You are a Capet, and I am of Montague. Sworn enemies, already at war. But as my wife, you become a Montague, too. Your family would have you marry Thibault and lose your lands to the rising sea, while mine would ask you to do no more than you mean to do already: rule Veluwe, and keep it safe."

Oh, that she could have such things with but a word, and a small one at that. Finally, Julia dared to hope. "And what of you? What would you have me do?"

Romein grinned. "First, I would have you kiss me, so that I might prove my love for you.

Later, after we are married, I would have you share my bed, instead of leaving me to sleep on the floor by the kitchen fire, as I did every night you slept in my box bed at the mill. I would have you in all of the thousand ways it is possible to pleasure a woman, or so the scholars say. There was a book in Queen Molina's library that was written by some sultan's eunuch, and I would delight in demonstrating all that I learned from its pages. Why, you would never want to leave my bed…"

His eyes followed her gaze to her bed, not three steps away.

"How soon may we marry?" Julia asked.

"Tonight, if you wish it. We can climb down the ladder, and head to Elst."

Her mouth was dry, but other parts of her felt alarmingly wet. Did she want more kisses? Did she want him to share her bed? Did she want…everything he offered?

"Yes," Julia breathed.

Thirty-Three

Waking Father Laurence when they got to Elst took longer than Romein had expected. Both he and Julia yawned in between their vows, and by the time they returned to her balcony, dawn was already breaking.

Yet as his eyes met hers, he wished he could stay.

"Must you go? It is not yet day," Julia said.

Romeo laughed. "The sun's streaks lace the severing clouds in the east. Night's candles are burned out. It is day, or near enough. Do not fret, for night follows day, and our wedding night will come soon enough."

"Not soon enough. Today, I find I hate windows, for mine let day in, and love out," Julia complained.

"The mill has no windows. Meet me there in the hour after dusk, and I shall make you the happiest of brides, I swear it." But he was as tempted as she. "Farewell, farewell…give me but one more kiss, before I descend."

Julia threw her arms about his neck and kissed him, with all the eagerness he could ever wish for. Oh, that night would fall right now…

But no. It was day, and he wanted to finish the windmill before she arrived. And she would need rest, for they would not get much sleep tonight.

He forced himself down the ladder, until his boot sank into snow. Then he allowed himself one last glance up at her, a moment to blow a kiss, before he seized the ladder and was gone.

Thirty-Four

Married. To Romein. No longer a Capet, but a Montague. Julia could scarcely believe it, but one look at Romein on the ladder below her, and she knew it was true.

Then dread's dark wings engulfed her, for as she saw Romein, so far below, for a moment, in dawn's faint light, he appeared too pale, like one dead in the bottom of a tomb.

She whispered a prayer that it was not so. She was a water witch, not a seer.

A soft knock at the door dragged her from the balcony.

"Lady Julia? I brought up fresh water, so you might wash. I shall have breakfast ready directly. Would you like me to bring it up, or will you take it downstairs?"

"I'll come down for breakfast, Amma. Leave the water jug outside the door. I'll just be a moment."

"Very good, my lady." The jug clunked to the floor, before the sound of Amma's footsteps died away.

Julia washed and changed into a new gown, wishing she'd had more time with her husband to enjoy being his wife. But that would come tonight, she promised herself, before she headed down to breakfast.

The kitchen was quiet, filled with the normal morning bustle as Amma and one of her daughters in law made bread and prepared a pot of soup to set on the fire for dinner.

"We are almost out of fish, Lady Julia," Amma said.

"If the weather is fine, I shall take the boat out on the river today, and see what I can catch," Julia said. She could not remember the last time she had sailed, aside from aboard Captain Balthasar's ship. One day, she must take Romein out on the boat, and teach him to sail.

"The first loaf is ready, my lady. Would you prefer butter or honey?" Nellie asked.

Julia wanted soft cheese, but until they replaced the dairy herd, there would be no fresh milk or cheese. "Honey," she said, for that was a fitting wedding breakfast, surely, on the first day of her honeymoon? Though she should be sharing the meal with her new husband…

On the morrow, she promised herself.

When she'd finished the bread, and washed the honey from her fingers, Julia turned to Amma. "I know we need fish, but how are our other stores? I mean to call by the mill this evening, so I will see what he can spare." She fought to cool the telltale blush threatening to burn her cheeks.

Nellie was too busy setting the new loaves in the oven, but Amma had surely seen. Then again, Amma had known she'd spent the night with Romein, so her cheeks would tell the housekeeper no tales she did not already suspect.

"We have almost no meat left, and the flour is running low. We have enough vegetables to last the week, but not enough to see us until spring. This is the last crock of butter, and while we have hard cheese enough to see us for some weeks yet, I fear it will not be enough if Sir Thibault is our guest for much longer."

From the thinning of Amma's lips, Julia knew she thought even less of Thibault than she herself did. She wished she could find some pity in her for the poor scarred man, but when he behaved like a…

"Julia! Why is there no ham? Or eggs? We are in the country – surely someone can go out and catch a pig or something!" Thibault appeared in the kitchen doorway, his eyes as red as his nose. He'd evidently drunk far too much wine last night, and was still feeling the effects.

Any other morning, she might have tried to placate him. But that was before she knew he'd eaten most of her winter stores, stores she'd bought from Romein. Now she'd married Romein, she refused to support the leech any longer.

"There are no pigs because we slaughtered and salted the last one in the autumn. There is no ham because you have eaten it all. And there are no eggs because chickens do not lay eggs when the days are so short and cold. And even if someone did go into the forest to hunt wild boar, they would need an experienced hunting party, and it would take at least a day or two to bleed and dress the carcass, before it could be cooked. What we have is bread, and some honey. If that is not good enough for you, then I suggest you return to Paris and dine with the other tourney champions. Or, better yet, return to my father, and his plentiful table!"

Pain exploded in her cheek. It took her a moment to realise that Thibault had struck her.

"If you ever speak to me again with such disrespect, my soon to be wife, that is just a taste of what I shall give you in return," Thibault spat. "It is your fault the cellars are so bare here. You have mismanaged this place for so many years, it is no wonder even your peasants do not know the first thing about farming. Why, the first thing I shall do when we are married is teach the peasants to do as they are told, just as you will. There will be no digging up fields covered by snow. No, they shall plough and plant in spring, like sensible people. I might not be a farmer, but even I know that crops sown in the dead of winter will die!"

Julia took a deep breath. Tonight, when he had drunk himself into a stupor, she would have the men carry him out and toss him in the river, just like she'd wanted to do when she'd first arrived in Veluwe. Then they would lock the gates, and never allow him to enter Veluwe again.

Luckily, Thibault stormed out of the kitchen, saving her the need to reply.

"My boys will take him to the nearest pigpen and toss him in tonight, my lady," Amma said softly.

Julia managed a smile, though her jaw ached from Thibault's blow. "And I will promise them a smoked ham as a token of my thanks, when we have one to spare."

Thirty-Five

When Romein reached home, he found Mercutio on his doorstep, whistling.

"What are you doing here?" Romein asked, pushing open the door and gesturing for Mercutio to precede him.

"Her Majesty the Queen sent me, with more designs for your windmill. New vanes and plans for a horizontal instead of a vertical axle, for a windmill is not the same as a waterwheel," Mercutio said, pulling papers out of his satchel. He spread them out on the kitchen table. "Look. Master Zimmerman said you get more power with the different axle, and the vanes." He pointed at the sails.

Romein shook his head. He did not regret his night's work, but he did wish he'd had more sleep, for he needed a clear head to make sense of these new sketches. "I would need an entire tree to make such an axle. I do not have a piece of wood so large. I'd need to take all the mill ponies and the cart into the forest for something like that..." But if it would make for a better windmill, it made sense to do it now, before he put everything together, for he'd only have to take it apart again. Romein swore. "Fine. I shall go woodcutting, but you must stay here, in case Lady Julia comes to visit. Tell her where I am, and what I am doing, and that I shall return as soon as I have what we need."

"Tell the lady that you have gone hunting, and will return soon," Mercutio said. "Now, you would not let a growing boy get hungry while he's waiting, would you?"

Romein sighed. He could do with some breakfast, too. "We have a loaf of yesterday's bread, plenty of butter and honey, and a wheel of soft cheese in the buttery…"

"Any more of that spiced sausage?" Mercutio asked eagerly.

Romein blinked. The half sausage that had been on the table only a moment ago was already gone. "I'll go get another," he said. For a well-fed Mercutio would be more inclined to be polite to Lady Julia when she arrived.

When he'd laid a veritable feast on the table before Mercutio, and swallowed a few bites for himself, Romein headed for the stable, to harness the pony cart. This would be a long day.

Thirty-Six

"Close the gates! Close the gates!" The shout came from Henk, as he raced into the bailey.

Julia hurried down to meet him. "What is wrong? Are we in under attack?"

Henk and Jan waited until they'd barred the gates before they turned to answer her. "Not any more. Sir Shouts-A-Lot has just come down to the orchard, ranting and raving about the proper way to plant crops. When we told him we were mining salt, not planting anything, he pitched a fit. Called us traitors and fools and all manner of unpleasant things. So Jan here told him it was all according to the miller's instructions, for the miller had been mining salt for months in his own fields. Sir Shouts-A-Lot said some even more unpleasant things about Master Romein, before rushing inside to put his armour on. Then he rode out the gates, swearing to teach that upstart miller – his words, not mine, Lady Julia – a lesson in manners."

"But why shut the gates? Surely you should be riding full speed to the mill, to warn Romein!"

Henk shook his head. "Master Romein can take care of himself, Lady Julia. He does sword practice every morning, just like you'd expect of a knight. Not like Sir Shouts-A-Lot, lazing in bed every morning and drinking late into the night, and shouting at people every hour in between." He winked. "When that lazy knight comes running back here from the beating Master Romein will give him, he'll find the gates closed and no welcome waiting. Mistress Amma said she would boil a pot of water and tip it over the palisades if he tries to break down the gate."

Julia wasn't sure whether to laugh or cry at that. But Romein. She could not let him face Thibault in full armour alone. Romein didn't even carry a sword. It was all well and good that he knew how to use one, but if he didn't have one on him and Thibault attacked him while he was defenceless – which she fully believed an honourless bastard would do – Romein would have no chance.

She would not lose her husband to Thibault again. Last time, she'd been too shocked to stop Thibault, but now…now she wished to strike a blow of her own.

Thirty-Seven

The next time Romein needed a beam this big, he swore to himself, he would pay a woodcutter to bring it to him. It was either that or buy a bigger cart, and horses who were used to having big lengths of timber hanging off the back of it. He'd have to give the mill ponies several apples apiece when he reached the mill, and in only a few hours, Julia would arrive…

Romein quickened his step at the thought of

his bride, wed but not yet enjoyed. Oh, such pleasure would he give her, so that she did not regret for a moment choosing to marry him.

He left the new axle outside the barn, then unharnessed the horses and put the cart away. He thought he heard raised voices, and headed for the mill, where the words became clearer.

"He's not here, I tell you. He's gone hunting. I'm merely the Queen's messenger, come to bring him a letter from Her Majesty." That was Mercutio's voice. Judging by his tone, he'd repeated this tale several times, and was growing desperate that his interrogator did not believe the simple truth.

Romein hurried up to the house. Whoever was looking for him was about to find him.

"Sir! You will call me Sir!" an unfamiliar voice roared.

Mercutio was one of the Queen's wards, a prince in all but name, much like Isaak. What title he held when he became a man, Romein did not know, but he would definitely outrank any knight.

"You are a rude brute, Sir, and no mistake!" Mercutio said.

Romein rounded the corner just in time to see Thibault, in full plate armour, punch Mercutio. The boy went down, his head striking the ground hard, and he did not rise.

Romein broke into a run, dropping to his knees beside Mercutio. "Are you hurt?" he asked.

Mercutio grinned, but blood stained his teeth, and his eyes would not seem to focus. "Aye, a scratch, a scratch. 'Tis not so deep, but 'tis enough to scratch a man to death. A braggart, a rogue, a villain…a plague on both your horses!" He wagged his finger at Thibault's horse.

The creature reared up, as if struck, and galloped off.

Mercutio shifted his finger to point at Thibault, as if he wished to curse him, too, before his hand fell to his side, as lifeless as the rest of him.

Romein closed the boy's eyes. He would

send for Father Laurence to say Last Rites, but first, he must see to the villain who had slain Mercutio, for this child beater could not be allowed to live.

"Mercutio's soul is but a little way above our heads, waiting for yours to keep him company. Either you or I must go with him, and I vow it shall be you!" Romein seized the knight's sword from its scabbard, and began to hammer its owner's helm. Within moments, he had it ringing like a bell.

"You brought him here, miller, and his blood is on your hands!" Thibault shouted, trying to dodge the blows, but in such heavy armour, he was too slow.

"Romein!" Julia's scream cut through his heart like a blade, distracting him just enough to give Thibault the advantage.

The knight bulled into him, using his greater weight to knock Romein to the ground, just as he had Mercutio.

Romein waited for a punch from that armoured fist to end his life, just like

Mercutio's, but the blow never came, for Julia came flying out of nowhere, crashing into Thibault and knocking him to the ground.

Thirty-Eight

Julia saw Romein on the ground, and she didn't think. She just threw herself at Thibault, desperate to keep him away from Romein. They landed beside a boy, another of Thibault's victims, judging by the pool of blood beneath him.

But Thibault recovered before Julia did, seizing her around the waist and lifting her into the air. "You will learn your place, bitch!" he growled, shaking her until her teeth rattled.

"Or maybe you are too much trouble. I had thought to enjoy you for a little while before you met your untimely death…poison slipped into your wine cup, and you would simply go to sleep and not wake…but now, I think it is better to end things now. I shall slip some coins to the priest, who will record our marriage on the day I arrived, so that when your father arrives, there is nothing to stop me from taking Veluwe as my own, as is my right. But first, I shall teach you to be silent." He carried her inexorably toward the rushing sound of the river, then shoved her in, face first.

Julia tried to scream, but all she did was inhale a mouthful of water instead. Water – the only element her magic could touch. She bit her lip, her lungs burning for a breath, and let out the last of her air with a whispered plea for the water to help her.

Coolness touched her face, like a soft breeze stroking her cheeks. Julia gasped, inhaling blessed air, before she convulsed in a fit of coughing, bringing up the water she'd swallowed. She was still under the water, held there by Thibault's heavy hand, but now, she could breathe.

She stopped fighting, willing her body to relax, as she tried to take deep breaths from the air bubble the river had given her. Surely Thibault would give up, and release her.

When he did, water seized her limbs, carrying her out of his grasp, and deeper into the river channel. She floated on the current, drifting in the murky depths, until she glimpsed a flash of silver. A fish, she thought, reaching for it, but it was colder, heavier than any fish.

No, in her hand she held a sword – the same sword Romein had raised to block her path on the day they met. A weapon that had lain on the river bed, waiting for the day Romein would face Thibault again.

But he would not face him alone.

Thirty-Nine

Romein wasn't sure how long he lay there, stunned by the bastard's blow. It might have been a second, or it might have been an hour. But his first waking thought was for Julia – he must protect Julia. He clambered to his feet, casting about for his wife, and for Mercutio's killer. Only to see them on the river bank – the knave on his knees, with her in the water, submerged to the waist, her heels drumming on the shore as he drowned her.

"I am your foe, not her! Fight me instead, coward!" Romein shouted, but the knave did not hear, so intent was he on holding Julia down.

Romein picked up a stone and threw it. It clanged off Thibault's back. He threw more, each ringing louder as he came closer, but still Thibault did not release Julia.

And then…Julia's feet stopped moving, and Romein's heart stopped with them.

Only then did Thibault release her, pushing her out into the water where she sank like a stone.

Romein lost all reason in that moment, for his mind knew only rage.

Not Julia. Not sweet, saintly Julia, who did not deserve to die by violence, least of all at the hands of her own kin.

He pounded on the knight's helmet, beating at his chest. Somehow, he lost the knight's sword, and fought with only his fists. Until an armoured fist landed deep in Romein's gut, punching the breath out of his lungs.

He was dimly aware of hitting the ground, snow cushioning his fall, a mercy it had not given to Mercutio, before the knight seized his feet and began to drag him. First along the frozen ground, then along cold cobblestones, until he realised they were on the bridge.

The knight hoisted him up over his head. Romein was no longer the skinny boy he'd been seven years ago – it took all the knight's considerable strength, and he could hear the man breathing hard inside his helm.

For seven years, Romein had racked his brain, wondering what he could have done differently so that he did not end up in the river with a broken leg and smashed ribs that day. He'd learned to walk, then fight unarmed, and with a sword, and yet here he was, about to fall from the bridge one final time.

Romein surveyed the river. Julia's body should have floated to the surface now, but there was no sign of her. The river that nearly took his life seven years ago would be her grave.

"Either you or I or both shall go with her," Romein muttered.

Mercutio deserved a companion with which to walk the afterlife, but angelic Julia deserved an honour guard to march her into heaven. Romein would share her grave, God willing, for it would be their marriage bed.

If only fate were not so fickle, he would find a way to avoid going into the river. And yet…if that was where Julia was, why should he fight?

All his work with waterwheels and windmills, with Julia, had been to save this river and the lands around it. After Julia's death and his own, who would save it now? Not Thibault, whose very presence polluted the land Julia had loved. For Julia's sake, he could not be allowed to befoul it any longer.

"Your or I or both must go with her…and I choose both!"

Romein could not stop Thibault from tossing him in the river – he never could – but this time, with his knowledge of weight and power, force and how to apply it, he would see Thibault fall, too.

Romein fastened his legs about the knight's neck, then dived for the water, dragging the knave in after him.

Forty

Julia's sodden gown weighed her down, and the sword slowed her even further, but finally, she made it to the river bank, and lay sprawled on the stones.

Romein – where was Romein?

A shout echoed across the water, and for one terrible moment, she saw Thibault lift Romein into the air.

No…not again…She pushed herself to her feet, using Romein's sword as a crutch when her numb limbs threatened to buckle beneath her. Cold…so cold…she could scarcely struggle to take a step, let alone make it to the bridge before Thibault dropped Romein.

Blood streamed down her hand – she must have cut herself without realising it. Shivering, she stepped up to the river's edge, holding her hand out so the blood dripped into the river instead. The river that had saved her, and now she paid the price for the blood magic which allowed the river to understand her words, as she prayed that the waters would protect Romein, too.

The river swirled, her blood eddying around in a dizzying circle, before a wave began to build. The sort of wave one saw on the open ocean, in a storm, but never on their quiet river without a flood to stoke its rage. Her blood fuelled this, she knew, for she could clearly see the red streaks in the foam as the wave rose up and up, higher than the bank, higher than the bridge, higher than the waterwheel…before crashing over the top of the bridge, Thibault,

Romein, stone arch and all.

And when the water had washed away…only the bridge was left. Both men were gone.

She stumbled along the river bank, desperately searching for Romein, but there was no sign of him. Weeping, she mounted the bridge, so cold she could scarcely feel the stones under her feet. She would throw herself into the river after him, and together…

A faint cough sounded down by her feet. Julia blinked, hardly daring to believe what she was seeing. Romein lay on the stones, wedged against the side of the bridge, as soaked as she was. He struggled to his feet, and pulled her close.

They stood there for a moment, too thankful to hold one another again to care about anything but each other, until a creaking groan rent the air.

The waterwheel had begun to move. Slowly, at first, before it began to turn steadily, as though Romein's sails still drove it. But there were no sails today — only the river current. This was the river's work.

The water around the wheel began to change colour. At first, it was just faint pink, before it turned to red, a spreading pool that streamed away in the current. And in the middle, a leather eye patch floated up, bearing the fleur-de-lis, before it was swept beneath the bridge downstream.

Forty-One

"We should get out of these clothes, and inside, where it is warm and dry," Romein said.

Julia nodded, leaning on him as they limped toward the mill.

Once inside, Julia headed upstairs to get some blankets, while Romein built up the fire. He stripped off his clothes and hung them in front of the hearth, then accepted a blanket from Julia.

"You know, we could just take these

blankets back upstairs, and start our wedding night early. I know of no law that says a man can only make love to his wife after the sun has set," Romein said.

"I do not know much about such things at all. Only that it is a wife's duty…" Julia closed her eyes. Her mother had called it a duty, but her brothers had called it a joy.

Romein took her hand. "Then I shall teach you what I know, and everything else, we can find out together."

She followed him upstairs, then climbed into the box bed after him, closing the doors behind them so that the only light was the flickering candle in a lantern, high up on the wall.

She opened with a kiss, as his lips met hers, until her tongue entered the fray, eagerly wishing to taste if Romein was as sweet as she remembered. Then his hands joined the dance, gliding over her skin beneath the blankets, until she had no further need of scratchy wool, for all she wanted to feel against her body was him.

Her pleasure at his touch started as slow tingles, bubbling beneath her skin like a breath blown out under the water, but it built quickly, turning into a raging torrent until she was overcome by waves so powerful, she was powerless to do anything but cling to him and cry out his name, until she surfaced from an ocean of bliss to take another life-giving breath.

Only to hear his own hoarse voice caress her name, a cry so rough and raw, and yet it was the sweetest sound she had ever heard.

And if they slept for a time, it was only to wake to the bloom of heat between them, as they made love again.

Forty-Two

Spring had melted the last of the winter snows, and the fruit trees in Julia's orchard had begun to bloom before another Capet came to Veluwe. But it was not Father, as Thibault had told her, or a company of his men. No, it was her oldest brother, Aran, and he rode alone.

"This is a strange country you live in," he greeted her, as he kissed her cheeks. "For the last day, I have ridden past a number of structures with sails. Never in my life have I seen sails on land before, and here, they seem to sprout like mushrooms. What sort of madness is here?"

Julia laughed. After the success of Romein's first windmill, they had built them everywhere, to drain the snowmelt away from the fields, first to mine them for salt, and then to plant crops for the next season. "They are mills, like horse mills, only the sails driven by the wind power them. Most of them pump water out of the fields, to stop them from flooding. The plans came from Queen Molina to my husband, and who are we to refuse a royal decree?" She shrugged, and her shawl slipped from her shoulders. It was a wedding gift from Lady Mona, woven swirls of pink and blue wool, and so large she could almost use it for a cloak.

"Ah, yes, your husband. Father had us all ready to set out to Veluwe for your wedding, but he was laid low on the very eve of our journey, and he did not recover." Aran hung his head. "Forgive me for being the bearer of bad tidings, but Father has passed to his eternal rest. His final words were of you, and how he intended to make Veluwe a wedding gift to you and your new husband. He made me promise I would give these lands to you instead. Yet he never did tell me what manner of man you married."

"He is a good man, and a noble one. Honourable, too, with a terrible thirst for knowledge. He is one of the Queen's favourites, and he has her ear. The Queen even sent us a wedding gift…" A book filled with the most lurid pictures of couples…and sometimes more than couples, abed. She dared not show it to her brother, for every picture made her blush so hot her cheeks burned. "He has been a great help, managing the estates at Veluwe, especially repairing the damage from the last floods. Father could not have chosen a better husband for me."

"And are you happy?" Aran asked.

Ah, he was as perceptive as William. If she lied, he would know.

"I have never been happier than I am now, as Romein's wife. For a time, I thought our fates so star-crossed that my life was doomed to tragedy, but Romein, with his windmills and other modern notions, has quite changed my mind. In fact, I would challenge anyone, man or woman, to deny that our life together will be lived any other way than happily ever after."

"Not I, certainly, for I wish you and Romein every happiness. Though I cannot imagine these windmills will remain in use for long."

"Fate will decide, as she always does, to the surprise of some, and the gratitude of others," Julia said.

But fate had already decided that this pair of star-crossed lovers had suffered enough, and their future held only happiness.

As for Thibault, no one ever did find his body, though his horse was found outside a lonely inn, a known gambling den, which the knight had often frequented in the past. The inn patrons merely shrugged, and played a round of dice to see who would claim his horse. And then forgot about Sir Thibault of Paris, tourney champion and Prince of Cats.

About the Author

Demelza Carlton has always loved the ocean, but on her first snorkelling trip she found she was afraid of fish.

She has since swum with sea lions, sharks and sea cucumbers and stood on spray drenched cliffs over a seething sea as a seven-metre cyclonic swell surged in, shattering a shipwreck below.

Demelza now lives in Perth, Western Australia, the shark attack capital of the world.

The *Ocean's Gift* series was her first foray into fiction, followed by her suspense thriller *Nightmares* trilogy. She swears the *Mel Goes to Hell* series ambushed her on a crowded train and wouldn't leave her alone.

Want to know more? You can follow Demelza on Facebook, Twitter, YouTube or her website, Demelza Carlton's Place at:

www.demelzacarlton.com